The Landowner's Secret

Sonya Heaney

16pt

Read How You Want
LARGE PRINT BOOKS, BRAILLE & DAISY

Copyright Page from the Original Book

Title: The Landowner's Secret

Copyright © 2019 by SONYA HEANEY

Published by
Escape
An imprint of Harlequin Enterprises (Australia) Pty Limited (ABN 47 001 180 918), a subsidiary of HarperCollins Publishers Australia Pty Limited (ABN 36 009 913 517)
Level 13, 201 Elizabeth St
SYDNEY NSW 2000
AUSTRALIA

romance.com.au/escapepublishing/

TABLE OF CONTENTS

About the author	iv
Acknowledgements	vi
Chapter 1	1
Chapter 2	19
Chapter 3	37
Chapter 4	60
Chapter 5	84
Chapter 6	105
Chapter 7	122
Chapter 8	142
Chapter 9	163
Chapter 10	184
Chapter 11	202
Chapter 12	217
Chapter 13	232
Chapter 14	247
Chapter 15	263
Chapter 16	285
Chapter 17	311
Chapter 18	330
Chapter 19	340
Chapter 20	363
Chapter 21	393
Epilogue	415

INTRODUCING

ROMANCE
.COM.AU

RURAL | CONTEMPORARY | FANTASY| HISTORICAL| PARANORMAL | ROMANTIC SUSPENSE | LGBTQI

All the books you love with all the romance you need!

Sign up to newsletter for all the latest romance news, romance e-book deals and competitions!

SUBSCRIBE NOW

The Landowner's Secret
Sonya Heaney

New South Wales, 1885

When Alice Ryan wakes to find thugs surrounding her cottage, on the hunt for her no-good brother, she escapes into the surrounding bush.

It is wealthy landowner Robert Farrer who finds her the next morning, dishevelled, injured, and utterly unwilling to share what she knows. With criminals on the loose and rumours that reckless bushrangers have returned to the area, Robert is determined to keep Alice out of danger, and insists on taking her into his home—despite the scandal it may cause. Convincing her to stay on with him for her own safety, however, is going to take some work.

What Robert doesn't expect is his growing attraction to the forthright, unruly woman staying in his home. Before either of them can settle into their odd new situation, their home and wellbeing come under threat and they will need to trust each other to survive. But they are both keeping secrets, secrets that have the potential to ruin their burgeoning love, their livelihood ... and their lives.

About the author

SONYA HEANEY began her professional life aged eight, as the Changeling in Queensland Ballet's *A Midsummer Night's Dream.* After many more years of hard work, even more blisters, and plenty of pretty tutus, one too many injuries forced her out of her pointe shoes.

Between then and now she has worked in a posh Dublin hotel (that didn't last long), pulled pints in London pubs (that lasted years), taught English in Korea (her apartment was broken into and her computer was stolen—along with many half-finished manuscripts), and worked on costumes backstage in various theatres (it was always chaos).

Sonya holds a Bachelor of Arts in Professional Writing, and spent years putting it to use in nonfiction fields before turning her hand to romance.

After working her way around the world, she once again calls Canberra, Australia's gorgeous capital city, home.

If you'd like to know more about Sonya, her books, or to

connect with her online, you can visit her webpage sonyaheaney.com, follow her on twitter @HeaneySonya, or like her Facebook page @SonyaHeaneyAuthor.

Acknowledgements

Thank you to my editor, Chrysoula Aiello, who understood my book at least as well as I did. Thank you also to Johanna Baker and the rest of the team at Escape Publishing and HarperCollins Australia. I am so grateful to Christine Armstrong for creating such a gorgeous cover.

Queanbeyan, New South Wales, a place I've visited thousands of times over the years, served as inspiration for Barracks Flat. I hope I've done you justice!

Finally, credit has to go to my family, who never once told me I was crazy for quitting a perfectly good psychology/law degree to study writing!

Thank you to Queanbeyan, New South Wales, my inspiration for Barracks Flat. And for my grandmother, Sophia Jacyszyn (1922–2015), who made the town her home.

Chapter 1

Southern Tablelands, New South Wales
Late April, 1885

Alice Ryan woke at the first shout, and sat bolt upright at the second.

With her mind still muddled by sleep, her body shook with fright before she even realised what was happening. She felt the unease, the disturbance in the night. This far out the bush was usually still, the quietness punctuated only by the odd scuffle of a possum or rustle of wind in the trees. But right now there was an energy that didn't belong.

Curling her fingers into the counterpane, she waited in dreadful anticipation.

There. A voice—faint, but distinct—reached her ears, becoming louder as she sat frozen in place.

Someone was out there, in the dark.

'Ian?' she whispered, uncertain. Who else could it be but her brother, and yet ... Some instinct stopped her from calling out and confirming she was home. And just as it took complete hold, a second voice joined the first.

Slipping free of the blanket and pressing her bare feet to the floor, she clutched the bed's footboard and waited. And waited.

The light of a flame—so dim at first she thought she'd imagined it—flashed not too far beyond the cottage's small window. It wasn't much, but it was so foreign in the darkness of the scrub.

She strained to make out any sounds that weren't meant to be there, but heard next to nothing over the pounding in her ears. Moments later the light flashed by again. It was closer this time.

Alice startled; clapped a hand to her mouth.

This was all wrong. Nobody had a reason to be there, on a road that led to nothing but her home. This far out she was all alone, except for—

Endmoor.

If she could slip out unnoticed, she could reach the big homestead beyond the trees on foot—thieves or troublemakers would be mad to try anything with Robert Farrer. The landowner was too wealthy, with too many men on his property, and no doubt he had better weapons than she did if it came to that.

Alice made her decision in an instant.

Moving fast, she struggled into her frock and grabbed her shawl from the end of the bed before slipping a hand beneath the mattress for the small packet she kept hidden there. She stuffed it down the front of her bodice, shaking with fright and determination.

Trying her best to be quiet, she scrambled across to press her back against the cool wall near the door.

One of the men spoke again but she still couldn't make out the words. There were at least two of them and they weren't just talking, but laughing. *Whacks* echoed through the night air, as though they were hitting at the scrub with sticks, and then she heard more laughter in amongst the other sounds of the night.

Whatever they were about, it was a game to them. Likely a drunken game...

Alice curled her toes against the freezing floor and hugged herself tightly, willing them to just *go,* just leave her be and make their fun elsewhere. The voices came more loudly from the front of the house. Her only way of escape was through there.

Cursing her rotten luck, her absent brother, and all the trouble life brought down on her, she took a big breath for courage and lurched past the window as fast as she could, scrambling in the darkness for the small knife she'd left on the table.

'Ian, you bastard!' The call came from so close by her heart nearly stopped.

Desperation took over then, and she chose speed over silence. Fumbling in the shadows with frozen fingers, shoving her way through the bits and pieces she'd left on the table that evening, she patted about desperately until they hit a strip of cold metal. *The knife.*

'Help me, help me,' she whispered to a God who'd never listened before, and gripped the handle firmly, her other hand shaking, while she once again backed up against the wall.

Bracing herself for anything, she pulled back the curtain only enough to get a glimpse of the clearing around the porch. In a sliver of moonlight she could just make out the figures of grown men dotted around the clearing. Further down the trail, near the road, she saw more forms and shadows. *Horses,* she realised with even more dread in her belly. She sure as hell couldn't outrun those.

Shaking more, she cast her mind out beyond them all, mapping herself a route of escape. If they were here for Ian, they were out of luck. As usual he was nowhere to be found.

She let the curtain slip back through her fingers and then bent to grasp the laces of the boots left beside the door. There was no time to tug them on, nor to find her stockings.

She nearly shrieked with surprise when something whacked directly against the outside of the house, but held fast and slapped a hand over her mouth again as she waited for what'd come next.

'Are you comin' out, or are we comin' to get you?' one of them called. It was not a familiar voice.

'We don't have all night!' yelled another.

There was more laughing. More jokes.

Alice rose carefully, quickly tugging the shawl more tightly around herself without letting her grip on the knife loosen. She edged the door open the tiniest amount, trying to peer beyond the intruders to find the fastest direction into the trees. The boots banged lightly against the old wood, and she pressed her lips tightly together in frustration.

'Maybe there's no one 'ere. I swear, James, if we're out 'ere freezin' our bloody arses off for no reason...'

'Someone's 'ere. There's smoke comin' from the chimney and I saw movement at the window just now.'

'Bloody *hell*,' Alice whispered, becoming number and shakier than before. 'Bloody, bloody hell.'

There was silence then except for the shuffling of shoes in the dirt. And then a third man spoke.

'Maybe it's the sister.'

'There's a sister?'

An awful pause followed. And then, 'Is she pretty?'

Alice wished the bottom of the floor would open up and swallow her whole. Fear icier than the chill in the air ran over her from head-top to heels. She knew more about physical fighting than any proper lady ever would, but she was still a scrap of a thing and not likely to get far before they...

'There's only one way to find out.' The first man said. 'James? Kick in the door.'

'Not bloody likely,' she whispered. She'd go to the devil before she let that happen or let a single one of them put his grubby paws on her.

And with those thoughts giving her fresh determination, she flung the door open and ran.

There was a shout of surprise, and then a bark of amusement at the sight of her, but all she focused on was the security of the trees ahead. She bolted like a barefooted colt for an opening between two old eucalypts.

Gasping in pain at the scrapes of sticks on the ground and—worse—the dull thuds of bone connecting with rocks buried in the dirt, in her urgency she almost smacked face-first into the nearest tree. A low branch scraped along her cheek as she slipped into the cover of the bush, and she sucked in a short breath at the sting.

She ducked behind a big gum tree and stared hard into the night, willing her eyes to adjust to the frightening, sudden darkness while more calls came from close by.

She needed those boots on before she ruined her feet too much to run. Stuffing the knife quickly into a pocket, she dropped down and slipped her bare feet into the worn leather; there was no time to bother with the laces. It was going to rub terribly, but she'd had blisters before and there were worse things in the world.

Rising with a hand against the trunk to steady herself, she knotted the shawl at her breast as tightly as she could, gathering her courage to leave the cover of the plants, and ran on.

The men tracking her had no such qualms about keeping quiet; she bit her lip hard when they spoke again.

'Ian, we saw you, you fool. Are ya goin' to hide in the bush all night?'

'Are you daft? That's not Ryan, not unless he's wearing a frock.'

That set them all off laughing. The whole night was just so much fun for the lot of them. And then they took up the chase with a thunder of footsteps as they dived after her full into the scrub.

Alice gasped for breath, the autumn chill in the air burning her throat, and only fear of stumbling into a dark ditch and breaking an ankle made her moderate her steps. This part of the land dipped and rose at the oddest times, which was why her father had never bothered with the clearing of it.

A rustle and a thud came from not far away, followed by a string of swearing. One of them had gone and smacked into a branch.

Using the cover of their shouts to pick up a little more speed, she darted to the left, taking herself closer to those horses the intruders had arrived on, hoping against hope they'd not expect that. She'd no real idea what her plan was, but surely making it to the road was better than being tracked through the trees for the rest of the night.

If those louts knew Ian, and if her brother owed them something, then none of this was good news. It wasn't as though the either of them had anything much to hand over.

Her pursuers veered off to her right and Alice realised she'd chosen the best path. With a pace increased to match her growing confidence, she picked her way along on the tips of her toes in an attempt to disguise her steps, and kept one hand outstretched to feel her way and not meet the same fate as the fellow with the branch, the handle of the knife in the other.

Don't go and stab yourself, Alice Ryan.

The boots rubbed at the backs of her heels, and she hissed and then hissed some more at the sting of it.

She was going to *kill* Ian the next time she saw him. And if she got back home in the morning and discovered those men had destroyed her neat house and eaten all of her food, she was going to board up the door and never let her useless brother back in.

The next shout stopped her in her tracks and ripped her from her temper.

It had come from *in front* of her.

Alice dropped behind the nearest bush and clung to its rough branches as an argument unfolded up ahead. The tone of the words was harsh, carrying across to her only in indecipherable sounds at first. She snatched her hand back from a prickle when she grasped a twig too hard as she strained to hear.

A crack of a branch and the shriek of a bat decided things for her: she used the cover of the quarrel to dart ahead, again risking sound for speed.

'You want to wait out the whole winter? You're daft if you do.'

'It'll be worth it, I reckon. Yes, I say we wait for the date like we're told to.'

'Madness. We don't need Ian Ryan's help for that.'

Alice covered another ten or fifteen yards before the argument became louder, shouts echoing across the night, reverberating around her, surrounding her and lighting up the shadows. She no longer had any idea where the men were, only that she couldn't risk running any more.

Panting desperately, her heart beating so fast she thought she'd faint, she collapsed on the ground by a fallen tree, clasped her little knife tighter still, huddled into a ball, and waited.

***

'Incredible, is it not, that the fellow survived the night?'

Robert Farrer grimaced and inclined his head in agreement as he and John, his closest friend, walked east along the town road. Between them Robert's heeler darted and weaved, nose to the ground as he investigated each and every new scent.

The fog had rolled in some time over the course of the night, the first one of the season, and now it was slow to clear. Sunlight had begun to force its way through the haze, and dewdrops sparkled on the leaves of the bushes around them.

Endmoor had been shocked awake hours earlier, long before dawn.

The gunshot that'd brought the night to life had echoed around the valley, setting the dogs off barking and the men scrambling for weapons and coats.

Confusion had reigned first. The Southern Tablelands were hardly a hotbed for violence anymore. No ... that'd all gone by the wayside in the Sixties, with the demise of the likes of Hall and Gardiner. Now there was a lot more peace in the region than there was excitement.

It was Robert himself who'd all but tripped over the wounded yet still living man soon after they'd set out. In the dim light he'd been nothing more than a slumped silhouette on the side of the road—but an ominous one. The fellow had had enough energy to demand that no physician be called for, just about making a run for it when Robert would have sent a message to town anyway, and then he'd fallen into a fever of pain they'd not been able to wake him from.

One man, one bullet wound, and nobody else in sight, bar the tracks of multiple horses that had only become visible some time later. The knowledge of how close it'd happened to Endmoor's gates sent another chill through him.

He and one of his farmhands had transported the chap back to the homestead and done their best to patch him up, and by the time John Stanford had ridden out to see Robert after breakfast, the whole property was alive with activity and unease.

'I wouldn't say he was out of the woods yet,' Robert said, glancing at his friend as they kept pace with each other, senses cast outwards, braced for anyone or anything to emerge from the bush.

In fact, Robert wasn't at all confident the fellow would see out the remainder of the day, God help him. It wasn't a pleasant thought, and his fingers flexed on his weapon.

Young, roughly dressed, and looking as though he'd not seen a bath for a considerable amount of time, the stranger was not a familiar face to Robert or to John, nor to any of the curious locals who'd poked their head into the staff quarters in the past couple of hours.

John grunted in agreement, jaw tight. 'It's a nasty wound, that one. Never heard of a shot like that meeting a happy ending.'

They trudged along, footfalls deliberately heavy in the dry, overgrown grass as a deterrent to reptiles that bit when startled. The sun climbed higher into the sky as the autumn mist gave way to another brilliantly sunny day. The new season had hit quite suddenly the week before, taking with it the worst of the summer heat, but leaving the land parched and brown and dangerous.

'Are we allowed to mention bushrangers yet?' his friend asked after another moment's thought. 'Or would that be too alarming a thought for our neighbours to hear at this point?'

Robert smiled tightly and without humour. For decades the Southern Tablelands had been infamous for armed highwaymen terrorising the roads, but they'd thought the gold rush had moved them on years ago.

'God knows. I've no doubt half the town will be speaking of it enthusiastically before the day is out, and the other half will be cowering in terror at the mere suggestion.'

A crack sounded up ahead in the trees, setting off a flock of cockatoos, dozens of them fleeing as one, their deafening calls blocking the men's ability to hear anything else.

They stopped as one, tensed and ready for anything.

Robert met John's eyes as the bush settled again and the birds departed, a streak of white across the sky. The dog, Hutton, paused too, alert for signs neither man could sense.

'It's all right over here!' a male voice came from deeper in the trees. ''Tis only us!'

'It's old Adamson.' Robert recognised the voice and shook his head, smiling in spite of himself. The senior most member of his staff was likely capable of taking on a gang of criminals alone.

Robert relaxed his grip on his pistol as they walked on. Boots crunched through the carpet of fallen leaves and bark. Hutton trotted onwards, stopping here and there to investigate a scrubby plant, a tree.

Up ahead was the Ryan cottage, the last stop before a man found himself well and truly out of town. He should probably check in there on the way back, Robert thought. He'd mixed feelings about the family and their patchy behaviour, but they were the closest thing he had to neighbours.

The men made it another thirty yards or so when the dog barked once sharply and darted off to the left.

'What is it, Hutton?' he called, picking up his pace as he changed direction to follow.

As the heeler led him through a gap in the prickly bushes nowhere near big enough for a man, he swore and then ducked around another way, keeping the wagging grey tail in sight.

The dog barked again, and then stopped suddenly, prancing in a circle once before bending to something on the ground.

Robert approached silently, just as John did from the other side, their tread careful and cautious. Together they stepped over the rocky surface, nearing whatever it was that'd captured the animal's interest.

He saw the boot first. Unlaced and sticking out from behind a fallen tree, it brought him up short. He paused a few seconds, bracing for sudden movement, and yet the dog only bent closer to his find, whining a little as he pawed at the figure on the ground.

Robert edged around the log, saw the sweep of serviceable grey fabric spread across the dirt, and finally registered what he should have before.

It was a *lady's* boot.

Chapter 2

'Hutton, that's enough,' Robert said once he'd ascertained there was no immediate danger, and then gently eased himself between dog and woman, kneeling beside her and placing his pistol within reach.

The dog subsided immediately, settling down beside them and letting out one final, low whine.

He knew this woman, this girl, Robert realised immediately, even if he'd never seen her like this before, with her wheat-blonde hair loose around her face and her skirts covered in debris and tangled around her legs.

With a surprisingly shaky hand he reached out to feel for her pulse, holding his hand there even after realising it was still beating, and was shocked by the warmth of her skin in the chill of the morning.

'She's alive,' he told John as his friend drew nearer, steps crunching dry leaves. He ran his eyes over her from head to toe, searching for obvious injuries, but finding nothing of the kind.

Terrible assumptions began to flood his mind as he regarded her yet he shoved them aside. A young woman alone and criminals on the loose was a dreadful combination, but he'd not draw the worst conclusions yet. Other than a small, reddened scratch on her cheek, its line leading up to her closed eyes, and a flush beneath it that stood in stark contradiction to the small shivers running through her, she did not seem too worse for wear. Except she'd not stirred at their arrival.

'Miss Ryan,' he said, touching a hand to hers. Her fingers moved slightly and he held tighter, curling his around her own and repeating her name.

'*Alice,*' he tried when he received no further reaction, and watched as a frown flit across her features before it could set in.

John knelt on the other side. He exchanged a concerned look with Robert, but didn't speak.

'Miss Ryan. *Alice.* Where are you harmed?'

She frowned again and then murmured with a sigh of annoyance, struggling her way out of unconsciousness.

'What...?' It was a whisper, but at least it was something. 'Ian?'

'No, it's—not your brother. Miss Ryan, where are you hurt?'

He received the smallest of shrugs and then she drifted back to sleep.

'Damn,' he said under his breath, and barely resisted the urge to shake her awake and tell her his name. Instead, feeling guilt at the need for it to be done, he moved his hands carefully along her body, not sure if he felt relief at finding nothing broken, or worry that she didn't react to the contact at all.

A sudden crack of a twig nearby had both men and the dog looking up, and no one relaxed until yet another cockatoo emerged from the foliage above, showering them with chewed-off debris from the branch where it watched.

It was a warning of their vulnerability.

'John,' Robert said then, full of new urgency, 'will you help me.'

Together they lifted her, Stanford untangling her skirts as dispassionately as possible while Robert got a knee and then his arms under her upper body. It was a struggle with the weapons they carried, and with a dog whose attempts at help involved enthusiastically winding his way around their legs, but they were driven by necessity and managed.

With Hutton finally giving up and trotting ahead, they made slow progress out of the bushland and back in the direction of the road. Robert swore once quietly as he stumbled over something he couldn't see, and adjusted his hold on the Ryan girl, hefting her higher into his arms.

'Go ahead and call for the physician,' he said when they came free of the eucalypts. 'I'll take her the rest of the way.'

John only paused a fraction of a moment. 'I'll go for my horse. Can you manage?'

'I'm determined to.'

His friend took one final look at the girl in Robert's arms, no doubt seeing the heated flush to her cheeks that

Robert felt against his chest, and nodded.

John was off then, jogging ahead with the dog caught up in the excitement of it all and bounding alongside him. Robert firmed his hold on Miss Ryan, scooping an arm under her as he broke entirely from the scrub.

Somewhere on the journey back he became aware of her wakening again, of the tension that entered her body, and the small noises of discomfort she made as he stepped over a rock here and a rut in the road there.

'I'm sorry,' he said under his spent breath, but already she was going limp again, a shiver wracking her.

Had he not seen her on his ride home only the day before? He was almost certain of it, but in Barracks Flat people tended to see their neighbours with such regularity that one day blended into another. If it *had* been yesterday, she'd not looked sick in the slightest. Whenever it was, she'd made it this far on her own.

'What happened?' he asked, not hopeful of an answer.

When he received none, he hoisted her higher, the fabric of her skirts tangling and her bodice crinkling, searching for a better grip on her legs so she wouldn't slip through his grasp.

As he did, with a cry of pain Alice Ryan finally came fully awake.

The suddenness of it nearly startled him senseless. He fumbled, recovered, and then looked down into grey-blue eyes awash with confusion and hurt.

'What is it?' he asked urgently, even as he put more speed into his tread. If he moved any faster, he was in danger of losing his grip on her, but his heart hammered so loudly it was hard to moderate his steps.

'Miss Ryan, what is it?'

Only, she was too busy trying to climb his body to respond, scrambling and grasping at his shoulders at the same time as kicking weakly with one of her legs. It was an effort to hold her when she was determined to not be held, her panic and stubbornness blinding her to sense. He hurried on, feeling the pounding of his feet on the compacted dirt and the way it reverberated through him, through her.

He just had to get her to the house, but still he was too far away to even catch a glimpse of the place.

'Ankle. Or ... foot,' she said on a couple of gasps.

The worst of thoughts hit him then, and he stopped still in an instant, dropping to the ground with her still in his arms. His knees protested the impact but there wasn't time to worry about that.

Dumping her unceremoniously on the dirt in his haste, he tipped the brim of his hat up and reached for her skirts, hefting them up to her knees.

'Which one? For goodness' sake, Alice, which one?'

He received his answer when he reached for her right foot and she instantly shied away. Grunting in frustration, he grabbed her by the unlaced boot when it was clear she'd not have any part of the aid voluntarily and held her firm. She wore no stockings—*had she had to flee that fast?*—and the puffy, reddened skin where her foot met her leg sent fear through him.

'What was it? Did you see what did this to you, what it was?'

She shook her head and looked very deliberately in the opposite direction. 'No ... idea...' she managed before taking a great gulp of air as though she would be sick.

'Are there marks?' she asked a second later, in an even smaller voice.

'Puncture wounds?' Robert bent closer and strained to see, but if it was a snakebite, it wasn't like anything he'd seen on the farm or heard of before.

'I don't think so.' But bloody *hell,* he just couldn't say for certain.

If a snake was the culprit, then he shouldn't be lugging her about the way he was and risk spreading the poison further, but what were his alternatives? Staying put was hardly a sensible choice.

'When did this happen? *Alice,'* he used her name again as her fear was overtaken by fatigue and her eyes fell closed once more. She gave him a brief, ferocious scowl as he woke her; he needed answers if he was to be of any use to her.

'Miss Ryan, when did this happen to you?'

It seemed as though it took all the strength in the world to answer; for a moment he didn't think she would.

'Don't know. It was dark.' A short breath and a ripple of pain came across her features, and then another.

'It was ... dark,' she said again. Her vagueness was alarming. 'Last night?'

An answer framed as a question, but Robert had no response for her. If she didn't know, he didn't have a clue. Storing the rest of his interrogation away for later, he bent over her leg again, trying to satisfy himself he wasn't going to do more harm by moving her further.

Up ahead John was long gone, and Robert prayed that he was already at his horse, ready to make the ride into town for help. Endmoor wasn't far from the heart of the community, but right then it might as well have been in Sydney.

Last night, when it was dark...

The sun had been up for a while, which meant that she had been out there for some time already. In Robert's experience fatal bites struck their victims down within the first few hours. If she'd not been taken away by it yet, surely that was good news.

He looked at her ankle another time before removing the boot entirely and then tugging her skirts back down. He still could not say for certain what'd caused the discomfort, the swelling, or the fever, but it was a sensible time to consider the worst possible scenario.

There were those who claimed he should suck the wound to remove the poison, and others who—Heaven help them both—claimed he should destroy the damaged area with gunpowder to save the rest of her. Yet if it was a snake who'd taken a bite there should have been two obvious puncture wounds, and there weren't. There was no chance he could bring himself to do such things to her without knowing they were absolutely needed, and at any rate they couldn't stay out there on the road for the remainder of the morning.

With no real option other than to continue on to the house, he slipped his arms around her again, taking a deep breath, eyes on the road ahead, and stood.

***

The jostling began again as the man carried her along the uneven road. Alice heard the slapping of feet against the earth, and the heavy breathing where she had her cheek pressed to the soft fabric of his waistcoat. The pain in her foot came and went, and then came and *stayed,* radiating from one spot that felt like it was on fire.

She tried not to make any more noises, biting her lip and drifting in and out of awareness as she shivered again and again. Fever or illness? She could no longer tell. Perhaps it was simply that she'd been asleep in the cool wilderness through the hours overnight.

The pain had first come before the sun rose, at some point in the endless night of hiding and waiting. She couldn't remember exactly when she'd realised the men had given up on the chase of her and left, but it was about the time she'd given into the unexpected pull of sleep.

The severe ache was worse now, though. From toes to hips, she *hurt.*

She was too afeared to ask the man—and she was vaguely aware it was Robert Farrer himself who was lugging her along—what time it was, or what day. Everything was muddled in her mind, and if his reaction to seeing her ankle told her anything, it was that the situation weren't so good. There were too many ways to be killed in the bush, and Alice was nowhere near ready for *death.* Life was hard, but she'd always thought she'd at least reach twenty years of age before she carked it.

Lost in her misery, she knew vaguely that he paused, and then turned a corner. Once more he hauled her higher in his arms, and she felt him fumbling with something—a gate, she thought—before continuing on.

After what seemed like an age, he started up some steps, and she forced her eyes open in time to see him carry her past the butler and through the front door of the grand house of the Farrer estate.

Of all the reasons to be invited inside, she thought, *it had to be because I'm dyin'* .

'In here, in here.' A woman's voice joined Mister Farrer's low murmurs, and she opened her eyes to see the rounded, motherly housekeeper approaching.

Her rescuer took a sudden turn and then Alice was placed on a bed softer than she knew a bed could be. She drew in a hiss of breath as her poor leg was jostled again, and then struggled up onto her elbows as the master and several servants carried on a low conversation about her.

'Pardon?' she said—or at least she thought she'd said it aloud. Nobody spoke to her directly.

'I beg your pardon?' she tried again.

But either they didn't hear or they didn't care to include her in the discussion. She closed her eyes in frustration and drifted a little, coming back to the present with a start of surprise when her foot was unceremoniously propped up onto cushions.

Alice only hoped the housekeeper, Mrs Adamson, knew what she was doing, because it seemed she was at the woman's mercy.

'What?' she tried when the conversation picked up around her again, giving up on her manners. It was hard to concentrate when her teeth chattered and rattled so loudly. *Fever,* someone mentioned. *Ankle,* someone else added. This was not new information to her.

Snakebite, said the only male voice in the room, and Alice shuddered and sent up a silent plea everyone would get that terrible notion out of their heads. A couple of years back a man around those parts been bitten by a brown snake, and the poor old bloke was dead the same day.

After that the voices fell to whispers, which couldn't mean anything good.

Alice shuddered again and tried lifting her foot. Now she was *determined* to see it, if only to prove them wrong, to prove that—

The sharp stab of pain took her by surprise and she groaned in discomfort, but at least the noise she made finally shut everyone else up.

'Miss Ryan, stay still!'

Mrs Adamson wasn't her mother, but a person wouldn't have known it by the tone. Within seconds she'd been deftly pushed back onto the bed to lay like a corpse and await her fate.

'What kind of snake was it?' she asked, but thought her voice sounded funny. Must've sounded funny to them, too, because she was asked to repeat herself.

When she finally made herself understood, the older woman shushed her.

'Nobody said it was a snake.'

Alice thought that unless she'd also lost her hearing overnight, that was a big bloody lie, but she couldn't say things like that aloud in such a fancy house.

Mister Farrer came up to the side of the bed then, and bent so that his face was close to hers. He had brown eyes, dark brown with black lashes—of all the things for her to notice at such a time.

'Miss Ryan, I don't think it was a snake. I didn't see the puncture marks I would expect if it was. Mr Stanford has gone for the physician, and we'll know more then. Do *not* panic yet.'

Alice should've asked when she was allowed to panic if not then, but decided that even with concessions made because she was ill, that was also too rude to say aloud.

The master of the house reached halfway across to her like he might touch her, and then drew his hand back and stepped away.

Pity, Alice thought as he left the room with another quiet word to Mrs Adamson. If she was going to be dead soon, she wouldn't've minded being touched by him one last time.

'You'd best be listening to him, Miss Ryan,' the housekeeper said once he'd gone, in a voice just as firm, but twice as loud. 'He's a clever young man. Tends to say how things will be, and then makes them so.'

Well, then. Maybe she'd still be living by the time the physician rode in, no matter how much she hurt all over.

Everyone knew Mister Farrer was the closest thing to a genius they had in the Southern Tablelands. He knew science and farming and crops, and had come from far away in England, and if not even *he* could find a snakebite on her foot, it was a good sign.

The maid entered the room again and handed the housekeeper a handful of fabric, and before Alice had a chance to snatch her foot away in fright, she was muscled into place and bandaged from knee to toe-tips.

'What's that for, then?' she asked through gritted teeth as the pressure became greater and greater. She trusted the lady, but surely that bandage was tighter than anybody with sense would recommend.

'I beg your pardon, my dear?'

It was a talent the woman had, to be speaking all polite whilst torturing someone.

'Why' do I need bandagin', d'you reckon?'

'It's only a precaution,' the older woman explained as she tucked the end of the fabric into the rest of it. 'You didn't see how swollen your ankle was?'

Answering was slow to come, because a flood of queasiness hit her so fast, it was all Alice could do to grab her belly and try not to moan too loudly. She saw swirls and sparks and had to force her focus to return to her torturer.

'Mrs Adamson, I might be dyin' right now. I didn't see a thing.'

Chapter 3

'My guess would be a spider bite. Though the severity of the reaction is an unfortunate twist of fate for the girl. In situations such as this, no one can predict who'll succumb to illness and who'll be able to go on almost as normal.'

'It wasn't a snake, then?'

'No.'

Walter Dunn, provider of any and all medical services in the Barracks Flat's district, placed his hat back on his head and adjusted his gloves while Robert thanked God he'd not given into his first instinct and made use of that gunpowder.

'She should not be moved from the bed for a few days, at the least. Unless...'

The physician—a fellow Robert had a fair amount of faith in—eyed him speculatively.

'Unless arrangements can be made to move the girl to a different location?' the man continued.

Which was something Robert's conscience would not allow, of course. Especially not now, considering all that'd happened overnight. His housekeeper and her husband were both in hearing distance, and Robert suspected there were a few other pairs of ears nearby that strained his way. No doubt each one of them would have an opinion ready to offer should he request it.

However he was the master of the house—allegedly—and it was his choice to make.

'I understand she lives nearby?'

'She does, but there is nobody there for her, so it wouldn't do.'

There was nobody as far as Robert was aware of at any rate; he'd given up trying to keep track of the comings and goings of the Ryan family. He couldn't help but wonder if the small house on the fringe of his property was even habitable. God knew, even *he,* a man who'd made a point of not noticing ladies' fashions for the past five years, could tell Miss Ryan's gown was clean but made as much of patches and darning as it was the original fabric.

'She'll stay here.' He added some authority to his tone in case any eavesdroppers thought to object.

'We have Mrs Adamson to care for her, and my sister will be home soon enough.' *He hoped.*

That made two people hurt and incapacitated over the course of the night, and both of them on the fringes of Farrer land. As Robert had suspected, the mysterious gunshot man's prognosis was not good, and there seemed little even Dunn could offer as a means to save him.

'It is in the hands of God now,' the man had proclaimed gravely after examining the wound, which hadn't seemed like the most helpful of explanations coming from a gentleman trained to use medical fact before faith.

Troubled, Robert cast a brief glance at the members of his staff hovering at a respectful distance off to the side, each one of them failing miserably in their attempts to look like they had a legitimate reason for being there.

Something had sent Alice Ryan out into the bush in the darkness, and Robert wanted to know what it was.

For her safety, for his, and for Endmoor's. For the town's too, when it came down to it. Even though it was said bushrangers were a thing of the past, that armed men had stopped roaming the countryside since the Victorian stand-off at Glenrowan nearly half a decade ago, incidents still flared up all over the colonies, and Australia was far too large to be properly policed.

If Miss Ryan wouldn't talk to him—he suspected he was in for a battle on that front—there was always Mrs Adamson to weed it out of her.

Swiping his hat off the railing, Robert thanked the older man, left him to his assistant and makeshift bodyguard waiting with the horse and gig on the drive, and stepped back through the front door of his house.

The interior was a dark, cool and swift change from the bright April day outside, and it took him a few moments before his eyes cleared of the sunshine.

'It is a spider bite, he thinks,' he repeated absently to the silhouetted figure hovering a few feet ahead. 'Is she any improved?'

'No.' His housekeeper stepped closer, a curious look on her face. 'But then it is very early to expect such things.'

He knew that, he did, and he trusted the woman over just about anyone to do all that was necessary to make the girl better.

'I suppose you're right.' Passing her at a stride, he started in the direction of the sickroom, and then common sense finally caught up with him and he stopped still.

What had he been planning to do? Sit by her bedside? They were hardly on that level of familiarity.

Choosing to ignore Mrs Adamson's scarcely concealed amusement at his dithering, he grappled for something sensible to say.

'Miss Ryan's father died not long ago, correct?'

'Yes. It's been a couple of years now. The mother's gone, too.'

'And so ... who is it I am supposed to contact about her illness?'

He was beginning to think the answer to that question really was *nobody,* as he'd told Dunn, as surely she'd have been missed already if there was anyone to do the missing. There was the brother, but Robert had seen neither hide nor hair of the fellow for months, and he knew for a fact the town milkman's position, the occupation Ian Ryan had tried after he found farm work to be distasteful, had been reassigned some time ago.

'Since you booted the brother off Endmoor, best I can tell the girl has been pulling in most of the coin herself.'

'Are you saying I should have kept him on, Mary?'

It was more than a little rude to address her by her Christian name, but it was an immediate reaction to the stab of guilt he felt at her words.

'Lord, no. If you pay a man, then he ought to be doing the work in return for it, correct? I never saw that boy put in an effort for more than five minutes at a time. His head was full of dreams of excitement. Thought he was too good for farm work, that one did.'

Robert fiddled with the leather braiding on the hat in his hands.

'And in town? Who ought to be told about this?'

When the woman did not immediately answer, Robert felt a terrible ache on behalf of the girl. He looked towards the sickroom, lingering a moment as the events of the past few hours caught up with him.

'There must be someone.'

'Oh, there's always *someone.* It is only the Ryans seem to have a talent for dying young. Or disappearing, at the least,' she added in an undertone, eyes flicking briefly in the direction of the bedrooms.

Why had it never occurred to Robert that the sister might suffer for her brother's actions? She couldn't be very old, by the looks of her, but she was a young woman now, rather than the girl he'd stupidly thought she still was. It was a consequence of knowing her in passing for as long as he could recall that she'd gone and matured without his notice.

'Word will get around town soon enough,' Mrs Adamson said in what he supposed was a comforting tone. 'For the time being I've no plans to stray far from this house for any period of time. Not with bushrangers running riot in the countryside.'

Bushrangers ... apparently Mary Adamson was one Southern Tablelands resident who'd no issue with reviving a buried and fearful word.

Her piece said, she patted him on the arm and brushed by to continue with her chores, the true ruler of the house no matter what posture he assumed.

Completely unable to get on with his day as planned, Robert spent the next five minutes pacing distractedly in the library. There was plenty to do but it felt insensitive to even attempt it when he'd two invalids on his property. At any rate he was poised for the day's next drama, whatever it would be. There was little point even trying to concentrate on the minutiae of consolidating his papers.

His pacing took him by his desk with its documents full of graphs and notes on vinification lying in wait. It seemed to him the pile had grown since the day before, and it couldn't be put off for much longer.

After wasting another minute or two glaring at the work, and listening to the increasingly intrusive ticking of the clock on the mantle, he realised he wasn't alone in the room.

'Thank you for everything, John,' he murmured, turning to his friend. 'You'll be thoroughly fed up with the ride to and from town by this point.'

The fair-haired man made a dismissive gesture with his hand and stepped further in, not bothering to hide his amusement at Robert's mood.

'I'm glad of the exercise,' he said, and grinned. 'One tends to ride faster when they imagine a gang of highwaymen hot on their tail.'

Still agitated despite his best efforts, Robert grabbed a book off the nearest shelf at random and shifted it from one hand to the other.

'It feels redundant to stay here through the day when I won't achieve a thing.'

'You make a good point.'

Tutting at Robert's fidgeting, John relieved him of the tome. 'And yet you *will* stay close by, because you intend to protect the household.' He glanced down at the book in his hands, rose his eyebrows, and snorted. 'Really, Robert? *The Atrocities of a Convent?* Instead of working, you'll waste the day reading about randy nuns?'

'Believe me, John, you've spectacularly misinterpreted the title.'

'So it's about regular nuns? The type with the rosaries and the canes? No doubt it's as boring as every other religious work I've been unfortunate enough to cross paths with in my life. I misinterpreted it deliberately, of course.'

'How predictable of you,' Robert said. He hadn't a clue what the book was about, and had no plans to read it in the near future.

The other man pressed a hand to his chest. 'Predictable? You wound me.' He returned the book to its spot on the shelf, shaking his head in disappointment. 'Come on. We can't stand about in here all day without going at least half mad.'

They left the room together and turned towards the front door in silent mutual agreement. Once they were free of the house, Robert rested his hands on the veranda's rail.

'They'd be mad to remain in town, those thugs, whoever they are. Surely they know they're being hunted.'

'And I suppose the girl will know incriminating information of some sort.'

Robert was certain of it.

'Miss Ryan? I suppose so, and I intend to ask when I can.' *If* he could.

Unfortunately, and no matter what he thought of Alice Ryan, with each hour his suspicions about *Ian* Ryan's involvement in the night's dramas grew stronger. As long as the man could avoid the noose, he'd be looking for an easier—and more exciting—way to earn his keep than honest work.

'Want to make an attempt at checking the plans?' John asked. 'I've a sketch of a layout for the vines, if you're in a mood to see it.'

'Yes,' Robert said, pushing away from the ledge, 'Let's do that.'

Their path took them past the various buildings that surrounded the main house, the space eventually opening out onto an expanse of fields and the gentle rises of the mountains beyond. Merino sheep dotted the land, partially hidden behind the dry, yellowing grasses that grew in the region.

Sheep and wheat: the two mainstays of the tablelands.

An outbuilding up ahead was home to most of their recent work. The place, looking a little worse for wear now, was the original house built on the Farrers' newly acquired land when Robert was just a boy. It served as home while the homestead was being built, and even though it'd seemed a perfectly fine house to Robert in the past, now it seemed to shrink with each passing year.

He bent to pick up a rock from the middle of the worn gravel path and tossed it far out into the grass.

'The police seemed at least as excited about all of this as they were concerned,' John said as they neared the door. 'It seems that brawls at the tavern and the odd lost cow aren't excitement enough for the magistrate, but short of the two of us stalking the hills for unsavoury sorts, I doubt there's much else that can be done for the time being.'

For a good ten seconds Robert seriously considered doing just that, and then dismissed the idea. He needed to be close to his home, not off roaming the Brindabella Range on a wild-goose chase.

He looked out at the mountains. The bushland covering the far slopes was thick and largely untouched, and from where they stood the eucalypts turned everything a deep blue. They could track that land for weeks and never see another soul.

He sighed and walked on as John pressed a hand to the old house's door.

'Come on and look at the plans and tell me what a genius I am. And if all goes well for the rest of the day—God knows, it can't go worse—we might open that bottle of Château Margaux you've been saving.'

It was then, when Robert had one foot across the threshold and had turned to say something to his friend that he'd immediately forget, that the shout rang out and footsteps sounded behind them, heavy and pounding the ground as one of the stockmen called Robert's name.

The fellow, Harry, skidded to a stop on the path, breathing heavily, all frowns.

'What now?'

'Kicked the bucket,' the man managed, and Robert's heart leapt. He exchanged a glance with John.

'I beg your pardon?'

'Died,' the fellow said, as though the expression was beyond Robert's comprehension. 'Just now. Can't say I'm surprised.'

He had to ask; he didn't want to ask.

'Which one of them is dead?'

'The—what? Oh,' Harry said, realising what he'd *not* said, 'It's the chap, not the girl.'

Robert let out a short, sharp breath. 'What happened?'

The man jerked his head back in the direction of the staff quarters and pulled a face.

'He's ... well, he's dead, isn't he? Made this bloody awful sound—' the man paused to demonstrate, '—and then opened his eyes, and that was it. He was gone. Took us by surprise, it came on so fast.'

Robert could've done without the theatrics, and might've said so if he wasn't so busy silently chanting *it wasn't the Ryan girl who'd died. It wasn't her.*

'Well,' John said, his standard humour gone from his tone, 'I suppose this'll change our plans for the day. You'll want me riding back to town again now to notify the police and such. Let's call our business cancelled for the afternoon.' He began to button his coat.

Robert scrubbed a hand across his face. 'Thank you, and do *not* get yourself shot on the way.'

John inclined his head. 'I'll do my best.'

That decided, and the place in turmoil for the third time in half a day, Robert pivoted back towards the homestead as his friend once again left calling for his horse.

***

Well, she'd done it.

Alice had lasted as long as she bloody well could before the queasiness won over her stubbornness and she leaned over the bed to puke all over Mister Farrer's fine wooden floor. She'd had enough sense to try and miss the rug, but no strength left to check if she'd managed it.

A whole day, an entire night, and most of the day after had passed since she'd been dragged out of the bush by one of the fanciest men in the region, and she was obscenely grateful she'd not had to spend that time alone, terrified of her own shadow.

But now it was time to be gone, before any well-meaning person tried to make her stay on.

Vaguely, she was aware she'd won a victory over what'd seemed like certain death the morning before, but she was far too miserable right then to feel much in the way of triumph. Later, maybe, once she'd got herself out of the homestead and back on the road home she might feel gladder to still be alive. However she definitely needed fresh air and sunshine for such feelings, and the sickroom's curtains were pulled closed.

So instead she lay back, collapsed across the mattress, too miserable to be mortified, and too exhausted to call for help. Closing her eyes, she remembered too late that was what brought on swirls and sparks dancing in front of her vision, but opening them again seemed too hard. Instead she drifted, feeling like she was spinning in circles, and waited for someone to come and discover her sorry self.

It was terrible being so cold but so hot at the same time, and right before she was sick on the floor both her feet had ached for a reason she didn't understand—they still did. Actually, right then *all* of her ached.

One good thing had come of it: in her trip over the side of the bed she'd found her old boots, which were going to be needed when she made her escape.

And escape she would, because voices carried a long way in the country and she'd overheard more than enough talk since arriving at Endmoor to know she and Ian were in some bloody big trouble.

Death—*murder*—possibly a robbery or two. All of them hanging offences in New South Wales, and so far she'd not a clue if her brother was one of the dead, or one of the fellows who'd be headed to the noose just as soon as he was caught.

Any way it worked she was pretty sure she'd lose her home, small as it was. Maybe her cow and her chickens, too. She had a vague recollection of being told someone from Endmoor was looking after the animals for her, and she sure hoped they were going armed with something more than a kitchen knife.

Once again she patted the front of her frock, hand trembling with illness. The staff must all think her mad with fever but she'd argued hard and long to be allowed to keep her clothes on in bed, and so far nobody'd managed to wrestle her out of them.

If they saw that money she was hiding they might think she'd got it by illegal means. No, they'd *definitely* make assumptions she had.

The papers crinkled reassuringly and she let out a little sigh. She needed that cash more than ever if she was going to make a future for herself. It wasn't much but she worked hard and might find some decent employment. *Ryan* was a common enough name in the colonies, and if she headed north surely she'd be able to outrun a sullied reputation. It was a lucky thing she was good with a needle, as it'd provided her with an income during Ian's many absences.

'I can't stand this,' she announced to the ceiling, as she'd done more than once in the past day.

Soon, she promised herself. Any hour now she'd find the strength to get up and get out of the big, grand homestead unnoticed—and without puking again.

More voices floated towards her from another corner of the house. It was not that the property was loud as much as that it was populated. There always seemed to be something happening and someone around. Such a big house and yet every corner of it seemed to be busy. Something clattered, and she caught a whiff of ... food? And—

'Oh!' Alice's eyes shot open and she clamped her lips together as tightly as she could, holding her hand to her nose against the smell.

She focused intently on the painting on the wall opposite. It was one of those pictures of the countryside that people with money put in their houses, or so it seemed in Alice's limited experience. But to her eyes it was painted all wrong.

There was a town with a church—definitely not Barracks Flat or anywhere Alice'd ever been. The fields were a mad shade of green, and the sheep's faces were black. Who'd ever seen a sheep with a face that colour? She saw Robert Farrer's Merinos most days; she knew what a sheep looked like.

Cross with the artist's fantastical imagination, she struggled up onto her elbows to take a better look at it, and then she—

'Ah!' The sickness swept back up and took her by surprise.

She rolled onto her side in the hope of curling in a wretched ball, but forgot about her throbbing bite. A sob escaped as she rolled back, more carefully this time, and used what strength she had to get her foot back up on the pillow.

Five minutes, she decided. She'd give herself five minutes to recover and then she'd come up with a proper plan for her escape.

Time passed, and then more voices came—men's voices that were low, but loud in that way whispers sometimes were.

It was Robert Farrer speaking she decided, the fancy tone of his voice different to every other in the household.

The voice that responded was rougher, less refined, and far more Australian.

'We haven't had a murder out this way in a long time. Wonder if they'll do the hangin' out here or take it up north.'

Good God, had they caught a culprit already? Alice pushed herself up onto her elbows. Was it Ian—please, please not Ian.

Could she let her brother hang if he was guilty?

The voices trailed off into the distance, and Alice was so busy fretting she didn't notice Mrs Adamson until she was in the room.

'Oh dear,' the housekeeper said, taking in the sorry situation. 'I left the bell there for you to use when you needed it—and no, don't you dare open that mouth to tell me again you don't want to be a bother.'

With deft, impersonal assessment, the woman ascertained what needed doing and called for Bessie and a bucket of water.

Good Lord, this was embarrassing. Alice rested the back of her wrist over her eyes.

'I'm sure I'm dyin', Mrs Adamson.'

There was a pause, and then the splash of water on the side table, and her hand was carefully removed and a cool cloth wiped across her forehead.

'No, you're not. As long as you can tell me you're dying, then you've the energy to stay alive.'

Well, that might've been the truth, but it didn't mean Alice didn't *feel like* dying right about then. She wouldn't, though. She had a relation to find and strangle some sense into before the authorities got to him.

'I'll clean it,' she protested when Bessie, a maid a few years older than she was, came back into the room, bucket sloshing.

'You certainly will not. You'll stay as you are and rest.'

'Oh, all right, but this is mortifyin',' she said in a meek voice, making the other two laugh.

Trapped. She was well and truly trapped for another whole day, she thought with more misery than before. As the people around her fussed and fixed and cleaned she felt the weakness pulling at her again.

But when she went to sleep it was with a plan forming in her mind.

Chapter 4

By the end of the second day of the Ryan girl in his home, Robert was giving up on propriety and made his way to the sickroom.

Something the whole lot of them had learnt over the course of thirty-six hours was that it was impossible to sustain the sort of fear and suspicion they'd all felt the morning before. No matter what else happened in the region, the animals still needed tending, the housework still needed doing, and the accounts still needed attention. With the dead—and still unidentified—man's body taken into the care of the police magistrate in town, there were a great many questions that needed answering, but for the time being, they all had to wait.

Another day was drawing to an end with an orange-tinged sky and a growing chill in the air, and Robert was glad to be stepping inside for the first time in many hours.

Perhaps Miss Ryan needed something. It had to have been half a day since he'd heard anything of her, and it was possible she'd been forgotten in the hive of activity around the estate since the drama began.

He was halfway to her temporary room when he heard the distinct splash of water in a bucket coming directly towards him and he ducked into the shadows of the nearest doorway. Bessie, cast all in silhouettes, emerged from a room, bucket clasped in both hands, and then rounded a corner, taking herself towards the back of the house, none the wiser she'd an audience.

Robert stepped back out into the hall.

'Good God,' he muttered, embarrassed with himself. What kind of man was caught slinking around the halls of his own home?

***

When he was certain the servants were all gone from neighbouring nooks and crannies, he gripped the handle of the partially open sickroom door and slipped partway inside.

Silence greeted him, though the air was full enough that he knew Miss Ryan was not only there, but alive and better than she'd been the day before. Embers from the recently stoked fire cast the space in a dim golden glow, the warmth of it in stark contrast to the increasingly foggy land beyond the shuttered windows, and it revealed the steady rise and fall of the blankets covering her.

All was well, then. Robert felt better for seeing it with his own two eyes instead of learning it from others' reports. He could go, then, and be satisfied if she was asleep.

At the last moment instinct had him turning back and stepping a little closer. Miss Ryan was not asleep after all.

Just as he'd suspected.

Though her eyes seemed colourless, their grey-blue indiscernible, in the shadowy room, he still felt that wary, near defiant stare as she took his measure—or so that seemed to be what she was doing, despite her illness and submissive position on the bed.

'Are you perhaps a little better?' His voice sounded rough in the heavy air between them.

She seemed to consider the question carefully before answering.

'Well, I'm not dead yet,' was the response he eventually received, and he fought against a smile.

'No, I can see that. Please, try and stay that way.'

The snort that it earned him was anything but ladylike, but it did coax his smile all the way out.

Again, he began to retreat from the room, feet dragging for a number of reasons.

He wanted to ask her questions; no, he had to leave the room. Working class or not, she was still a young lady and he a man who'd no place in there.

'Sir?'

Robert paused, turned back, raising his brows in query.

'It weren't just two of 'em out there in the bush. I dunno how many there were, but more than two.'

'You knew them?' Surely it wasn't this easy to get the facts out of her. He'd been prepared for a battle.

She *barely* hesitated before answering, but it was still a hesitation.

'Can't say. I reckon they were drunk. And I bet they weren't so interested in me as in money. I'd say they were idiots for pickin' me—*my* house out for that.'

If she wasn't so ill, Robert suspected she would've laughed at her own comment.

'Someone died here yesterday,' she continued. A statement, not a question.

Another young lady and Robert might have lied. 'They did. Who told you?'

'I've a fat ankle, not deaf ears. If it were a secret, I'd say you all ought to speak more quietly.'

Oh dear.

Robert glanced over his shoulder at the empty hall and then folded his arms.

'Yes, someone died. So far we don't know who he is.'

'And they've arrested someone else?' She sounded sleepy, but content to continue the discussion.

'Yes. Another man whose identity we still don't know.'

He didn't miss her audible breath at that little piece of news.

She shifted to look at him more squarely, and immediately winced.

'Don't move on my account. You need to rest and get better.'

Of course she shifted anyway, and Robert winced with her the second time.

'The rest of those men wouldn't be stupid enough to stay about these parts, right? They'd be on to Captains Flat or Goulburn or even Cooma by now.'

Those light, feverish eyes probed his hopefully. 'Am I right?'

Oh, she certainly wanted to be right, he could see that.

'You may be. Until then, we'll stay cautious.'

He hadn't a clue if he'd reassured her or not, but she closed her eyes then, and Robert stood there an unaccountably long while—obscenely long, if he were thinking straight. It was rude on his part, but he was taking stock of Ian Ryan's sister as her own person for the first time.

He wondered when Miss Alice Ryan had gone from the girl he used to pass on the town road—all plaited hair and big eyes, staring at him as if he were a prince rather than a mere landowner—to ... this...

Good God, he supposed he'd changed a great deal in the past five or so years, too. He'd buried himself in his work on purpose, needing the distraction.

A bark from one of the dogs drew him back to himself, and he went in search of his evening meal.

Later, he would realise he should've been more interested in the fact the invalid was wearing her day dress, clearly poking out in various places from the blankets.

***

Robert hardly slept. He made a go of it sometime long after the household had settled for the night. But there wasn't much point trying when each rustle of a branch in the breeze outside had him assuming the worst, and so his mind refused to settle.

He was beyond the point of tiredness, and had entered that odd state where the more his body demanded rest, the more alert he became. Not even the wine at dinner had helped dull his senses. Frustrated, he flipped onto his stomach, and then onto his back once more. The high-pitched cries of a colony of Chiroptera crossed the sky.

'Bloody bats,' he said to the ceiling. The creatures had been scared inland years earlier, back when he was a boy and summer fires took over the coast. There was no getting rid of them now.

He cast his senses out, listening for anything out of the ordinary. He was acutely aware of the guest in his house, and of the otherwise emptiness of the place, with his sister away in the city for so long. At night the distance from town always seemed so much greater.

In his youth the bush had been both exciting and terrifying. The threat of animals so alien to him after the squirrels and otters of Cumberland was adventure enough in those first weeks in New South Wales. Learning what creatures' bites would cause death, and which would only cause a temporary but unholy pain, was a process of trial and error—and sheer luck on his family's part.

Then there were the floods and the fires. The dry winters and sudden frosts that killed off most of what they planted, and the droughts and the extreme heat in the summer months. They were all threats in their own way, especially when a man relied on the land to make his fortune.

What he wouldn't give for a threat like that now instead of those that they faced; a challenge he could understand and tackle with confidence.

Despite everything, and unlike his parents, who'd sensed danger at every turn in New South Wales and been happy to return to England, after only a few weeks in Australia, Robert had felt he belonged.

Distracted, and fully awake, he considered the days-old newspaper on the desk near the lamp, and then discarded it. He didn't need news of the panic arriving from South Australia and across the Tasman Sea. The so-called *Russian scare* striking fear into people all over the colonies—as far as New Zealand—looked like it would amount to nothing, despite plans to build fortifications along the coast just in case.

For the time being he had enough immediate problems.

Groaning loudly as sleep continued to elude him, Robert tucked both his hands behind his head and settled in for a long, dull night.

***

'What are you doing?'

Alice nearly clean jumped out of her skin at the sound of a man's voice behind her. She whipped round on unsteady feet, a hand pressed to her chest. The papers crinkled, and she waited in dreadful anticipation, certain the man behind her had heard.

'Lord,' she said when she recognised the fellow. Young for a butler, with the hair to match his name, Albert Brown's present expression made him look more like a schoolteacher than the boy whose bare arse she'd seen a time he'd swum in the Murrumbidgee only a few years before.

She strove to collect herself. 'Don't scare me like that, Bertie.'

She straightened to her not considerable height while he winced at the childhood name, trying, *trying* to look innocent, as though it was perfectly normal for an invalid to be creeping out the door at daybreak.

'I'll see you later,' she said when he didn't make a grab for her, injecting as much confidence as she could into her voice. Turning to continue on her way, she silently prayed that he wouldn't do anything rash like ... slide neatly in front of her to block her way.

Bertie raised an eyebrow at her, and Alice wished she weren't so small.

'Where are you going with your foot like that?' he asked, but she knew he knew.

She sighed, and—despite her best intentions of looking strong—reached out to use the small hall table for balance. That awful pain in her leg was back again, even if the puking had stopped, thank God.

'I'm goin' home,' she informed him in the strongest voice she could muster. 'And I'd thought to do it before the whole household caught me makin' an escape.'

At the risk of toppling over with dizziness, she let go of the table and held her arms out for inspection. 'I've not taken anythin' that's not mine, if you're worried.'

Her piece said, the weakness came back in a surge and she got a hold of that table again.

Bertie's face dropped and he gave her an odd look. 'I know that, Miss Alice.'

He might have said more had he not swivelled at the sound of a clatter some distance from them, in a different part of the house. The place was already coming to life for the day, which meant the escape plan was already beginning to unravel.

Alice took advantage of the butler's moment of distraction and shoved away from the table and towards the front door. The pain streaked up her leg sharply, and she almost turned back and begged her reluctant pursuer to carry her off to the nearest bed.

But no. She wasn't the responsibility of any of these people, and she was likely putting them in some danger, and she had to find Ian ... somehow...

When she was home she'd be shoving the old trunk in front of the door and sleeping with the fire poker next to the bed, but it was all right. She'd a strong enough arm to whack an intruder pretty well, she reckoned. It couldn't be much different to chopping wood.

Cool air met her when she stepped outside, and she grimaced as she made her way down the few steps to the ground. Turning carefully, like a drunkard pretending to be sober, she faced the butler once more. He watched her warily from the top of the steps.

'Bertie, will you do a favour for me?'

'Of course,' he said, hovering with his hands half extended her way, like he might grab her, given the opportunity.

'Will you wait ten minutes before you go runnin' to tell them I've made me escape?'

He grumbled something she was probably lucky not to hear, and then he got that stern look again.

'Of *course* you'd ask for that.'

'Will you? Promise?'

He grumbled under his breath again and then nodded jerkily. 'All right.'

'Thank you,' she said, and set off.

When Alice next looked over her shoulder he was still there, holding his ground, but at least he hadn't run off to tattle yet.

'All right,' she muttered through gritted teeth as she put her mind to getting one foot in front of the next. Gravel shifted with each step. 'Good.'

It would've been better if she'd asked Bertie for half an hour to make her getaway, because she was certain somebody had doubled the length of the drive overnight. Even reaching the end of the carriage loop seemed an exhausting improbability.

Alice's vision narrowed, her belly roiled, and the impossibility of making a speedy getaway was made clear to her with utter, miserable clarity.

'Bloody rich people and their big houses,' she muttered, but it did nothing to distract her from the sharp burning in her ankle.

Once more, she glanced over her shoulder, dismayed to see how little progress she'd made. Her leg nearly gave way on the next step, and she said something vile no lady would ever have heard before, angry and irritable as she was.

Maybe she ought to have requested *two hours* to flee.

***

After passing into an exhausted doze somewhere between midnight and first light, Robert found himself up and about far earlier than he needed to be, uncertain if he'd slept more than mere minutes at any point. He washed and dressed quickly, not bothering to stoke up the fire against the slight chill the sun was yet to chase from the air, and then made his way quietly past the other bedrooms.

His sister Elizabeth's stood empty and silent. She'd been gone to Sydney several months, enjoying the society Barracks Flat would never provide, and Robert was loath to call her back.

The gurgle of a magpie outside signalled the day had begun, but the dimness held and the private rooms of the homestead stayed silent.

Too silent.

Stopping in his tracks, Robert listened hard—*harder.* Suspicion growing, he doubled back and stopped outside the third of the rooms, the one he'd left Miss Alice Ryan in two mornings earlier.

He paused at the closed door, straining to hear, not wanting to make a grave mistake and intrude.

However...

He rested his hand on the doorknob and grimaced as he eased it, opening the door the smallest of cracks. Cool air greeted him, as if the fire had been all but extinguished some time ago. He saw the foot of the bed and the blanket folded neatly on the end of it. Odd; he'd have thought Mrs Adamson would have it tucked all around the girl if—

Suspicion gave way to certainty and he stepped fully into the room.

There was no body silhouetted under the covers, not even the small figure of Alice Ryan. There was nobody in the room at all.

'Oh, bloody hell.'

Whirling, Robert strode down the corridor, glancing into darkened rooms as he searched the house in a hurry, knowing full well he'd not find her there.

He brushed by a sleepy and very surprised Mrs Adamson as he rushed for the front door.

Pausing again on the carriage drive, he wondered if the girl was mad enough to attempt a walk home along the town road. He couldn't shake the gnawing fear she'd have come face to face with the very people he'd kept her at his home to protect her from.

The gravel of the drive crunched under his feet as he strode past rosebushes and sun-bleached lawns in the direction of the gate.

If he could catch her before she reached the—

'Here. I'm here.'

The voice stopped him in his speedy tracks, and he looked incredulously at a particularly large wattle bush to the right of the drive.

Mildly amused, mildly concerned, and just a tad frustrated, he rounded the plant and caught his first glimpse of Alice Ryan's fair hair, braided down her back and shimmery in the morning light.

'Miss Ryan?'

One of those boots of hers was tied firmly on her foot. The other sat beside her while her bandaged ankle poked out from the end of her grey skirts.

'My *God,* what were you thinking to be out here at this hour?'

He knelt beside her on the grass and ran his eyes over his wayward invalid, wondering if she'd collected any more injuries in the thirty or so yards she'd travelled between his door and his garden. He saw no new wear or tear, but her pale face was twisted just a bit with pain.

'Has anything else happened to you?' he asked, just to be certain.

'Other than a cold bum?' she responded tartly, surprising a bark of laughter out of him. 'It's damp out here this mornin' and you took your good time comin' to find me.'

'Oh, *forgive me,*' he rejoined with the best gallant bow he could manage from his position on the ground. Come to think of it, his knees were beginning to soak through. It was their first truly dewy morning of the season.

'I thought you were in the middle of a breakout,' he continued. 'Generally escapees don't wish to be found in the middle of such things.'

She snorted at that but said nothing more, avoiding his eyes with what he decided was an appropriate amount of guilt.

A noise reached Robert's ears then, the distinct sound of a horse's footfalls breaking the stillness of the morning and coming their way. But where else would a rider be headed so far out? He tensed on instinct, but there was no great speed to the animal's gait, and it was a single rider by the sounds of it.

He touched Miss Ryan's shoulder.

'Stay put a moment. Can you manage that?'

She met his eyes with that request—that *order*—and her own flashed back at him. Wisely, however, she merely nodded.

Slowly, Robert rose and then groaned aloud as he recognised two things at once: the great, black mount, a fortune in horseflesh—only one man in the district purchased anything and everything based on looks and expense.

He hardly needed to see the slightly stocky, upright posture of the rider—a man past his prime but with more than enough confidence to disguise it—to know that his morning had just become rather a lot more complicated.

Bloody hell.

Horse and rider were still only at the gate; perhaps he could get Miss Ryan back inside before they were discovered. Bar the priest himself, there was nobody within a fifty-mile radius who he'd rather have been caught by in that moment.

He bent to her again, trying to disguise his urgency.

'Can you put your arms around my neck? Yes, like that.'

She wasn't much to lift, and he had her up, in his arms and headed towards the house within moments. And all the while he carried her he felt her wary gaze.

'I'll have you know, I'd already decided to turn back before you got here.'

'Turn back?' he asked with an arched brow, not quite willing to believe it.

'I was plannin' on getting back in the house before anybody noticed ...

this...' she unwound an arm from his neck to wave a hand at herself.

Twice more she started to speak, and then stopped. Just when he was about to ask her what the issue was, she said her piece.

'I didn't nick the silver or anythin', in case you're worried.'

'It never even occurred to me you would.'

She scoffed her disbelief, and Robert belatedly remembered the family she'd sprung from.

'It truly didn't,' he insisted.

The *clop, clop, clop* of the horse's hooves seemed to echo around the morning.

'Is your leg all right?' He kept his voice even, casual. They were at the stairs to the veranda now and Robert started up them.

'It's been better. But it's also been worse.'

'And no doubt it would have been better still if you'd not taken yourself out for a stroll before sunrise.'

She was not feverish and shivering now, not as she'd been two days before. Her heavy sigh though ... It spoke of someone carrying a big burden.

The horse had reached the top of the drive by the sounds of it; Robert could all but feel the breath of the beast on the back of his neck.

He wouldn't be fast enough. He was well aware of it.

Old Adamson, still tucking his clothing more or less into place, emerged from the back of the house in a hurry to meet their premature guest and his ride. He looked Robert's way sharply as he passed, but Robert hardly needed the warning.

He stepped over the threshold and into the still-darkened house. It was straight back to the sickroom for Miss Ryan, and Robert made a point of tucking that extra blanket about her as though it would help to keep her in place.

He made an attempt at stoking up the fire but in his rush it was a lost cause. He'd have to call a maid to do a better job of it.

'I'm fine,' the invalid in question said from the bed, sounding better than she had only moments earlier. He turned to a face that was all wide eyes and worry.

'Go an' greet your guest.'

He moved closer to the bed.

'You'll stay put this time? At least until we can discuss our situation?'

She seemed to give it some thought and, amused despite himself, Robert resisted telling her the choice was already out of her hands.

'All right. I'll wait a bit. Don't think I've the energy for two escapes in one mornin', anyway.'

Robert smiled slightly at the grudging admission, and—barely—resisted the urge to brush a few freed strands of hair back from her forehead. He watched as she carefully grasped her lower leg and moved herself into a more comfortable position, and then he walked to the door, pausing just a moment to deliver his rebuttal.

'Miss Ryan, you didn't even have the energy to escape *once*.'

***

Robert left her to the care of Mrs Adamson, who was bustling her way down the hall, looking harried for once as she hastily tied on an apron and ducked into the bedroom to watch over the runaway.

Bracing himself for the worst, he made his way back through the house to greet his unwelcome and supremely early guest ... He all but skidded to a stop when he found Tom Wright—rich, pompous, unwelcome Tom Wright—had already invited himself inside.

For a long beat the two men simply watched each other, neither one willing to give in first. There was far too much bad blood between them for that.

'I'd heard rumours,' the older man finally said, in that rough voice of his that would never carry the lofty tones he aimed for, eyes giving nothing and everything away at the same time.

Robert kept his shoulders squared and waited for the inevitable.

The older man's pale eyes fixed squarely on him. 'It's disappointing to discover they're true.'

Chapter 5

Robert would not admit guilt when there was none to be had. He would *not.* However, there was a world of suspicion and—yes—triumph within the glint in the other man's eyes, evident even in the low light. If Robert knew one thing about Tom Wright it was that he'd never pass up an opportunity to work a situation to his advantage.

'You felt the need to come here at dawn? Is there an emergency I'm unaware of? The roads are dangerous, Tom. I'd not be out alone at the moment, no matter how well-armed you are, nor how fast your mount.'

Wright's mouth thinned at the dual insult of his questioned ability to protect himself *and* the use of his Christian name, but Robert would not apologise to a fellow who'd had no trouble delivering thinly veiled insults in their shared past.

The man glanced beyond Robert, blue eyes flicking with something calculating. Instinctively Robert moved away from the door, drawing his investor's attention away from the hall.

'There's nothing more to worry about.' Wright dismissed the danger with a wave of his hand. 'They've caught the third chap responsible for that business. He was hiding down by the tributary, looking like he was running south to Heaven only knows where. That's all there is to it, and we've more important business that can't wait.'

Well. This was big news.

'When was he found?' Robert wouldn't dismiss things so easily.

'Overnight, it seems. One of the landowners to the south of town was concerned about a campfire on the edge of his land—the area is a big bloody tinder box right now, what with the drought.'

'As I well know.' Robert shuddered to consider what might happen to his own property—and to the town itself, for that matter—if a fire was left untended, or the man who started it failed to fully extinguish the embers. They'd had close calls in the past.

Again, the older man looked to the hall, another silent message Robert was struggling to understand. Surely Miss Alice Ryan went beneath his notice or care; God knew the man considered even Robert himself to be of little consequence.

'They're certain there was just one other involved? It seems odd for one to turn on the other. Nobody I know of has reported a theft, so it can't have been over money.'

He received a disinterested shrug for that. 'Young chaps. They don't change, and now none of them will grow up enough to prove me wrong.'

'You mean he'll hang? Charged with murder, I suppose?'

'Seems pretty cut and dried to me.'

The fog of the morning was lifting rapidly, and sunlight streamed in through the window, defiantly hotter than it ought to be by that time of year. Robert couldn't understand the cause of it, but he had the feeling he was on the edge of something monumental.

'Of course, when the railway reaches us we'll all but have wiped out bushrangers,' Wright continued, pulling Robert back from scattered thoughts of a ragamuffin in the bush.

'They're hoping it'll be here by Eighty-Seven,' Wright was saying. 'I reckon it's optimistic, but they're laying those tracks faster than I initially gave them credit for.'

Things were changing, but the Molonglo and Murrumbidgee River regions were the end of the line at the moment, quite literally. Things in the region would change fast only two years from now.

'It's a good deal harder to rob a speeding train than a stagecoach. However,' Robert crossed his arms, 'this news alone didn't drag you out this way at this hour.'

There was a telling pause.

'No. No, it did not. I'm off for Captains Flat after here, but I thought it was my duty to stop and tell you what's happening in town.'

'There's more?' Robert frowned. This was becoming absurd all around. However, the frown was swept right off his face a moment later when Wright grimaced.

'There've been...' the man paused for obvious dramatic effect. 'People are curious what all this is about with the girl you've got stashed in the house.'

'I beg your pardon?' As confused as he was annoyed at the turn of the conversation, Robert did his best to explain himself, feeling far more like a chastised child than he ought to a man who certainly had no claims as his father.

'For the love of God, Robert,' Wright interrupted eventually. 'What were you thinking with Elizabeth away? You had to know there'd be talk.'

'I was thinking I'd rather not leave a girl to die alone in the bush.'

This was madness. He was hardly a man known for debauchery, and even if he was, it was nothing of the other man's business.

'What is this really about, Tom?'

Eyebrows rose slightly at the repeated casual address, but Robert hadn't the time or patience for games.

Wright lowered his voice. 'People're bound to talk when there's an unmarried girl living in your house.'

'For only *two nights?*'

'It's more than that, though. Nobody can say how long she's been living here. Some're saying it's much longer than a night or two.'

'That's ridiculous. Total nonsense.' Robert had a fair idea of who was behind these lies. And behind his calm façade, he was fuming.

'The truth doesn't really matter when people's imaginations've run away with them.'

'These rumours were started by whom?' Robert ground out, even though he knew—yes, *he knew.*

The culprit in question fiddled with a sleeve, checked his pocket watch, and then shrugged with a great deal of nonchalance.

'Small communities. You know how these things happen.'

Indeed he was aware. Robert knew that Tom Wright was delighting in this, that he had devoted half his life to bullying his way to the top of the pecking order. If he wanted the people of Barracks Flat to believe Robert had taken a mistress in the form of a poor young neighbour, he'd manage to convince enough of the community for serious damage to be done.

The question was *why.*

Despite his substantial property and family standing, and his admirably close ties to England, Robert wasn't the one holding all the cards here. He wasn't the richest man in town—he was probably the second or third. What he was missing was the clout to get his and John's burgeoning winemaking enterprise off the ground. It was the only reason he didn't speak his mind freely then, as he was twitching and clamouring to do.

Instead, he took a few steadying breaths, looked beyond the man to the promisingly bright day outside, and then forced himself to meet Wright's eyes again.

'What would it take to end these stories being spread, whatever they are?'

Another nonchalant shrug.

'A man might do the honourable thing and save the girl's reputation.'

A charged silence stretched between them. *Good God.* There was no doubt the man was serious. And flirting with insanity.

'That's absurd, Tom. She's a simple invalid, living in a household that—may I remind you—already includes a *female* housekeeper, and will soon be overseen by my sister.'

'Your sister Elizabeth?' the other man said with some incredulity. 'She's in Sydney with my daughter, as you well know.'

'Not for long. She's on her way home as we speak.' A lie but a necessary one.

Wright grunted and shifted his weight.

'Then I'll look forward to seeing her again. My Martha will stay on in town, of course.'

'Of course.'

The man's only daughter wouldn't dare defy her father on anything. She'd stay in the city and better herself in better society whether she liked it or not.

'I'll be off then. It's going to be a long day out and back.'

Wright extended his hand, clasping Robert's tightly enough in warning it was all Robert could do to not roll his eyes, and then brushed by him.

'This whole situation is suspicious. It doesn't look good for investors,' he delivered as a parting shot, which seemed more to Robert like a nail in the coffin.

It was only when he heard hooves on the drive that Robert groaned aloud, barely resisting the urge to smash something. He had to get to town and telegram his sister before his whole bloody business plan crumbled out from under him.

***

'She calls Albert *Bertie,*' Elizabeth told him a week later.

They finally had a moment alone after the initial chaos of Robert's sister's return. Elizabeth was now pottering about, settling herself back into the house and dividing and ordering her purchases, some of which would go to the new Salvation Army outpost in town.

'*Bertie,*' she repeated as she inspected a blank canvas, shaking her head in bemusement.

His sister had a talent for painting, such as her opportunities were where they lived. It would be a long time—if ever—before Barracks Flat would be known for the arts, but Elizabeth persisted with her passion, producing works worthy of more than the walls of Endmoor.

Even with materials and training in short supply where they lived, nature could not have provided better inspiration.

Robert found himself fighting yet another smile. He was feeling oddly transformed in recent days, despite everything that was going wrong. 'I know she does. I suspect it drives the fellow mad, but he's far too amiable to say as much.'

Elizabeth grinned back at him and held up her hands: *what can one do?*

'He does not seem offended by it, only mildly ... resigned to his fate.'

It was approval Robert heard in her voice, for more than just the silly name, and he all but sagged in relief. He hadn't truly thought Elizabeth would insist on the removal of their houseguest, but it was good to be certain all the same.

Miss Ryan was better. She'd been improved enough she could have returned home days ago, but nobody—not even Alice—was denying there was still danger around them. She'd seemed as unconvinced about the matter of the outlaws being resolved as Robert was. Even so, he'd been mildly surprised she'd accepted his offer to stay on a little longer so readily.

Elizabeth gestured at a vase that'd appeared in the corner not long after Miss Ryan's first, and thankfully only, attempt to bolt from his house, filled now with late autumn blooms in a violent shade of crimson, dotted with red berries.

'While I've no complaints about my own education, she certainly knows more about the garden than I do.'

'That couldn't be true. You're always out and about—'

'I only *paint* nature, Robert. I wouldn't be surprised if Alice could tell you all the Latin names for those,' she pointed at the vase, 'and no doubt how to grow them to perfection. Lord only knows where she learnt so much. You'd best watch out for that one; she seems to absorb facts without even knowing she's done it.'

While Robert considered that and decided it was likely the truth, his sister went back to her unpacking.

'You might think I've overspent,' she said to him over her shoulder, perhaps in reaction to his silence. 'However I've been frugal.'

A stray curl of hair the colour of his own slipped about her shoulder, drawing his attention to her gown. Dark in colour, he realised it was one he'd seen before, not the newest Sydney fashion.

'I'm not the least surprised. We're doing well enough, Elizabeth; I'd not have worried if you'd come home with more.'

For all of a moment a cloud passed over his sister's face.

'What is it?'

'Nothing, truly nothing.' But her hastily bit lower lip told him otherwise.

Voices from elsewhere in the house had them both turning guiltily to check if they'd been overheard. After several moments' stillness they resumed their discussion.

'She'll need things,' Robert said, turning to practical matters and realising he was floundering. 'I—uh, I am not sure what those things are. Things women need. Clothes and such.'

The words earned him a sudden grin.

'Oh, it's a *very* good thing I've returned, I'd say. *Clothes and such,*' Elizabeth muttered, and bit her lip again, this time—he was sure—to hold back a laugh. 'I take it that means she's staying on?'

He hadn't a clue. 'For the time being, yes. She has an absconded brother I'm almost certain is involved in the recent crimes around here, and a rundown cottage to get through the winter in on her own. It feels wrong to send her on her way.'

Elizabeth touched one of the berries in the floral arrangement.

'And how do you think she will react to being kept?'

'*Being kept?*'

Christ. Even his sister was making it sound like he'd a mistress. His words must have come out harsher than he intended, however, because he drew her attention back to his face.

'I only meant she strikes me as extremely independent. The present danger, though...'

'I shouldn't have asked you home at this time,' he admitted. It'd been done in a panic, in the short space of time between Tom Wright's visit to deliver barely veiled threats and the moment he'd spoken to Alice Ryan again, the worry in her eyes convincing him the danger was far from over.

'Oh, nonsense. I'm here in one piece, am I not? And I've had my fill of the city for the time being.'

'I suspect she *is* a little scared to go home,' he said pensively.

'As she ought to be.'

Robert glanced at the flowers again. 'Perhaps I'll employ her as my gardener if she demands a reason to be here.'

'You could do worse.'

'I'll leave you to it,' Robert told his sister, 'and see you soon for dinner.'

***

'I feel like I shouldn't be takin' any steps in it in case I ruin it.'

Alice felt like a princess all dressed up in someone else's frock, but she knew better than to say so; Miss Farrer'd implied more than once it wasn't anything fancy.

'Clothing is made to be worn,' Robert's pretty sister pointed out, and tugged at something at the back of the gown, drawing excess fabric out of the way.

At least the colour was practical, Alice supposed. It was a shade somewhere between moss green and bronze, something dark enough for her to wear without ruining it too fast. It reminded her of the colours of the bush. The fabric shone a bit, and made a *swishing* noise when she moved—she'd never worn anything special enough to do that before.

Even though the mirror in the bedroom was far bigger than she was accustomed to, Alice wished it to be longer still so that she could see her reflection top to toes. She felt like the bloody Queen, and wanted to smooth her palms down the silk skirt but dared not.

Eyeing Mr Farrer's sister surreptitiously, she tried out the lady's name in her mind. *Elizabeth.* Well, there were plenty of Elizabeths around, but Alice wasn't sure she'd be fine with calling this one by her Christian name just yet. She'd been invited to do so, but she struggled with it.

Elizabeth held herself in a way that stirred up one of Alice's few memories of her mother. *Sit straight and shoulders back,* she'd tell her when she was a girl, but it was never a scold. They'd played princesses together even though it was ridiculous.

'I doubt there's any damage you could inflict on it that couldn't be fixed,' Miss Farrer said with confidence.

Alice plucked reluctantly at a tiny corner of the fabric and grimaced.

'You'd be surprised what I can do.'

That earned her a chuckle, but then Miss Farrer immediately sobered while she studied Alice from one end to the other.

'It's a little long in the skirt, but that can be easily adjusted. The colour is lovely on you, better for you than for me. Yes,' she nodded and moved to the pile of gowns on the edge of the bed, 'that one will do. Let's see what else I can find.'

'But ... what for? This frock won't survive milkin' the cow, and I've a dress good enough for church already. Not that I'm ungrateful, but...'

She trailed off and dared to touch a deep blue ribbon that lay atop a pile of others in every colour. She straightened it out, letting the silky coolness send little bumps across her forearms. In amongst the ribbons were a few scraps of lace much finer than Alice had ever had a need of.

Mister Farrer's sister brushed by to pick up another frock and give it a good looking at.

'You ought to have more than one thing to wear if you're to stay.'

Alice's head snapped up.

'If I'm to...? I beg your pardon, Miss Farrer, but I'm goin' home soon. Tomorrow,' she decided immediately. 'I should've gone back already.'

Instead of trying on things she had no business wearing, she should be shoving her fear aside and being brave enough to head home.

'Um, you might want to talk to Robert about that. I was given the impression you'd be here a little longer. It was the reason he called me home, I am certain of it.'

'Because I need chaperonin'?' Alice laughed up at the ceiling rose. The mere idea of it...

And then she abruptly stopped when she realised she was laughing on her own. Confused, she gently touched the silk of the skirts again. Elizabeth briefly rested a hand on her forearm, drawing her attention again.

'My brother is *not* happy about you being on your own yet, not considering the crimes that have happened in the region. And we all need clothing, and I've more than enough to share. Luckily we are close enough in size.'

In fact Alice looked weedy and rather short next to Miss Farrer, but she wasn't mentioning it if the lady wasn't.

'I can't just sit here in this house, doin' nothin'—*nothing.* It's more than charity; it's ridiculous.'

'Well, funny you should mention it. If you're willing, our garden has been awfully neglected. It wouldn't be charity to have you work on it during the day, in exchange for a place to sleep at night. At least until we know you'll be safe in your home,' she coaxed, perhaps sensing Alice weakening at the thought.

All the things she could do with the Endmoor land ... It wouldn't be work. It'd be a gift.

'Oh, I wouldn't dare. And I doubt your brother'd agree,' Alice said, even though she was already taken by the idea. What she might do with the better soil—not rocky and dry like over at the cottage—it was so tempting.

'Yes,' Miss Farrer replied after a moment's smiling consideration, 'I believe he would.'

She returned her attention to Alice's dress, speaking in a deliberately casual voice as she did something with the overlong hem.

'Do you have any other family around? Other than your brother? Or perhaps a friend who is like family?'

'I know people.' Alice knew everyone, really, which was how things went when a girl lived in a small community. Too many of her childhood playmates had married or moved on to other towns for employment, and in the past two years her life had become one of isolated hard work.

'I help Mrs Hobson down at the shop sometimes.' As Miss Farrer would know, being an occasional customer.

They both dropped the conversation then because a figure—a tall and dark-haired and well-dressed figure—had stirred from the doorway.

Robert Farrer took in her improved appearance, and she was *not* going to imagine it was approval in his eyes, no matter that she wanted it to be. His dark eyes met hers then, and his face relaxed into something that was almost a smile.

'Come for a walk with me,' he said.

Silence reverberated around the room, and it took Alice a long few seconds to realise he was asking *her*, not his sister—or not even her *and* his sister.

'I beg your pardon?'

He offered an elbow in invitation, like they might stroll down the corridor arm in arm.

'A walk. You assure me you've recovered, and it's a beautiful afternoon.'

She stared uncomprehendingly. 'Why?'

He smiled outright. 'Why not?'

'I can't walk in this frock yet. It's too long.' She lifted the skirts a little to demonstrate, saw his attention drawn to the ankles he'd already once had a bloody good look at up close, and quickly dropped the fabric back into place.

'Then wear your other. Will you come?'

Painfully aware of the rapt attention of Miss Farrer, and also of her idiotic belly that was doing flips of girlish excitement, she forced herself to stand straight and sound normal.

'All right. But first I need to change.'

Chapter 6

They went in a gig most of the way, which hardly classified as a walk, but Robert was uneasy with Miss Ryan—*Alice, if you can manage it,* as she'd told him more than once—on foot.

His travelling companion said little on the trip out, which was not the usual way of things with her, but Robert did not try to force conversation.

The road was a rather rocky, uneven one, still only used by locals out of necessity. They bounced along in the little vehicle, with *Alice* dutifully snapping her leg back whenever a rut bumped it his way. It was a sunny day, warm, even. His companion resorted to covering her eyes with her hand when her tiny, fashionable borrowed bonnet proved to be too small to do the job. It effectively shielded her from *him,* too.

They passed an older couple Robert knew by sight and Alice knew by name heading the other way in a sturdy wagon. After a brief exchange of greetings before both pairs moved on, she became even quieter, if such a thing was possible. Bracing his legs, and wishing for better suspension to go with a better road, Robert fell into thoughts of his own.

He really ought to not constantly be seen with her alone if stemming rumours was the plan of action, but he kept allowing it to happen all the same. He could also not keep her locked inside the house for ever, and there were things that should be done and discussed without the audience of a chaperone—even one as forgiving as Elizabeth.

'Oh,' she said when he brought them to a stop, arranged the reins, and hopped down, reaching a hand up to assist her.

Robert waited until she was on the ground.

'*Oh,* what?'

She smiled, tried to cover it, and her smile became bigger as a result.

'I was wonderin' if we were goin'—*going*—to walk at all. Or if the gig was how fancy ladies did it.'

'Did what? Walked?' he asked while he went about the business of offering his arm, and then tucking her hand through it himself when she stared at it like she'd never seen such a gesture before.

'Yes, *walked.* I thought, with those nice frocks 'n all, maybe ladies couldn't go for walks. Why are we headin' to my house?' she continued before he could inform her about the finer points of walking with a gentleman.

He'd tell her later about Elizabeth and her preference for long walks across Farrer land, because, yes, they were indeed moving down the dirt track that lead to the Ryan cottage, and an edge of unease settled around them.

Robert surreptitiously patted at the weapon concealed in his coat, and then guided the girl beside him over a large, dead eucalypt branch that had fallen since either he or Alice had been out that way. Once they were clear, he answered her in low tones.

'My sister walks all over the station on a near daily basis. And as for your question, we are here for two reasons. Firstly, because I thought you might like to see the cottage again. Secondly, because it might give me a chance to convince you to stay on with us.'

'Because I'll get a look at this place and remember how bad it is?'

'No, *goodness.* Don't think that.'

He looked sideways at her, appalled by the obvious—accidental—implication, only to find her smiling again. It wasn't forced, either. She truly was teasing him, and she continued in a conversational tone.

'It's probably true though. *Lord,* look what happens to this place when I'm gone a few days. Branches everywhere, which probably means there's a dead tree or two about to topple and fall right through me—*my* roof. And I reckon the grass has grown ten feet since I last saw it.'

'Well, maybe only eight or nine feet,' he suggested. It was more like a single foot, thanks to a rare dose of rain the other morning, but the exaggeration seemed to fit the situation. The bush *was* swiftly taking over the place, leaving a feel of a ghost house up ahead.

'I've been wonderin' if the thieves came back after that night. There's not much worth thievin' but some criminal sorts like to make a mess before they move on. Not,' she added hastily, 'that I'm an expert on the matter.'

'Thieves, hooligans, pirates. Always making a mess. They ought to be outlawed,' he said, trying, and succeeding, to make her smile.

'Pirates?' She scoffed at the suggestion even as her tone hinted she was taken with the notion. 'Here, inland in Australia?'

Their boots crunched old leaves and skidded over the occasional knobbly gumnut. The cottage was in plain sight now, looking every bit the abandoned ghost house Robert had thought it to be.

'The pirates might have come by ship up the Murrumbidgee,' he suggested.

'Must've been a skinny boat.'

'Perhaps it was a tiny ship. Or perhaps they changed vessels along the way. At some point the river connects to the sea.'

Alice gave that a moment's thought. 'I reckon they couldn't've come any further than from New Zealand in something so small. Absolutely not from somewhere like Penzance.'

Penzance? The mention of a place at least ten thousand miles away drew him up short, their connected arms causing her to stop, too. He searched her light eyes with genuine curiosity.

'What do you know of Penzance?'

'Oh,' she said. 'Nothin', I guess. It's just a name I've heard.'

Their silly trail of conversation was broken as she darted sideways a couple of steps to kick aside some debris that'd either fallen from yet another towering eucalypt or been dislodged by a bored bird, muttering to herself as she did, clearly unhappy with the state of her home. When she joined him on the path again, his thoughts had returned to the serious.

'You know that we'd like you to stay on at Endmoor. I know Elizabeth would appreciate the company. And, even if you were determined to be back here at your family home, I think we can both agree it needs clearing up,' *and more security,* 'before you could do that.'

'It's not that bad here,' she said immediately, but she sounded unconvinced.

'I'd be uneasy if any young lady—yes, *lady,*' he said with emphasis when she laughed outright at the moniker, 'was on her own out here, especially after what has happened recently.'

They walked on, more or less in step, though Robert's strides were naturally larger. A breeze rustled the treetops up above, but didn't reach them on the ground, where the shade turned the atmosphere chillier than it'd been out on the town road.

'Elizabeth said you might need a gardener,' Miss Ryan said tentatively when they'd reached the clearing surrounding the cottage.

'I think the homestead needs one, but it shouldn't be construed as me luring you into slave labour. Nor as an insult. It's not compulsory, but I thought it'd be something you'd enjoy.'

She looked up at him, all earnestness. *'Construed?'*

He searched his mental dictionary. 'Interpreted as. Understood as.'

'Oh.' Her attention drifted to their surroundings. When she made a dismayed sound, he knew he'd lost her attention once more.

Robert bent to pick up an entire fallen branch of a dying tree, and dragged it across the clearing, the leaves trailing curled patterns through dust and dirt.

When he'd finished his little task, Miss Ryan had taken off ahead of him.

***

The house looked terrible.

Alice muttered a few words she was certain Mr Farrer knew but would never use in front of a lady—or her—while she took in the scene in front of her. Luckily he wasn't in earshot.

The porch was a sea of scattered dead leaves and other mess that'd blown in over the days she'd been away. She could have sworn that the wooden planks forming the building's front walls had rotted, dried, and splintered all in the time she'd been gone, but more likely it'd been that way a fortnight ago. She'd been living like a princess for a little while now, and suddenly, mortifyingly, all she could see now was how the place looked through the eyes of others.

She really did believe Mr Farrer when he said he hadn't brought her out here to show her the difference in their positions, but she was feeling awfully self-conscious regardless. It was one thing for him to know where she'd come from, but another for him to see it with his own eyes. He'd never been in her house before, and she didn't want him there now.

She picked her way over rocks and twigs, putting some space between herself and the handsome fellow in question, a little relieved he gave her the distance she needed as she approached the house.

'Miss Ryan, wait for me!'

She looked over her shoulder to Mr Farrer, who had started off after her.

'Why?' she called. She couldn't let him in there, she simply could not.

'You never know who might be around. After everything that's happened.'

He was almost on top of her, and she quickly held up a hand to stop him.

'Whoever's been here before is long gone, I promise. Even if they robbed me blind, all they could've taken was the cutlery, and some stockin's.'

He didn't look convinced, and she tried harder.

'It's a small house, with no shadows to hide in. Isn't it better you stay out here, standin' guard?'

'All right,' he told her after a long, long pause. It was a pause so lengthy that Alice had time to remember she shouldn't be mentioning stockings to a gentleman.

'Call if you need me.'

Someone—and she was betting on that bothersome possum that was fond of cackling bloody murder during the nights—had taken a liking to the autumn berries growing over to the far side of the building, and had made a meal out of them right at her front door. Alice used the toe of her boot to kick the scraps aside, and then bent to pick up a stick to bat at the big new cobweb that'd been cast across a quarter of the front of the door. It was thick and strong and all but glued to the wood.

Spiders ... She'd never loved them much, and as she fought her silent battle with the web she could all but feel one at her nape, climbing into the layers of her frock. Shuddering at the imagined sensation, she eased the front door open and stepped inside.

The dim light was the first thing she noticed, so quickly accustomed she was to the bigger house down the road. Next, she bent to inspect the surprise of a pile of meat dumped on the table in the middle of the room. Something cold and ominous crept up the back of her. She knew exactly what that meat meant: Ian was here.

Alice straightened, and wished against all knowledge and sense she was wrong. However, her traitorous eyes made out his silhouette in one corner.

She sighed, turned to pull back the old curtain and wave her reassurance at Mr Farrer through the window, and then let it fall into place as she faced the brother she was disappointed to finally see.

'What're you here for, Ian?'

She heard a sigh bigger than her own, and then he was stepping towards her. He came into a shaft of light so that she saw him properly: a much taller, lankier version of herself.

All those lonely nights of wishing he'd return, and now here he was, and she wanted him gone.

Dismayed, she saw that the wooden cabinet had clearly been rifled through, and thoroughly. She edged closer to it, eyes adjusting to the dimness, and hoped against hope that Ian hadn't found the hidden compartment at the back.

'You thought I couldn't take care of you? Alice, you don't need that rich family up on the ridge, you've got me.'

'Fat lot of good that's done me so far.'

'What's that mean, then?'

'Ian ... You can't go away for days or weeks and then just come home with a few pounds of lamb. Thank you, but it's not going to help me next week when you've upped and disappeared again.'

'No. It won't be like that anymore. I've got friends now, connections. And as long as you keep your head down and keep quiet about it, then we're set.'

'*Criminal* friends? *Criminal* connections?'

His silence was confirmation enough. With a frustrated sound Alice moved further into the house, taking it all in with an eye for anything damaged or missing. Like the outside, it just looked scruffy.

'You wantin' to be arrested, is that it? Or killed while you're tryin' to make money in a hurry?'

'It's only while I set us up, Alice.'

Did he realise he was a brother, not a husband? Did he really think she would be there forever to keep house for him? She absently picked up a spoon that had fallen to the ground and been left there, polishing the dust off it with her skirt and then putting it away with the others.

It was a good opportunity to check the cabinet more closely.

Her heart all but sank when she saw that the compartment *had* been pried open. A look over her shoulder confirmed Ian was watching the window—not her—warily, and so she slipped her hand in, praying silently it was there, but knowing the necklace was gone.

The pain she felt was immediate and so strong she didn't hear the beginning of what her brother said next. Something about how he'd be bringing pounds and more pounds home soon, and then she could fix up the house however she liked.

Yes, then. Ian probably did think they were a pair for life. She should tell him she'd other plans for *her* future, but she minded her words; something about him was scaring her.

'It'll all be over by Januarius,' he said with confidence.

'What? What's that?'

'Januarius? No bloody idea, but I've been told that's the night it'll happen.'

'*What*'ll happen?'

Her brother visibly closed up. 'Nothin' for you to worry about.'

'Ian ... Business as in ... robbin' people?'

'*No,* Alice. It's not for you to know.'

Alice turned cold, and silently committed the word to her memory. *Januarius, Januarius, Januarius.*

'All I have to do,' Ian said with an odd gleam in his eyes, 'is lie low around these parts until I'm summoned.'

'That doesn't sound good for anyone, Ian.'

'Even if it's only once? Well, Alice, these people have enough money they can stand to lose some of it.'

Alice felt sick. 'So it *is* theft, then.'

He looked guilty, but then did he not always seem that way? She watched him fidget under her gaze.

'I promise you, I've no bloody idea.'

The subtle sounds of Robert Farrer moving around the clearing then had them both tensing. Alice went back to the window and drew back the curtain a fraction. He was still a distance from them, but had turned to look at the house.

She slowly dropped the fabric back into place.

'I have to go, Ian. I can't stay here at the moment.'

He flicked a glance over her shoulder.

'What's *he* doin' here, anyway?'

Alice nearly explained herself. She nearly gave into old habits and family loyalty. And then she remembered the last time she'd been in that house, and the reasons she'd fled from it. Turning to take one last good look at her brother, she changed her mind, and moved to the door.

'He's takin' me home.'

***

'Have you drawn any conclusions? Come to any decisions?' Mr Farrer asked her as they got back up into that gig and turned around the way they'd come.

Tell him about Ian.

Alice stole a look his way. 'I reckon I might've. But only with conditions.'

He spared her a quick glance before turning his attention back to the bumpy road.

'Conditions?'

'Yes. Like the gardenin'. I don't know if you were bein'—*being* serious about that or not, but I'd like to do it. And mendin'. I'll do that, too. And ... I don't know what else yet, but I'm sure there's more.'

She thought he'd argue with her on it, but he was silent and thoughtful for a while—considering, she supposed.

'All right,' he eventually agreed. 'All right, we can come to an agreement on that. I take it that means you'll stay on for the time being?'

Tell him about Ian!

Alice twisted her hands and felt miserable. Her mother's necklace was gone, and her brother wouldn't have kept it for any sentimental purpose. She was about to accept charity from this handsome man beside her because it was her best option, even if it was selfish of her.

They were almost back, and she felt stupidly happy on seeing the gate. She glanced at the man beside her once more and heaved an exaggerated sigh.

'It'll be an awful hardship to stay here, but it seems I must.'

Maybe if he hadn't rewarded her with a quick grin then she'd have told him why she'd made her decision. But she was a chicken, wasn't she? Terrified he'd take the invitation back if he knew.

She'd tell him about her brother another day, maybe...

Chapter 7

'Just ask me, Alice,' Elizabeth Farrer said a few afternoons later. She offered Alice a small, friendly smile and turned a page of her book, eyes going back to the text. It wasn't the first time Elizabeth tried in the past few days, but so far Alice'd not the courage to do as she asked.

It was much like—she thought wryly—a person coaxing an animal to trust. Little advances and then a pause. Not pushing her to speak, but waiting patiently for her to do so all the same. She appreciated the patience, but the craven part of her wished the other woman would give up on it.

'Ask you what?' she said eventually, playing dumb, though it fooled neither of them.

Elizabeth's fine, pale fingers, darkened by charcoal in a spot or two, rested on the page, holding her place as she returned her full attention to her companion.

'You should ask me whatever it is that's been bothering you. Whatever it is that has you working your way through our library at all hours of the day and night. I'm in earnest when I say I don't mind helping—if I can, that is.'

Alice frowned and considered her options. For days now she'd been wondering—*worrying.* She'd raided the Farrers' book collection and tried to make sense of words and phrases that weren't familiar to her. It had been a frustrating exercise when her education was minimal. She needed to grow the collection of words in her head but wasn't sure there was time for that.

She felt like the village idiot, but some things were too important for pride, and so far nobody had laughed in her face. She'd a mystery to try and solve, and it was something of an emergency. Even so, she was reluctant to show her scribblings to anyone.

If she couldn't find the answers she needed in the books, she was going to have to squeal on Ian. It was the right thing to do. It'd been the right thing to do from the start, but she was still a chicken, and she still thought blood counted for something, even if it was the unpopular opinion when it came to the Ryans.

Briefly, she wondered what her father would have thought of her lack of family loyalty, and honestly couldn't make up her mind. And her mother had been gone so long she didn't trust herself to know her mind on such things at all.

Alice shrugged and then opened her mouth.

'I've been readin' through so many books, but I still don't know...'

'Know what?'

At Alice's feet a trail of ants were busy coming to and from a home they'd made between the paving stones of the path, which happened to be near where she sat. Not wanting to end the afternoon with stockings full of biting bugs was motivation enough for her to get up and hand Miss Farrer the paper, self-consciousness nearly making her snatch it right back.

Elizabeth put her book aside and glanced at what Alice had written before accepting it with a slight incline of her head. Alice's cheeks heated as the woman looked down at her partially legible scrawl.

She would not be ashamed...

The paper had some dirt on the edges, each muddy mark in the shape of a fingerprint. Even though Alice had worn gloves for the past hour she'd been digging in the ground and clearing dead twigs and sticks away, the soil was a little damp and she'd not managed to keep *all* the muck off.

'Of course it's spelt all wrong. I tried it lots of times, but it's still wrong.'

She leaned across and pointed. 'Maybe you know what this is. Januarius? At least, I think that's how you say it. I thought maybe the second try was the right spelling. Or maybe the fifth.'

'Mm,' Miss Farrer said, reading through the dozen attempts Alice had made of the word, looking as blank as Alice felt.

'It sounds Latin, does it not? But I can't think of what it could be.'

She looked at Alice over the paper. 'Where did you hear this word?'

Tell her. You really should tell her.

'I heard it somewhere or other, I don't remember,' replied the chicken with the muddy fingertips so quickly she sounded guilty to her own ears. 'Don't worry about it.'

Elizabeth watched her closely for a while longer, and Alice put her gloves back on and picked up her little trowel. She'd get back to work so she wasn't caught squirming at her lie.

'You should ask my brother,' Elizabeth said. 'It might be the sort of thing he had drilled into his memory in his school days. I'd wait for our guest to leave, however.'

The guest in question was that pesky Mr Wright with his expensive vehicle and his rude looks that told Alice all about his opinion of her. She wished the men—Mr Farrer, Mr Stanford, and the toff—would finish their meeting, and that Mr Wright would set off to wherever he needed to go to be rude and disagreeable next. Only then Alice could have access to the room and the books.

It was a mean thought, but she knew snobbery when she saw it: the man was an expert at thinking himself better than others.

'I wish he would leave *soon,*' she muttered, and bent to brush off a line of ants that had begun a parade up her leg.

***

By midway through the afternoon Robert found himself wondering why he'd not seen the cliff he was toppling off long before he reached the edge.

The meeting he and John had with Tom Wright had been bizarre, awkward, and full of an odd dynamic that had John looking askance at Robert more than once. They made little progress in the hour they'd been talking in circles, and Wright had shown only the mildest interest in the papers they'd compiled to show just how ready they were to proceed with riesling production.

Now—at Wright's request—John had left the two men to a private conversation that took them around the side of the house and towards the paddocks. Merinos bleated and baaed some distance away, the sound carrying across the open space and surrounding them.

'The warmth is holding out despite the change of season,' the man beside him said as he held his imported pipe in Robert's direction, always trying to impress, and as though they'd nothing better to discuss in private than the autumn weather. Robert supposed it was some sort of grunt he made in response.

He thought back to the conversation he'd conducted with Wright in town several days earlier, when he'd called on the man at the risk of running into the rest of the Wright family—something he was loath to do—to find out why he was stalling on news from South Australia. They needed the help from there if the vineyard was to ever get off the ground, but so far all they'd heard was deafening silence.

What he did not need in his way were the machinations of someone who'd been manipulating his life however he wanted for close to a decade already. On the other hand, it was becoming clear that the man who held all the cards was keeping them very close to his chest.

'Say what you came here to say, Tom. Please,' he added as an afterthought, aware he sounded as sarcastic about it as he felt.

The man beside him stopped walking abruptly, and propped a booted foot up on the low rail of the fence.

'If we're to have a business arrangement, Robert, I won't have my family tainted by your behaviour.'

It sounded like a scold from a frustrated parent. Robert suspected it was exactly the way it was intended. He rankled, and worked hard to rein his temper in and find a reasonable tone.

'Good Lord, what am I reported to have done now? Overstayed my welcome at the pub and swum naked in the Murrumbidgee? Debauched one of the more upstanding members of the Ladies' Auxiliary?'

With that Robert earned himself a quelling glance.

'You know what I'm referring to.'

'Yes, I do. And I assume you're here to once again warn me of inflated rumours that will be the end of our business venture. It's Stanford you're causing trouble for, too. All for what?'

The man's lips thinned, and—if possible—he managed to look more like a stern father than a moment before.

Damn.

Wright, whose smoking had begun the moment they'd left the confines of the house—presently giving Robert nightmarish visions of stray embers sparking a bushfire—took another draw on his pipe, staring off into space while he exhaled slowly. The smoke curled about his whiskers and then trailed off into the bright afternoon.

'When I *first* saw the girl on your property, she was more than capable of walking, of getting herself around. Why did you keep her here?'

And why does it matter to you?

'Apart from the obvious danger? Is that not reason enough? I'm not leaving a girl alone in the bush while there are bushrangers around.' Robert lifted a boot to the fence, matching the older man's position. He fixed his attention on a wayward sheep in the shade not too far off, steeling his temper into something manageable.

'You don't care about this, Tom. Not really. What is it you're trying to get at here?'

Wright took another puff, and Robert suffered the frustration of being made to wait. A kernel of anxiety had formed in his belly, but he'd be damned if he would let the other man know that.

'I have to make a commitment soon,' Wright began. 'I have to think of my own business, my family, you know? And I have to make a decision where the best place is for me to invest.'

He glanced at Robert.

'I've requests from beyond here, you know. There's talk that the land up in the Highlands is more favourable for what you're intending to try here with those wines. I've plenty of reasons to proceed nearer to Moss Vale or New Sheffield...'

Investments the man had *not* been investigating until the very recent past. Robert knew it with absolute certainty.

'And what would it take to make you keep your backing with us?'

But he already knew. Damn the bastard, what had he ever been thinking taking a verbal commitment from this particular man as a true one? He should've chained the fellow to his office desk weeks ago and kept him there, a starved and unhappy hostage, until he'd legal documentation of their agreement.

Robert muttered something unpleasant and gripped the railing. The harshness of the climate was getting the best of the wood. Gloveless as he was then, he was likely to pull away splintered, but in that moment better the fence than Tom Wright's neck.

'You are going to deny us the funding and the support because I helped a sick girl? Have you run *mad?*'

'I wonder, that's all. And I have my own reputation to be concerned about.' A sharp sideways look preceded his next words. 'There's my family to consider, too.'

Yes, the man's damn family and the pampered jewel at the centre—his daughter—around which the entirety of the world seemed to revolve. *She* was the real cause of all this bluster and fuss and fabricated scandal. Of course she was.

Wright drew on his pipe and then exhaled, and another trail of smoke swirled up between them. It was as practised a mannerism as most of his others, and as much a part of the man's act as the expensive imported fabrics he dressed his family in, and the obnoxiously expensive barouche in which he'd travelled to Endmoor that day. It was a perfectly impractical thing on the poor roads in the area, and especially so with so few people about to appreciate its high price.

Robert and John were both twenty-eight, had worked hard and held better positions in society than most. But to these older men like Wright, they were still boys to only be taken seriously if they had the right connections—and money. They were to be toyed with for amusement now, it seemed, and there wasn't a bloody thing Robert could think to do about it.

He'd the education, the inheritance, and the years of practice behind him to make his attempt at growing rich green vines instead of wheat worthwhile, if only he could gain the attention of the bigwigs in Sydney and Melbourne and other parts of the colonies to listen to him. That was where the old guard of the region came into it, and that was precisely why he couldn't afford to antagonise the likes of Tom Wright.

Robert was a landowner, and like all other men in his situation he was rich in some ways and poor as a church mouse in others. Just as it was back in England, where his father had taken back over the reins of the Farrer lands some years earlier, they owned vast swathes of property, but only profited from it if it was managed well.

The Farrers were far and away the most British—and therefore, in the eyes of many, the most impressive—people in the district, and yet they'd not made their money through the gold rushes. Unlike the Wrights and the Stanfords, they had not come to the tablelands to build themselves a fancy town house and live off investments.

It was precisely why Robert was now in such a bind. He wanted, more than anything he'd ever wanted before, to branch out on his own. Sheep were reliable and Australia had long ago won the battle with Germany to become known internationally for their wool, but sheep were sheep were sheep.

What the Germans found success in was wine, and that was where Robert's—and John's—passion lay. John, raised well thanks to his father's wealth, was more than ready to branch out on his own, but was still cultivating the funds and connections that only came with age and experience, just as Robert was. The Farrer name had something of a pull locally, but it was not enough.

'What is it you expect me to do to earn your backing and get that signature I need?' he ground out.

The wayward sheep roused itself out of its stupor and dawdled off in the direction of the others as Wright's smoking bout drew to a close, with a lone last half-baked curl of smoke drifting away, leaving only the scent of the tobacco behind.

'To gain my backing? Tell me, Mister Farrer, what would a gentleman usually do when a girl has been brought into his care and compromised?'

Cold realisation washed over him as the goal of the man's scheming became all too clear. There was that crowning jewel in need of protecting, and what better way to do it than this?

Anger—no—*fury* reared up so fast it was almost impossible to control. This was utter ridiculousness, but then he hadn't brought a rational man out with him that afternoon.

Wright didn't think Robert would do it. He thought he could tidily remove himself from a deal with the Farrer family by making outlandish threats. Robert was being tricked *out* of the deal, not into it. A social climber such as Tom Wright wouldn't be capable of conceiving of someone doing what Robert, in that moment, resolved to do.

Grimly, determinedly, he pushed away from the fence, effectively ending the conversation on his own terms.

'I thought you had another property to call on before the end of the day.'

'That I do.'

They parted ways at the carriage drive, and Robert didn't bother seeing the man off on his way, instead taking a few minutes to himself in his office.

He knew why there'd been no communication from the Germans in Bethanien in South Australia, nor even from Adelaide, where communication was not difficult these days. There was nothing wrong with the telegraph or the post; Robert had been receiving regular correspondence from all over New South Wales and beyond.

Frustration and a deep-seated anger boiled up inside him as his mind framed an image of chess pieces falling neatly into place.

Checkmate, Tom Wright. The man moved fast.

Robert wasn't aware of how much time passed as he sat there at his desk, staring at the figures in front of him until they blurred, and then giving up and looking off into space.

He thought of Endmoor, and the legacy his parents had left in his young hands when Australia had become too much, too harsh for them and they'd returned to Cumberland.

He thought of his sister, who was his charge, his friend, his confidante all in one, and how that she would one day soon make a match. He hoped for a good one.

He thought of John Stanford, and the hard work the other man had put into their shared dream of turning the tablelands into a producer of good rieslings. It had been proven to work; Australian wines were already beating their more favoured French and German counterparts in blind tastings in international competition, even if the prizes were being revoked the moment the judges discovered the provenance. Nobody yet seemed able to believe colonials could produce something so crisp. In time, Robert was certain they could achieve that, too.

As long as he had the backing to bring...

And then he thought of exactly what he was being pressured to do in order to achieve those dreams—not just his own, but those of all he felt responsible for.

The sunbeams lengthened across the room, and still he sat idle, his dreams of the view beyond the windows filled not with Merinos but German vines precariously close to fading. Somewhere close by Hutton was barking with excitement at something. It was probably Miss Ryan, who'd taken a liking to the dog as surely as she took a liking to almost everything and everyone.

Somewhere further off a cacophony of birds announced the change in the day. The days were growing shorter as winter approached, and soon there'd be no light at all by the evening meal. That last thought triggered him into action, and he pushed back and got to his feet.

He came to a solid decision between the veranda and the path that veered west from the house, and had made up his mind absolutely before he even passed his mother's roses. The girl in his thoughts had worked a miracle of sorts after taking the suggestion of gardening to heart, coaxing things out of the soil that he'd have thought were unachievable on the cusp of winter.

It wasn't hard to find her out on the drive, as she was laughing in delight at the dog's antics. She turned when she heard his approach, quickly and shyly rearranging her skirts, her hair, into something a tad more presentable.

No matter what he wanted, Robert couldn't help but make her uneasiness grow as he took a chance to study her, this girl who'd exploded into his life—and stayed. Perhaps once he'd found her nondescript in that way one tended to be when they hadn't the funds to emerge from the drudgery of poverty, but since the day he'd been led to her boot he'd seen flashes of something else.

She amused him, to be honest, entertained him. It wasn't what he'd have thought he'd want, but there it was—a man could be surprised. And, in another borrowed gown from his sister's wardrobe, she had a dignified prettiness about her, the Cambridge blue of the fabric a complement to her colouring and frequently cheeky smile.

He wondered what she thought of *him,* if anything. In social standing he outmatched her a thousand times over, but did she see anything beyond his authority and his vast property?

He supposed he was about to find out.

Finally, resolved to it, he extended his hand to her, and waited with as much patience as he could muster for her to tentatively slip her fingers into his palm.

'Walk with me again,' he coaxed, and after giving Hutton a final pat she fell into step.

Chapter 8

He took her in the opposite direction to the last time, again in the gig. The sun bathed the yellowed grass of the paddocks in light, and currawongs called to each other across the valley.

As the horse clopped along, he told her of things she hardly understood, and yet he didn't speak to her as if she were stupid. He talked about his plans to make wine, which seemed mighty extravagant to Alice, except he told it as though he already had it all planned.

'It'd be easier than shippin' it here from France,' she eventually conceded.

'Cheaper than coming from the Rhineland, too, which is the market I hope to compete with.' He drew her back to the conversation with that statement, which invited her to ask further questions.

'I think I understand. Mind, I've no idea of the meanin' of half the words you're sayin'.'

He grinned.

'Believe me, that's not uncommon. Forgive me, but I've been studying like a schoolboy on this topic and tend to forget not everybody finds it as fascinating as I do.'

'It's not that I don't find it interestin'. In fact, I keep picturin' how the town will react. If it's not wheat here, it's sheep. You're not supposed to be different.'

'And it's deathly boring, is it not? John Stanford is in on this with me, so the town will have to panic and tut at the antics of not one but two of us. The horror!' he finished with rather a lot of drama in his tone.

'And this worries you?'

'Not at all. At least, it won't bother me once I find my German expert to come and battle the scorched land with us and teach us how to achieve our miracle.'

'What's that word you keep usin'?'

'Viticulture? It's the harvesting of grapes,' he explained patiently. 'Just a fancy word for it.'

'And you can make it here? Wine, I mean?' Alice didn't mean to sound as doubtful as her tone, but she *had* grown up in a world of wheat and sheep, and this was beyond anything she'd ever thought to imagine.

'I don't know for certain,' her companion said easily. 'However, I certainly intend to try.'

Alice considered all of what he'd said, thinking she should say something intelligent about it, but not knowing what. And then something off to the right caught her attention.

'We ought not to be out like this, I reckon. People are watching us, Mister Farrer.' Alice was mightily aware of the nearness of her companion. She hadn't any idea how to act normal when pressed so close to someone so powerful. In fact, she felt a fool, trying so hard to appear unmoved by him that she'd become a statue.

'*Robert,*' he corrected, as he always did, shifting beside her, seemingly all confidence and ease. 'What people are watching? I see none.'

'We just passed two in the paddock out there, and they gawked.'

'Surely they were kangaroos, not people.'

'In *hats?*'

He didn't respond to that, only smiled. Alice knew there was something different about him that afternoon, though. Now she dared to give him a closer look she saw his smile was so tense it was almost false, and she suspected his meeting hadn't gone the way he wanted it to. Mr Stanford had implied as much when he'd taken his leave of them, a farewell that had included an odd glance Alice's way.

It was another one of those *walks* that had so far been conducted while seated in a vehicle, but Alice wasn't complaining. They'd covered ground in a direction she hadn't been before, and as awkward as she felt being alone with this man, she was enjoying the journey.

'Didn't Elizabeth want to come with us?'

'Ah, well. She is familiar enough with my driving skills to know better.'

They passed expanse of grass after expanse of grass, the view occasionally broken by stubborn old gum trees that grew haphazardly in various directions. The mountains seemed to stay off in the distance no matter how much closer they came to them.

'I think it's the road,' she said after some consideration.

They'd gone mostly in silence on their little journey, long enough that Alice was beginning to get suspicious about the bland look on her companion's face.

'I beg your pardon?'

'I think it's the road that's bumpin' us around like this, not your drivin'. Look at that big bloody hole there, for Heaven's sake.'

Belatedly—very belatedly—she realised her choice of language, but by then it seemed a little late to be gasping and apologising profusely as other young ladies would have done. Instead, she gave him an expectant glance, waiting for him to berate her for it.

He did not, and they continued on, neither of them any worse for wear for her words.

A moment later, she spotted the flowers. Squinting to bring them into greater focus, suddenly the blues and the purples and the pinks running the length of the road had her sitting straighter.

'Oh stop, Robert! Stop here a moment.'

***

This wasn't precisely the outing Robert had planned.

Before he even had a chance to assist her, his companion had clambered down from the gig. It was lucky he'd stopped soon enough, because he rather thought Miss Ryan would have flung herself from a moving vehicle, she was suddenly so full of excitement. If in her haste she stumbled over her new skirts a little, she was oblivious to it, so intent she was on her mission.

He followed her as she waded into the bushes running along the side of the fence, and watched with baffled amusement as she bent to admire one of the wildflowers growing there before plucking it to hold up for inspection. It must have passed muster, because she dived for another, and then another.

'What's that you're picking?'

'Crowea,' she said without stopping her task. She made a grab at her skirts as though she expected to find an apron there to hold them in, grunted in consternation when she recalled she'd removed it before they set out, and transferred the bunch to her left hand so she could continue plucking with the right.

'I haven't seen them for so long, I almost thought they'd stopped growin' around here.'

Robert reached out and relieved her of her quickly growing burden.

'And you need to pick them here?'

She looked up at that and after a second's thought sprang back onto the road and away from the plants.

'Is this someone's property? Of course it is. There's a fence.'

'It's mine, actually,' he said with a quick smile. 'Pick as many flowers as you want. I could probably do with an education about what's growing on my own land.'

She stared at him, light eyes uncomprehending at first.

'This is *still* your land?'

He nodded, and she lightly touched a finger to a purple petal of one of the flowers he held.

'Bloody hell, how much of it do you need?'

He laughed, and then gestured to the sheep off in the distance.

'How much land? Animals need space to graze.' And his property was tiny compared to many; his interest in expanding his numbers of Merino nowhere near that of his interest in the introduction of riesling production to the region.

The land in the valley was a little more fertile than some in the southern areas of New South Wales, and his family had been lucky to purchase it before its value was discovered. However, it was not English soil; it was a much harsher thing than that. Rain was much scarcer, and rarely did anything planted seem to obey as it ought.

He watched Alice watch the view, saw her comprehend just what she would be marrying into if he ever managed to ask her.

Robert pointed into the distance. 'My land ends at the rise, see there? Where that distant tree seems to be growing on its own?'

She nodded, shielding her eyes from the harsh late afternoon sun with one hand. He gave her a few moments of contemplation, and then her attention was inevitably attracted by the flowers once more.

'I could really pick more?'

'I don't see why not.'

It was all the encouragement she needed.

'My mother used to have these, when I was young,' she told him as she continued with her self-imposed task. 'I always meant to have them again, but I haven't seen any for a long time. Around here it's always bluebells, which are nice, but ... I ought to come back soon and clip them properly. Maybe they could be grown nearer to the house?'

'You're the one who knows their flowers, Alice. Do whatever you think is best.'

She shrugged her shawl off and used it to wrap the stems in, adding those he held to the combination, creating a bouquet.

'These're rarer than bluebells.' Satisfied with what she had, she turned to him with an artless smile.

'All right, we can go,' she said as though granting him permission, and he grinned as she went to the step of the vehicle and reached up to hoist herself into the seat alone and one-handed at that.

Robert extended a hand to stop her.

'What?' she asked when he removed the makeshift bouquet from her grasp and put it up in the gig.

'What's wrong?' she asked when he took her arm and led her slightly away from vehicle and horse.

'Miss Ryan,' he began tentatively, in a tone she'd never heard from him before.

'Alice,' he started again.

'What's happenin'?' she asked when he found himself stuck.

And then, as if her question finally freed those words, he presented her with his proposal.

***

Time seemed to stretch on. Robert's possible future fiancée was looking at him in what he could only call dismay, but if it was for herself or for him, he wasn't sure.

Was this the most unconventional of matches? Yes. Would his parents—when a message eventually reached them in Cumberland—be shocked and possibly horrified? Undoubtedly. Would the people in town think him odd? Well, of course.

However, in the trip out that afternoon Robert had found he was fine with all of that. He'd always known he'd marry at some point, and perhaps a wife such as Alice Ryan wouldn't be frightened off from the country as easily as someone more ... well, more delicate and refined.

'It is not such a terrible idea, Alice.'

'Who for!'

'We get on, and we've plenty in common.'

'Certainly. I've a stash of ball gowns back home, and I know all about afternoon tea.'

'There's not that much to it. You pour tea; you drink it. There might be a biscuit or two, or something baked if the staff are attentive.' He smiled. 'As ours are.'

She gave him a little shove of protest, just a little nudge, and then snatched her hands back when she realised she'd touched him.

Robert tried not to grin again and give her the impression she amused him, regardless of the fact she did. Some instinct told him she might not enjoy that information now.

Instead he reached out for her, taking her hand in his and feeling a little stab of triumph when she let him. Her hand was small, but it was as deceptive as the rest of her; she was strong in ways most women of his acquaintance had never had to be. He knew there were calluses beneath those gloves she wore.

'I'm not saying we must rush to marital bliss. In fact, I assume we'll have to get our courting done after we've exchanged vows, but I can be a patient man when I need to be. We've time to muddle through the details.'

'After we've rushed into a weddin', you mean.'

'We *are* already living under the same roof, Alice. There's talk we should shut down now, for all our sakes. You will like it here, I think. You like my sister, at least?'

She scoffed at him.

'She's a princess next to me.'

He'd tell her one day about the social cuts and the relentless references to her colonial roots that had made Elizabeth's visit to England a couple of years earlier a nightmare in many ways. A princess of a rural outpost on the far side of the world she might be, but his sister had been humbled time and again in her life and knew better than to put on airs.

Was the marriage to be viewed as unbalanced and even scandalous? Of course it was, but he had confidence both that the scandal would pass and that someone as tough as Miss Alice Ryan would overcome it.

'It's warmer at Endmoor in the winter. You'd not have to chop your own firewood anymore,' he coaxed, and even though it was the silliest of reasons for a marriage, he didn't miss the flare in her eyes at his words.

He'd been to that cottage twice now, and he couldn't fathom how someone as small and slim as her could survive that bone-chilling air inside when the night took hold. Winter in the region was only at its cusp, and there were months of cool to come before the searing summer heat returned.

Already, her animals—chickens, a cow—had been moved in with his. The new pecking order had been established in the pens, and in so many little ways their lives were already intertwining.

'That's not so romantic, Mister Farrer.'

'*Robert.*'

A sigh. 'Robert,' she repeated obediently.

He'd tried love once, and it had gone terribly and all come to nothing. He and Miss Ryan suited well enough, God help them, and no matter what she thought of herself she would always stand up to him, always be a match. It was not the worst plan, no matter what outsiders would think.

'What does your sister think about this?'

It was a fair question, however ... 'I've not talked to her about it yet.'

'You ought to have.'

'Would that really be romantic? It's a decision between *us,* is it not?'

On the other hand, if Elizabeth had insisted on accompanying them that afternoon instead of directing knowing looks his way and disappearing inside to ensure they went alone, he would not be in the situation he was now.

If she'd put up any objections, or perhaps yanked him aside while Alice was removing her apron and searching for gloves that matched to tell him he was a madman, he might have found that excuse he needed to not proceed with his mad plan.

Alice returned her attention to the flowers—the *crowea*—that lined the fence.

'You could marry anyone.'

'Well, not quite. I am, however, asking *you,* Miss Ryan. *Alice.* What do you think?'

***

What did she think? Alice stared at the man in front of her and wondered why she hadn't yet burst out laughing. She was certain she wasn't dreaming, but none of it made any sense.

The man was loony, and that was one thing about him she hadn't realised before. She shouldn't marry a loony, no matter how much money he had.

Could she...?

Maybe he was the sort of man who was only a lunatic *sometimes.* Perhaps it was a manageable type of madness. Realising she was crushing the petals of a flower in her agitation, she pulled her hands back and pressed them against her belly, wishing it would stop churning quite so much so that she might concentrate on the bigger problem in front of her.

Studying him closely, she wondered if he'd taken more than a little wine with his most recent meal. She surreptitiously leaned in a bit to study his eyes more closely. It was too sunny for her to be fully sure, but she didn't think they were red-rimmed.

Sober. He was sober, she was almost certain.

'What do I think?' she parroted absently.

It made her mercenary, to be sure, but there were advantages to this madness of a marriage. Waking up to fresh water, waiting for her in her room. No more frosty mornings hauling it up from the river, trip after trip after trip.

And the food. The warmth. The help.

The *company*—that was most important of all things to her. She wasn't designed to be a solitary person, and she'd known that about herself long before the Farrers had presented her with a solution to her loneliness.

'You know all you have to do is say yes, and it will be settled.'

It wasn't a grand romance, this craziness between them, but Alice had never thought her chances of a grand romance were all that high. She'd never counted on having one herself, and she'd not miss something she'd never dreamt of in the first place.

'Are you drunk?' It had to be asked.

'I beg your pardon?'

'*Drunk.* What'd you sneak into your teacup this afternoon?'

His eyes took on a glint of amusement.

'A great deal of whiskey. And of course there was the gallon of ale I drank before coming to collect you for this outing.'

'*Robert!*' she thumped him lightly on the chest—again. Any intention to not use his Christian name had disappeared the moment she realised he was at least as daft as her brother. 'I'm bein' serious here!'

Somehow that hand of hers stayed where she'd put it, and he raised his own to cover it. It felt ... nice, actually. A little thrill went through her. Even though she'd had her hand held a time or two in the past, this was different.

Staring at their hands then, because the new sensations made it hard to meet his eyes, she thought about that big, beautiful garden, hers to do whatever she wanted with.

'You think I have to be drunk in order to propose to you?' His voice had lowered to a murmur. Even though they were completely alone out there on the road, the tone made her feel even more like this was a time and place just for them.

They'd be linked forever if she agreed, and that implied all sorts of intimacies she didn't yet understand.

'Of course I think that,' she told the buttons on his waistcoat.

'Well, I'm not drunk, and you're undervaluing yourself, but that can be remedied later. If you say yes, that is.'

Her fingers flexed under his touch, and he squeezed them and then turned her hand so she clasped him back. Hand-holding was pretty nice actually, but in summer it would probably be hot and sticky.

Maybe if they got married they would do other things on hot days.

'But won't folks laugh at you?' *And at me?*

'There're plenty of people around here who could do with being laughed at. The two of us would have to do something more scandalous than get married to deserve that honour.'

Sometimes he spoke in words she never used. Which meant sometimes it took her a second or two to figure him out. That was fine, though, because Alice thought she was a pretty good learner. If Elizabeth Farrer and her friends could learn to use big words, then Alice Ryan could too.

She'd have a lot to learn in this new life, but they were living in the country, not in a big city with a big society.

'I'd need some time. To learn, I mean. I don't want to go to parties with elegant people right away. I'd embarrass you.' *And myself.*

'Time is something we have plenty of.'

'Don't really seem that way when you're in a rush to wed.'

'Call me an opportunist. I don't want you escaping back home and forgetting about me.'

'Not bloody likely,' she said under her breath, but the look on his face said he'd heard.

Robert leaned down, his scent special. It was something she'd noticed even that first horrid morning when he'd carried her inside, her foot ruined by that spider. He'd shaved that day, but even so a stray strand of her hair had caught in his whiskers. If she was a little braver, she'd touch him there now, to properly tell what it felt like.

'All you have to do is say yes,' he whispered, and she tilted her head enough so she could look into his eyes.

Brown, they were, but there were flecks of gold there too. So different to hers, just like she was different in every other way.

But she thought about those meals, and the way a physician just came when he was needed. She hadn't had to treat the bite herself, nor the illness that came afterwards. It was such a luxury.

She thought about how pretty her new frocks were, those that Elizabeth had talked her into trying.

She thought about that funny way her stomach now turned when she was near this man. And she thought about how when she was younger she couldn't help but steal glimpses of him from afar as he rode along the town road with a strength and grace that snagged her attention and wouldn't let go.

And then she thought about her little house that was running low on firewood.

And—God help her—she did say yes.

Chapter 9

Robert's fiancée of twenty seconds looked like she was going to cry. This was not the beginning anyone would envision for a betrothed couple, but before acting on impulse he searched for some sense.

'You're not jokin', are you?' she asked rather belatedly.

'I wouldn't do that.' He grappled. 'This is a good thing, Alice.'

She nodded jerkily, lips pressed tightly together, which was hardly any more convincing than the expression on her face moments earlier. Robert gave her the time she needed to recover her wits. It was only seconds but seemed an age, and he devoted that time to swatting at a fly that'd taken a liking to the dark fabric of his coat.

'Tell me what upsets you,' he coaxed, which earned him a look so baleful it was nearly comical.

'Won't it embarrass you though, bein' married to me?'

She'd already asked that, but he was pretty sure she'd ask it again, and again. 'Should it?'

'Well, yes!'

He should kiss her, he thought. Betrothed people tended to do such things. However, he didn't think it would be particularly welcome yet, so instead he offered her a hand again, and helped her up into the gig. She devoted plenty of time to arranging the flowers in her lap while he gathered the reins.

By silent mutual agreement, they turned for home.

The vehicle rocked and wobbled along, occasionally kicking up a spatter of mud on either side of them from a new puddle below. Robert checked to see if it bothered Alice, but she seemed more concerned with her flowers, her grip on their stems tighter than strictly necessary.

Since his proposal the light had altered again. It was time to be home. They came over a rise long enough to spy one of the small shacks dotting the land, but there was another rise ahead, blocking their view of any of the buildings scattered across the station.

Though they were drawing nearer and nearer to civilisation, the landscape helped to create a cocoon around the two of them.

'Robert?'

The sound of his Christian name coming so easily from her lips this time drew his gaze to her face.

She'd been thinking again—that was plain to see. He'd not known many, if any, people whose head was always so full of thoughts, but whatever was on her mind now had swiped the dismay she'd worn earlier from her face.

'Yes?'

'Are there really pirates in Penzance? It's in England, isn't it?'

A huff of laughter escaped him at the unexpected question. The girl had knowledge of the obscurest of things.

'Penzance is on the English coast, yes. I've never heard any stories of pirates rampaging through the streets in recent years, but that doesn't mean they aren't.'

He ducked his head to study her face briefly before turning his focus back to steering the horse over the next little hill.

'What makes you ask?'

'Oh.' She looked a little embarrassed all of a sudden. Flustered.

She shrugged. 'Mrs Hobson's son married a—well, it's not important. But they went to Sydney for their honeymoon and they went to the theatre, and—'

'Saw *The Pirates of Penzance?*'

'Actually, don't know if they did, but they told me the story afterwards. Is Penzance near where you're from?'

Only the whole length of England away. He'd show her on a map that evening; he suspected she'd enjoy studying the thing.

'It's in the same country, at least. A long journey, though nothing to travel in Australia.'

'Is Sydney terribly busy? Have you been to the theatre there?'

'It's much busier than here, that's to be sure. As for the theatre, yes, I've been. But never to a comic opera like *Pirates.*'

'Oh,' she said again, sounding astonished by the possibility he'd not had every experience in the world already.

'I doubt the show is an accurate depiction of daily life in Penzance,' he said a little apologetically.

She considered that. A breeze picked up loose strands of her fair hair, and she brushed at them absently, one hand still clutching the *crowea.*

'Ah, well. I won't ever know the difference.'

'And in reality there's considerably less singing,' he admitted.

Robert was aware that there were many lives in New South Wales much smaller than his, but never before had it been so keenly illustrated. He almost asked her where she *had* been, but the chances of her answer putting even more distance between them seemed high.

They would go to Sydney as soon as he could manage it, he decided then and there, and he would show her something beyond sheep stations, bushland, and the dusty, rutted main street of town.

He grappled for a change of topic, but—rather predictably—she presented him with one all on her own.

'I won't be singin' for anyone at any time, I'll warn you. You'll be thankful of that.'

'Why would I require you to sing?'

'Isn't that what ladies in parlours do?'

'Not in my parlour.'

'Good,' she said with a great deal of satisfaction. 'I'm sure I'm terrible at it.'

The afternoon had reached that point where the warmth disappeared as suddenly as it had arrived. Robert caught an involuntary shiver from his companion, and he picked up the speed ever so slightly.

'So, we're agreed on this then?' he asked once he'd opened the gate and brought them through, heading up the drive to the house.

She waited until they'd come to a stop to answer, and he nearly fainted in surprise when she took his proffered arm to descend to the ground.

Progress...

She tipped her head back to study him for a short time, the fading light casting shadows across her face, and giving angles to the rounded cheeks, making her seem more mature than he usually took her for.

'Seems we are.'

'Excellent.' It seemed too proper for the situation, but he was suddenly overwhelmed with a surprising amount of relief.

They walked to the house as one, leaving the matter of horse and gig to Adamson with a murmur of thanks. Robert couldn't avoid the involuntary thought they seemed like a pair already walking down the aisle of the church, with Alice's bouquet on display, the effect only ruined by the appearance of Hutton at their heels.

'Now, to tell Elizabeth and Mrs Adamson. Shall we go and find them?'

Her jerky nod was identical to the one she'd given him before, when she said one thing and thought another. There was a hesitation in her step, but she came with him, up the stairs and into the house, and all the way down the hall, following the feminine voices drifting out from the sitting room.

**

A trip to town wasn't anything special—or at least that was what Alice told herself the whole way there the following week, knowing it was a big whopper of a lie. She stayed almost entirely quiet on the journey, leaving the talking to the Farrer siblings and their fancy English tones, only piping up when she was asked a question directly. She supposed she answered correctly each time, though she barely heard what was said.

The road seemed to have shrunk since she'd last made the journey. She was not at all ready for the sight of the first church spire at the crossroads, and nor was she ready for the cheery rows of two-storey terraces that had been popping up along the busier streets the past few years.

What she'd needed was another mile or twenty added to the road, so that she might have a little more time to compose herself and find the courage to hold her head high.

Were those people on the side of the road staring at her? She snapped her face straight ahead and refused to even peek. Likely they'd not even know her dressed as she was, and surely there were better scandals to be gossiped about in town than her recent betrothal to the man sitting across the other side of the carriage.

'Alice Ryan,' a voice from the street said none too quietly as they slowed to turn a corner, and she automatically swivelled at the sound of her name in time to see they were passing a gaggle of ladies she knew mostly from the church.

Who was she trying to fool? She *was* the best gossip in town at the moment, which was why she'd been shaking in her boots—well, the slippers she'd been wearing about the house that morning—for the better part of the day while her belly flipped over a thousand times at the thought of the spectacle she'd make of herself that afternoon.

She spared the ladies one glance, and then lifted a hand to wave when she saw them staring.

'Good afternoon,' she called loudly and with as much cheer as she could muster, startling the lot of them into stammered, rushed greetings that were only half done when their vehicle carried them away.

'Nicely done,' Elizabeth said quietly, and Alice didn't think it was sarcastically said.

Once round the corner, the town of Barracks Flat stretched out ahead of them, a place that'd grown steadily since its foundation five or so decades earlier. Mills lined the river at the street's other end, and at the rate development was taking place, soon they'd be matched in number by public houses.

Some fine homes had been constructed along the banks of the Murrumbidgee where it snaked around the settlement before drifting east towards the sea. Gold, silver and lead discoveries had flourished only briefly in the Fifties, but the people had come in droves, and plenty had stayed.

Set in a valley surrounded by gentle hills, with the larger mountains beyond hidden from view from most perspectives, it was a place that tended to extremes.

Alice winced at the sight of *Wanted* posters that'd been plastered across more than one shopfront, tattered now from being up so many days and subjected to the weather. But she couldn't help turning back to try and make out the illustrations of men's faces.

She couldn't be certain, and really, she only managed a glimpse, but none of the vaguely menacing faces seemed to resemble Ian.

'Word is the men have long since left the area,' Robert said to her in an undertone. 'It's being said the roads are safe again.'

Alice relaxed marginally. Still, though, there was the warning from her brother to worry about, and she bit her lip too hard until Robert brought them to a stop.

***

At the sight of the Farrer vehicle with the man himself in it, several people called out a greeting as their arrival on Monaro Street was registered, and Robert handed the women down. He returned the sentiments politely but without giving anybody a chance to chat, aware of the curious looks he was receiving, and *well* aware that Alice was holding her head high, even as people who'd never before have given her the time of day were suddenly scrutinising her in a new light.

'Will you be all right for an hour or so?' he asked, directing the question at his sister.

She smiled at him, and glanced briefly at Alice, who looked enormously confident until one peered more closely. 'Oh, I think we'll manage.'

They parted ways, the women to pick up something frilly for a bonnet—at least that was what he thought had been discussed the day before—and Robert for the post office, where he had communications to make with both Sydney and Adelaide.

He crossed the street, kicking up dust with each step of his boots. He raised a hand to a man he knew more by sight than acquaintance, and then tipped his hat to a couple of ladies a decade or more his senior, removing it entirely as he reached his destination.

He had his hand on the post office door when he spotted two familiar figures across the road, and he froze.

'Oh for Christ's sake,' he said more loudly than he should have.

There was no reasonable explanation as to why this kept happening. If God was up there watching him, He must be laughing heartily at Robert's constant bad timing.

Tom Wright led a lady down the walkway on the opposite side of the street. Their heads were close together in discussion, and they were seemingly oblivious to their surroundings. It suited Robert perfectly.

The lady turned then, before he could slip inside and hide, and Robert felt as though he'd been hit by the carriage they'd driven in on minutes earlier.

'Damn,' he whispered, because that was not Mrs Thomas Wright hanging onto his nemesis's arm: it was the younger version. And Robert's life had just become even more complicated.

Overcome with a new urgency, he threw himself inside the building with so much speed he came close to pulling the door from its hinges. From his position at the window he watched the lady like an inept spy.

The pair had stopped at a shopfront on the opposite side of the street, but only Wright was looking at the wares on display.

His daughter, who wasn't meant to be *anywhere* near Barracks Flat at the moment, stared across the street, at the exact place Robert had just stood.

She'd seen him.

'Damn,' he said again, his blasphemy unheard under the conversation going on at the counter.

The father lost interest in the shop's display—likely nothing expensive enough there for his elaborate tastes—and again held out an arm for his daughter. Martha stared towards the post office for a beat too long, and then marched her father off at a too-fast pace.

Sighing, and thanking God the Wrights had turned in the opposite direction to Elizabeth and Alice, Robert made his way to the counter and forced his thoughts in the direction of riesling and Germans and the Rhine Province.

***

Business done within the hour, including a drink taken at *The Dog and*

Stile, where he smiled through the sly congratulations aimed his way, Robert found the two women waiting for him when he returned to collect them for the trip home. Alice was in the process of stuffing parcels into the carriage, and he overheard something muttered about wasted money.

They made a pretty sight, sister and fiancée, though he knew better to tell them as much and be disbelieved as an empty flatterer.

It astonished him, really, that he was thinking such things about Miss Ryan. Never in his life had it occurred to him to think of her anything other than a distant neighbour, and yet here she was, fair hair catching the light beneath that little hat, eyes alight with one strong emotion or another—presently *amusement* as she struggled to balance the packages.

Yes, she was a little less put together next to Elizabeth, and there was no mistaking the swear word that escaped when she nearly tripped over her skirt and upended herself on the pavement, but she was...

She was charming him. And it seemed that when a man was charmed by a person's countenance he was capable of being charmed by her in other ways, too.

How had he not noticed before that there was a pretty girl beneath that scruffy exterior?

'You're staring, Robert,' Elizabeth said, sounding abnormally pleased about that development. It was enough to bring him back to his senses.

'It's unusually hot for May,' he said, ignoring her snort of amusement at the pathetic excuse. 'My mind wandered.'

'Oh, you poor fellow. Shall I drive us back if you're feeling that peaked?'

He supposed the glare that remark earned was answer enough; he wasn't going to honour it with words. Of course, that made his sister laugh at him outright.

Alice was stuffing more parcels into the carriage, and he overheard something else muttered about wasted money.

'Leave her be,' Elizabeth advised in a low voice. 'I think she's secretly pleased with her purchases, even if she's unhappy about the cost of them. I couldn't talk her into spending more than what was absolutely necessary.'

'Of course you couldn't.' He was actually surprised at his sister's success in convincing Alice to buy anything at all.

Before he helped Elizabeth up, he leaned closer still and spoke in a tone lower than a whisper.

'Did you know Martha Wright is back?'

The shock on his sister's face was his answer enough.

'She isn't. She couldn't be.'

'I'd beg to differ—I saw her walking on this very street less than an hour ago.'

'You saw her?' Elizabeth shook her head slowly, confused. 'How could I not have known she was coming home?'

'I saw her. She was across the street from me, walking with her father. I thought she might have written to let you know.'

Whatever was happening between the Wright and Farrer men, Martha and Elizabeth had been the closest of friends since childhood.

Elizabeth glanced quickly at Alice, who'd loaded her purchases to her satisfaction and was standing slightly off to the side, politely waiting for the two of them, in her mind still the outsider.

'I'm sure she has her reasons,' Elizabeth said. 'What are you going to do about her?'

'About Martha? She has nothing to do with whom I'm betrothed to now.'

Irritated by the behaviour of the Wright daughter as well as her father, and frustrated on his sister's behalf at the snub by her friend—even if he had his suspicions why it'd happened—Robert left it at that for the time being.

He shook his head. 'Every time I think I understand what that man's up to, he pulls another trick.'

Elizabeth shrugged, deceptively dismissive of the whole thing.

'I suppose we'll find out in time.'

As irritated with himself as much as anyone else, Robert assisted his sister into the carriage and turned to his fiancée, who was again about to hoist herself up without any assistance.

He took her arm just before she'd have done it, and Alice hastily stepped back, stumbling a little, making him smile inwardly.

'I'm meant to let you help me,' she recited to him, 'so that I don't get me foot stuck in a skirt and end up on me—*my* arse in the middle of the street.'

'Well, yes, but...' he took her slightly aside and lowered his voice beyond the reach of Elizabeth's hearing.

'Need help with any more parcels?'

Alice looked at him, lips pursed against a smirk. 'You could've asked a couple of minutes ago.'

'Ah, but you were doing such a good job I wouldn't want to have interrupted.'

She didn't believe that for an instant, but didn't call him out on it. Robert glanced down the street. They'd drawn a few spectators out of various shops, but everyone was keeping a polite distance.

'How did your afternoon go?' he asked, turning his attention to his fiancée's heart-shaped face.

Alice drew herself up, looking like a young lady about to tell a huge lie, and then visibly reconsidered.

'Nobody knows how to speak to me anymore.'

He could imagine. Most liked people to stay in the position they were born, not raise themselves higher, on purpose or by accident.

'Should I have gone with you today?'

'Oh, no. I just smile at them 'til they feel uncomfortable and have to speak to me the way they speak to Elizabeth.' She frowned, but it was a fleeting expression. 'In time it might be fun.'

She was unique, this one. 'You'll do,' he murmured, more for his ears than her own, and then helped her into place up beside his sister.

'So we passed the test, would you say?' he asked breezily as they set off northwards. 'You're still going to marry me, yes?'

'Mister Farrer, you made the offer and now you're trapped. Of course we're still gettin' married, even if you've finally come to your senses and realised you're mad.'

Chapter 10

Alice wasn't stupid. Or at least, she didn't think she was stupid too often. She was to be married in only an hour or so, and she knew what she was getting herself into.

Mostly.

Robert Farrer was a nice man, and she didn't think that'd change after they married. He certainly was handsome with those dark eyes, and strong enough to lug her about when she was ill. Maybe that part was a little embarrassing, but it also gave her little shivers when she remembered it—good shivers, not fever shivers.

She smoothed a careful hand down her skirts, noticing how it tremored as she did so. The gown was the most beautiful thing she'd ever worn, not fussy or frilly, but so fine it made her afraid to move. It wasn't white, but then that wasn't what she'd wanted. The copper-coloured silk *faille*—as Elizabeth had called it—was so very, very pretty.

After having dressed her hair and heard too many declarations of her prettiness, Mrs Adamson and Bessie had disappeared to take care of some wedding breakfast matter or another, giving Alice a few minutes to herself.

The reflection of the girl in the mirror did sparkle just a touch, thanks to her new brooch. Her face seemed paler than usual, but her eyes were bright.

You'll do she'd heard Robert say a few weeks ago. She bloody well hoped she'd do today.

A moment later she stiffened at the sounds of voices down the hall. Soon someone would come for her, but nerves she hadn't wanted to admit to kept her feet rooted to the wooden floorboards of her room.

Last night had been her final one sleeping in this place, in this bed. Probably. She wasn't all that sure about that part. She hadn't much of an idea about what came next, but she was certain it'd be surprising.

She'd fancied herself in love with Declan Greaney from the other side of the river for two full years before she caught him kissing that Annie girl from the farm out west. She'd discovered them behind the church, so involved in each other they hadn't even noticed Alice standing there, mouth gaping and mind confused.

It was only then she'd realised how Declan's ears were a funny shape, and noticed how he always spoke like a genius when he really didn't know much about anything. It turned out to not be the grand romance she'd imagined, and anyway, it was not long after that she'd begun to notice how handsome the local landowner was when he rode past her house most afternoons.

A cockatoo began screeching like a madman near to the window, and there was something so ridiculous about the bird that it helped to settle her nerves.

Alice almost smiled.

Maybe Mr Farrer didn't love her any more than Declan Greaney did, but she didn't mind as much as she should. It was a good match for a girl like her, even if it was a terrible one for her future husband. He didn't love her, and if she loved him a little, he didn't need to know about it. It'd be her little secret, and not for all the tea in China would she ever let him know.

She was smarter now than she was the afternoon she'd walked home crying because Declan had his hand up Annie Wilson's skirts, and she weren't going to be stupid about Robert Farrer. There were better reasons to get married than love.

She touched a tentative hand to her hair, just a brush to make sure the curls were still as they were supposed to be. She'd won a battle with Bessie and only had a few styled on the front of her head, even though she'd been told current fashion called for a lot more of the things. *Josephine curls,* they were apparently called.

When the curls had first been suggested—or, rather, when Alice had been ambushed that morning—she'd been dubious. Especially so when her transformation began.

'I don't know who this Josephine lady is, but I hope those curls look better on her than they do on me,' she'd said as she studied herself in the mirror.

Elizabeth had been more enthusiastic. 'Ladies in the towns, and back in England, buy their curls and simply pin them on.'

Alice had thought about it.

'They pin things on the front of their heads? Don't they fall off?'

'I'm sure they do on occasion.'

'That must end up bein' embarrassin'.'

Maybe the fancy ladies from town wouldn't think her fashionable, but she'd prefer her hair to look antiquated than to look like one of Robert Farrer's sheep.

Maybe, she decided, she wouldn't disgrace anyone that day after all.

'Are you ready?' a now-familiar voice came from the door, and Alice started ridiculously.

'Lord,' she said, pressing her hand to her chest in shock. 'Mister Farrer, you sure aren't meant to be in here.'

'Robert,' he corrected with a whisper and a hint of a smile, and seeing her as ready to go and be wed as she would ever be, he stepped across the threshold and offered his arm.

She took it, and moved to leave, but his feet stayed where they were. Glancing up at him in question, she found him studying her close enough it made her insides squirm.

'What's wrong?'

'Nothing's wrong,' he said immediately, but continued to stare. Alice brushed at her face anyway, wondering if she'd a smudge or something.

'Somethin' sure is, the way you're starin'.'

That seemed to amuse him. 'You look very pretty, Alice. That's all I was thinking.'

While she blushed and stammered, about to deny it, he continued.

'I've ordered a book,' he told her.

A book?*What in the world was he on about?*

'It's coming from Sydney—a book of saints. Catholic saints, of whom I'm not all that familiar.'

'Catholic saints? What d'you want with them?' Alice couldn't be certain, but she thought there were Catholics in her family somewhere along the way—she'd the Irish name for it—but that'd all been lost at a time she was too young to remember.

'*Januarius*,' Robert murmured. 'The word triggered a memory, and I think I might be onto something here.'

That cockatoo took up its squawking again, and Alice spared it a quick glance.

'Couldn't you ask the priest in town?'

'I did.' Her soon-to-be husband smiled wryly. 'He wasn't a great deal of help. However, let's leave it at that for now. I think we've something more important to do today.'

He'd have started off then, had Alice's feet not rooted themselves back into the floor. Her sudden panic surprised her, but she had something else that needed to be said before they could go ahead with this mad marriage, something needing to be clarified.

And so she looked him straight in the eyes and said what needed saying.

'Robert, I think my brother has gone and become a bushranger.'

***

'I know.'

Robert felt that he should be the one making confessions, but the deep concern in Alice's eyes touched something inside him.

'What do you mean, you know?'

'Well, let's say that I strongly suspected. It was the main reason I insisted you stay here instead of returning home.'

She stared. 'All right, that's it. You're a bloody dingbat. You should've sent me home immediately if you thought that.'

'To live alone, possibly in danger?'

'Uh, Mister Farrer, stop deliberately missin' the point. What makes you think *I'm* not an outlaw, too?'

'You're not,' he said immediately. The idea of it was preposterous, even hilarious. She was a victim of circumstance, and everything he'd learnt of her so far told him she did everything she could to stay out of trouble, not run towards it like her relations.

She pressed her lips tightly together and shook her head. And then she touched a place near her throat.

'I hadn't much when I came here. He took me mother's locket—Ian did, I mean. Not that I've proof, but where else could it've gone? I had it hidden and now it's not there anymore.'

'We can get you another one,' he said automatically. 'Not that it would be the same...'

He ought to have been outraged that the man could sink that low, but he knew his type, and had seen first-hand how greed and lawlessness and even desperation fed off themselves until any morals a man might have been born with evaporated entirely.

'Never really thought I'd marry,' she said more to herself than to him. 'But I always thought I'd wear it if I did.'

Robert nearly offered her a replacement to wear to the church then, but caught himself. An instinct he was beginning to develop about her told him it would only add insult to injury. Instead he strove for a happier tone.

'So, you're certain you won't jilt me, Alice? I'd hate to be embarrassed at the altar,' he said, adjusting his jacket.

She laughed at him, and reached out to grab his hand in such a spontaneous gesture that it affected him immensely.

''Course I won't, even though this is all madness. You're not marryin' me for a dowry, are you? I know we're not madly in love, but I suppose that'll be better. We can be sensible about this.'

He flipped his hand so that he was holding hers, and used his thumb and forefinger to learn the joints and bumps, the rough pads on her palms, and the surprisingly smooth skin running along the back. She'd worked hard her whole life, but there was softness at surprising times. Her gloves waited for her on the dresser nearby and he was glad she'd not yet put them on.

He heard her breath catch at the touch. They were going to be married, and this was the most intimate they had ever been. Robert felt an element of shyness about it all, as though they'd missed a few dozen steps to reach this point. He supposed they had.

When he spoke again, his voice sounded odd even to him. 'What do you know of my deal with Tom Wright?'

'Enough that he's a pest to you, and we wouldn't be marryin' if it weren't for him.'

He should have told her she was mistaken, but he couldn't bring himself to lie to her about that.

'Don't blame yourself for choices I made, Alice.' He touched a finger to the space between her brows, smoothing out her frown. 'We'd better be off. I believe we've something important we shouldn't be late for.'

'But—what about my brother? What if he—'

'Tomorrow,' he told her firmly.

'But ... we'll be married tomorrow, and then it'll be too late if you decide—'

'I won't,' he said before she could finish. 'When we're married we'll worry about these things. Together.'

Finally, he urged her forwards, pausing only for her to gather her gloves.

'This seems strange, to be goin' to the church together,' she said.

'We're being revolutionary. I take it as a good thing, not a bad omen.'

She snorted at that.

All the voices of the people waiting for them dropped to low murmurs at their appearance, and then together they suffered through a cacophony of compliments and a few very hard stares.

Elizabeth, dressed in a fine but plain gown in dark blue, one Robert knew for a fact was chosen so as not to outshine the bride, offered him a private smile, and then she took over, ushering everyone from the house.

'Well,' Alice said with a wobble to her voice, almost masked by false bravado, 'let's go and be wed.'

***

They were discussing her bridecake again.

Alice kept the smile on her face and her groan firmly hidden behind it as the conversation swirled in circles, always coming back to the enormous concoction of fruit and flour that dominated the reception room.

She'd been led to believe a wedding breakfast wouldn't take so long. In fact, an etiquette book she'd stumbled across in her search for Latin translations had told her as much.

Everyone ought to have gone home long ago, but apparently this far out in the country people weren't too fond of following rules. A little desperately, she looked across the room at Robert and his closest friend, accidentally catching John Stanford's eye and then looking quickly away again.

Her hands tightened around the glass in her hands.

'Only the best would do,' one lady to Alice's right said as she helped herself to another dainty bite of her slice. Only parts of the cake could be eaten, as the rest was a construction of pillars and sugar and small figurines that Alice had marvelled at when it'd been delivered all the way from Sydney.

It seemed a ridiculous extravagance to her, but at least it'd turned into a greater spectacle than she was herself. If the guests insisted on staying all afternoon, then she'd rather them stare at the cake than at her. For the moment she was more than happy to sit to one side, temporarily forgotten, and watch.

Elizabeth had gone from the room minutes before to fuss over some arrangement or another. *'Tomorrow it's my job to do all the worrying,'* she'd told her the night before, as they'd sat side by side on Alice's bed, avoiding serious talk about what was to come once vows were exchanged and registers signed. *'You're to move about and perch on various chairs and look decorative and pleased with yourself, even if the food turns bad or the room catches on fire.'*

At least Elizabeth had made her laugh.

Robert passed her then, bending to whisper in her ear. 'We're close to done with this nonsense,' he told her. 'I'll make sure they head home soon.'

'Mr Farrer ... perhaps you ought not to say it that way while your guests are still here.'

He sighed melodramatically. 'I hope I'll now be Robert in private, at least,' he said softly, and then his name was called by another man. Alice hadn't a clue of the fellow's name.

'Go,' she coaxed when her new husband hesitated. When he was off again she looked down into her glass. Nice as it was for Mr Stanford to provide wine for the afternoon, she only wished it'd not been a syrah from Victoria. To drink red wine while everyone was watching her? She'd likely end with it spilt down the bodice of her frock—or forming an overlarge purple smile on her face.

And so it went on. Alice smiled her sympathy each time one of the Farrer siblings was drawn away, did her best to perch decoratively, and ignored her growing anxiety about the mystery of the night to come.

She was glad of the Wright family declining to attend. Even though she'd be seeing plenty of him in the future, Mr Wright's was the one face she'd absolutely not wanted staring back at her over the course of the day.

With the light now drawing long shadows across the ground, surely the guests would be off soon. Oughtn't they to have gone by now? Oh, she wished they'd all just go. After the comments about her gown and her good fortune, and her handsome husband—and that bloody cake—most of the guests had all but run out of things to say to her and drifted back to their friends.

What would happen next? She didn't know, because she'd drifted through the whole day so far on other people's instructions.

Suddenly Alice wasn't yet sure she *wanted* the guests to be off. She wouldn't complain if she was forced to wait a couple more nights to find out what occurred when a man closed himself off in a bedroom with a woman. She was suddenly so very aware all the married folks in the room knew what they were about to do, whatever it was.

It didn't help one bit that Robert now looked at her differently, with something in his eyes she didn't understand. It was as though he suddenly saw *more* of her, and she had to try hard to resist checking her frock was still buttoned properly and that her skirts weren't suddenly revealing something they shouldn't. She wasn't sure she could be brave about it for much longer.

Another half hour went on, and Alice watched as the sun stretched longer still across the ground, and then suddenly the mood of the room changed. The guests started murmuring about the time, and about making it home before the road was clogged with kangaroos crossing at dusk. Before she knew it they were all rising and moving to the door, and Alice made her way out to the carriage drive and through a series of *congratulations* and *farewells.*

In the midst of it all, Elizabeth disappeared somewhere without Alice even noticing...

And all of a sudden she was alone with Robert, and fervently wishing all the guests back.

When her husband offered her his hand, she took it, calmness curiously settling in. And when he turned back for the house, she went with him.

'Are you hungry?' he asked when he'd closed the front door behind them.

Alice considered her options, and then decided to be honest. 'No.'

He met her eyes, and must've seen something there, because then his expression transformed.

'Well, then. Shall we stay down here or head up?'

'Let's...' Lord, it took so much courage to say it, but she did so with a nod, 'go up.'

Chapter 11

'My goodness,' Robert said from the opposite side of the main bedroom once the sound of Mrs Adamson's footsteps had disappeared from the corridor. 'That was hardly subtle.'

The housekeeper, eyes bright, and if possible looking even more sprightly than she'd been that morning, had just abandoned the pair of them for the evening, claiming fatigue. Mrs Adamson, in other words, was a terrible actress.

Alice resisted the urge to call her back, and only because she couldn't think of a good reason to do so. What'd she have her do? Stoke the fire? It was already toasty in the bedroom. Smooth the blankets? Sweep the floor?

She couldn't hear the woman anymore, and she knew it was far too late for excuses now.

Robert rose then and came to her. She watched him warily, trying to appear steady when she'd gone all wobbly inside and out. Something was happening now, or would happen very soon, and it was a bloody good thing she was seated, because she wasn't sure how standing would go with her legs turned to jelly.

He came onto one knee in front of her and then stroked a finger along her wrist, continuing the touch all the way down, until his fingertip came to rest on the gold ring on her left hand, the one he'd put there only that day. Alice watched with a mix of apprehension and wonder as he gently drew the shirt she'd been sewing up a hole in from her hands and set it aside.

'That's better. I can't watch you do mending on our wedding day. Surely that's against one of the rules in that housewife's book of yours.'

'I dunno. I never finished readin' it.' But the library at Endmoor was turning out to be full of help in many forms. Just not *this.* If there were books on what was about to happen, Alice was yet to find them.

'Trust me on this one, Alice. It *is* against the rules.'

He took her now empty hand in his own, his touch light, careful.

'But you've a hole in the sleeve,' she felt the need to argue feebly. 'It needs fixin'. How'd you do it, anyway?'

'The hole? Caught it on a nail when I was chasing a wayward Merino. There's no need to worry about it now, though.' The tone of his voice changed, deepened. 'Some days aren't for chores.'

'There's *always* mendin' to be done,' she said, hearing mild outrage in her tone. Robert heard it too, and smiled.

'There's no mending on your wedding day. If necessary we'll all wear holey clothes tomorrow.'

'Oh, that'd be a great way to maintain your standin' in society. People'll laugh at you behind your back.'

'They'd better bloody not,' he rejoined, shocking her into a laugh of appreciation for his poor language.

She was still grinning at him, more relaxed than she'd been in days, when he took her other hand as well, and closed the distance between them, drawing his face within an inch of her own.

They hovered there, one uncertain how to proceed, and the other expert at drawing out a precious moment.

He was so very manly. Such a strong jaw, and just a little bit of stubble at such a time of the evening. The glow from the lamps and the fire, which was nearly unnecessary as the house was warm enough without it, framed his features in even a stronger light. His eyes always seemed so strongly focused on whatever it was he'd turned his attention to in that instant, and right then it was on *her.*

Right when Alice thought she should pull back before she blushed any harder, he captured her chin with a soft touch of four fingers and a thumb, and kissed her.

His kiss was all controlled power and encouragement. Light at first, but with no question he knew what he was about and how to encourage her to join him. Alice fought the instinct to close her eyes, and instead kept them focused on his, waiting for cues she didn't quite understand, and watching the golden flecks of his irises as he used increasingly insistent pressure to coax her into responding.

Oh, this wasn't at all like she'd thought.

Alice hadn't been aware there was more to kissing than pressing her lips against the man's and then being done with it. Robert caught her bottom lip briefly between his own, and then bent to press the chaste sort of kiss she'd been expecting at the corner of her mouth.

He stayed there, close like that, and she felt him smile suddenly, lips against her skin. As he spoke, the small puff of his breath was warm against her cheek.

'There's someone lurking about in the hallway. I think we'd better stop before we give them too much to gossip about in the servants' quarters. Though I don't doubt that's probably the intention,' he added in a wry undertone.

Alice hadn't any idea when she'd come to be grasping him by the shoulders, but she instinctively pulled him ever so slightly closer for an instant before common sense took over and she let go.

'Who was it, do you reckon?'

'My money's as much on our respectable housekeeper as on one of the maids,' he replied, chuckling.

'And you're so sure it's a woman? Mostly it's men interested in...' she nodded at him, attention on his lips. 'In *that.*'

'So I'm often told.'

Robert rose and helped her to her feet. He edged the door open ever so slightly and peered out like a naughty little boy wanting to avoid an adult. Alice surprised herself by giggling as she clung to his hand and stayed back, hidden by his larger form—as though nobody around would know what they'd just done or what would come next.

'She's gone,' he told her in a tone barely more than a whisper, and then looked back at her.

Oh dear, Alice thought as he closed the door and turned to face her once more.

It's really going to happen now.

***

Alice hadn't told anyone that the peck in the church that morning had been her first kiss, clammy with anxiety as she'd been. It was hardly the sort of thing a lady yelled at the congregation the moment after the berobed man before her declared she was now a wife.

That kiss had been over and done with before she could worry about how well she'd done, and she'd been far too aware of their sizeable audience to think of anything else. Everyone in town seemed to have packed into the place to witness the oddest wedding they'd ever known.

Now, though ... When Robert set about kissing her again it was her second *real* kiss, and it was infinitely different.

He'd shaved well that morning, but he was still a little prickly as he moved his lips from hers to press soft little kisses along her cheek. Stupidly, the bristly feel of his stubble against her skin as he moved from her lips and bent to her throat was a surprise, and one that raised bumps on her arms and put more knots in her belly.

Uncertain about what she was meant to do, she rested her hands tentatively on his chest, and then curled her fingers into his shirt as he brought his lips back to hers, pressing more firmly, nudging her lips apart and then surprising the devil out of her by brushing the inside of her mouth with his tongue.

He drew back a tad when he felt her startle, and looked down at her, his arms looped around her waist.

'All right?' he asked softly, and Alice realised her fingers were still curled into him; she couldn't seem to let go.

She nodded, but followed it with a shrug.

'Mister Farrer, I *really* don't know what I'm doin'.'

His smile was sympathetic, but not mocking. 'I say you're doin' fine.'

That loosened her grip. She gave his chest a little thump.

'Don't laugh at how I talk!'

'Who's laughing? Who says I don't like it?'

She was about to tell him he was a bloody bad liar when she noticed a few things. Namely, he wasn't breathing quite normally, and there was a look in his eyes unlike any she'd seen before—a look for *her.* And, secondly, he was looking at her lips like he wanted to be doing more of that kissing.

Even if her speech was strange and uncultured, apparently he *didn't* mind it.

'You really are a madman,' she told him, and then rose up onto her toes so their mouths aligned and gave kissing another try.

She knew she wasn't doing it properly, but Robert guided her with small touches and nibbles of his lips, silent encouragement in the press of a hand to the small of her back, by bringing his hips closer to hers.

'Sorry if I do it wrong,' she told him once he broke free of her lips with another kiss to the corner of her mouth, and then went on an exploratory trail along her cheek, back to her neck.

'There is no right or wrong in this.' His voice was a whisper against her skin.

Alice tried not to snort, but lost the battle. 'Oh, I bet there's a rule or two I'm goin' to break.'

His head snapped up and he smiled into her eyes. 'Well, that'll keep things interesting.'

She was still sceptical and shaky with anticipation of whatever was to come, and she still worried enormously that this was going to be the disaster of her life, but she allowed him to continue as he wished, shivering as he removed pins from her hair, and sighing with the relief of him unfastening the tight hooks and ties on her gown.

Clothes were shed faster than Alice's nerves could keep up with. Not that Robert was in a hurry, but he kept stopping to distract her with small kisses here, and nibbles along the tips of her ear there, and her mind had gone wandering.

He unfastened the front of his shirt to reveal a fascinating few inches of skin she'd not seen on many men before. There'd been old Tom Brown, with his saggy skin where Alice had breasts, and Mr Peterson, who had had a stomach sticking out like he'd swallowed a ball. And of course, there was Bertie in the river...

Her new husband was a little hairy there, and she bet that if she'd been a bit braver she'd have touched him to see if he was wiry or soft.

Maybe next time, she decided, keeping her hands uselessly in front of herself and wondering if she looked as silly as she felt.

He paused in disrobing, and she was glad of it when he gathered her back up against him and cupped the back of her skull, pressing her close from the tips of their toes to where her cheek met his chest.

Not soft, she decided. But *not wiry,* either. Warm, though. So warm. She rubbed her face against him just a little bit and decided it was different, but not bad.

'Do you know what is going to happen?' he asked, preoccupied with combing his fingers through her hair. He seemed fascinated by it, which was something she didn't understand. It was just hair.

Nobody had played with her hair since she was a small child, and she found she liked it very much. It was the reason he had to repeat his question before she brought herself to answer.

'Oh, you mean—Well, you mean did I understand what Mrs Adamson was all in a bluster about explainin' to me before?'

'She was? I almost wish I'd seen that.' He made a sound in the back of his throat that was almost a laugh, and despite the nerves that churned in her belly Alice laughed aloud. That entire conversation was one she wished she'd never been a part of.

In fact, she wasn't sure she knew enough about *it* to get by, but it was too mortifying to admit. Mrs Adamson, face as red as a beetroot, had been in such a state trying to explain what was to come that Alice had taken pity on both of them, suggested she already knew all there was to know—a gigantic lie—and they'd left it at that.

'Maybe I can catch up with some help from you.'

'If that's the way you want it to be.'

She nodded against his chest and then ran her hands along his upper arms, feeling the lean bulk of muscle, and the way it tensed and then twitched at the lightness of her touch.

She'd never touched a man there before either, and even if it wasn't anything special for him, it was for her. Leaning back enough to fit her hands back between them, she returned her attention to his chest.

Maybe he was ticklish, she thought, maybe he didn't like it, and withdrew it back in a flash. He made a sound of protest, and then took hold of her hand gently, squeezing it lightly once before replacing it to his skin.

'Touch me wherever you want,' he encouraged in a low voice, and then buried his face against her shoulder, kissing her over and over until she shivered at the sensation of it.

***

Time passed as they learnt each other's bodies, breaths and whispers their only conversation. Somehow, without her quite sure how it happened, Robert walked Alice to the bed until the backs of her legs met the mattress, and then she was scrambling up onto it, moving back as he again closed the space between them.

He caught her foot in his hand, and held her steady as he had once before, on that morning back in April that held only hazy memories for her, memories punctuated with bursts of terrible pain.

She allowed it, knowing she was about to allow a good deal more once the rest of her clothes came away, and realised immediately what he was about right then.

'The ankle's fine now,' she told him while he paused in the peeling off of her stockings to inspect the place she'd been bitten. 'It was a long time ago now really, and—*Robert,* will you stop staring at it!'

Smirking, he stared a little longer, and then pressed a kiss to the spot, surprising her into temporary submission.

'I'm actually disappointed,' she told him in a near-steady voice, her head tipped back on the counterpane as she stared at the ceiling and willed herself not to blush.

'With me? I'd better try harder, then.'

'No, with the bite. I thought there'd at least be a mark to remember it by.'

He looked across at her, over the slight curves of her body.

'You want a scar?'

'Well, no, not really. But look how much has happened because of it.'

He tilted his head a moment, considering that, and then brushed his thumb over the place again.

'And it doesn't pain you anymore?'

'No. It's as if it never happened. Except that—'

She broke off and stared harder at the ceiling.

'Except that now here we are, where neither of us expected to be.'

'Exactly. So,' she said, and looked at him again, belly leaping in fright and anticipation, 'show me how this is to be done.'

Chapter 12

With her mind set to learning the task as they went, Alice's practicality took over, erasing the worst of her nerves. Even when the last of their clothes were gone and she was delivered one of the great surprises of her life, she managed to keep her wits about her.

Even so, it wasn't possible to look away from the most obvious thing in the room.

She'd seen a few men's willies in her life, but—*holy Moses*—never one that looked like *that.* It was a good thing the light was dim, because Alice rather thought it was better he didn't see her blush.

Only, *of course* he noticed.

Robert took one look at her face, and then he was gathering her to him with a restraint that surprised her. If he wasn't straining with … need, was it *need?* … If he wasn't straining with need, then she might've thought he just wanted to cuddle her, but there was the matter of the hard thing between them, hot and pressing against her skin.

'Here, we'll wait a moment,' he said, careful even though she knew he was ready for more. She was no expert, but some things were obvious. Alice took her moment's reprieve, and then drew back, reaching up hesitantly to touch his cheek. His colour was high and his skin very warm to the touch.

'Robert...? I am all right. We'd better do the rest.'

Despite his tension, he grinned at her.

'The rest?'

Did he know his hands had started travelling up and down her hip, and her thighs?

He repeated a brush along her leg, but firmer and closer to ... she shivered, and her legs parted just slightly, as though they had to.

'I'm not sure I know what *the rest* is,' she reminded him, tensing when the back of his hand brushed at the curls between her legs.

Had he meant to do that? She didn't know there'd be this sort of touching involved in the matter. Why were hands involved at all? Were they usually? Did they need to be?

It was all taking much longer than she'd expected, and—

Alice gasped when he repeated the motion. His hard, muscular thigh, and that other hard thing she couldn't stop noticing and feeling against her side, were warm and pushing more insistently against her.

It was all very embarrassing, but for some reason she didn't want him to stop.

Robert pressed his lips to her temple as he gently but resolutely encouraged her to part her thighs more, his hand working between them. She jumped at the first curl of his fingers in a place she'd never before imagined anyone touching, but he was determined, and with a soft murmur he continued as he wanted.

Alice wasn't sure how long it went on for, the touches that became firmer and more intimate. She had no idea at what point she became brave enough to reach down with an uncertain hand and then touch him, the part that'd surprised her so much earlier.

Suddenly shy about her boldness, she was about to snatch her hand back and wait for further instructions when Robert groaned. It did not seem like an unhappy groan.

Encouraged, oddly triumphant, and even bolder now, she continued to do what he appeared to like, though it became increasingly difficult when his own fingers probed deeper, shocking her at the same time as her body responded of its own accord, hips pushing closer to the sensation.

What an odd thing to be doing, she couldn't help but think. Did everybody know about such things?

There was the whisper of the blankets as Robert shoved them aside, and the soft sighs Alice vaguely recognised as her own.

The fire flickered and crackled, casting warmth across them even though Alice no longer felt that she needed it.

She'd not a clue how she ended up on her back with her new husband rising above her.

She was in far too much of a daze of newly discovered pleasure when it occurred to her the part she'd expected from the beginning was happening.

Robert was careful with her, but the intrusion into her body was beyond what she'd ever expected. The reality of him coming into her widened her eyes and cut short any frivolous comment she might have attempted to make light of an overwhelming situation.

He took his time, pressing forwards and retreating, murmuring quietly, tensely as he encouraged her to open to him. Unlike what had come before, this was not particularly comfortable, but Alice had been prepared to not like everything that happened that night, and allowed it.

Finally, finally he was completely inside her and sighed, lowering his cheek to hers briefly before turning his face to kiss her as he began to move.

Time passed and the discomfort gave way to a new sensation she'd not experienced before as her body became accustomed to his. It was still all so strange and new, and he was still such a stranger to her, but it was not as unpleasant as at the start.

Alice wanted to ask how long such a thing took, as she'd thought it a much faster and simpler activity than it was turning out to be, but she wasn't yet certain she ought to talk.

After all, Robert did seem rather busy.

She jumped a little at a loud *crack* from the fire, but her husband was too distracted to notice.

What *was* he doing? His movements became faster, and she hooked her arms around his shoulders to hold on as he became more frantic. He strained for something like he couldn't reach it, and she didn't know precisely what it was.

Did he need her help with something? Should she speak now and ask him? Oh goodness, she'd no bloody idea what she was supposed to do.

He pressed his face against her tangled hair and sped up more, breaking the kiss to gasp against her ear. Alice instinctively moved with him, but there was something ... something...

'Robert? Robert, what am I supposed to do. Help me to—'

Through it all he heard her whispered question and he rose up enough to slip a hand between them, touching her where it felt good, so good, and then it was Alice gasping and straining.

All too soon afterwards it was over. Robert strained against her one final time, and then came to relax, his weight on top of her long enough for him to draw in big gulps of air, and then he was gently extracting himself from her body and shifting onto his side.

Still they lay touching, his feet tangling with hers, and Alice self-consciously, tentatively, tugged at a corner of the blankets until she was half covered.

'Thank you,' he said to her then, bending to kiss her forehead, and she nearly laughed at the sentiment.

She didn't so much drift in the aftermath as she did lay still and mull things over.

So, this was the way things were to be from now on? She'd only thought as far as the wedding and the night that would come afterwards, but now they'd be sharing that bed and doing ... *that* often, she supposed.

It was a new reality she'd take time to become accustomed to, not that she minded it.

Well, there was the embarrassment, but surely that was normal. Maybe if she thought about the nicer parts of it ... It was almost ridiculous, such an odd thing for a man and wife to do, and she again came close to laughing as she wondered how anybody had even thought of it in the first place.

Tucking her amusement away for later, she leaned her head on his shoulder and sighed when he ran a lazy hand down her back.

'You're awfully quiet,' Robert murmured into the peace that followed.

Alice rolled her head to the side so that she could make out his profile in the dimming light. He looked strong like he always did, but he also looked different somehow. *Hers.* He might be big and strong and make people quiver in their boots, but right now she wasn't scared of him at all.

Not even after ... after what they'd just done.

Before she could stop herself, a little laugh escaped. Clamping her hands over her mouth, she tried to stop it, but the second laugh came soon after the other one.

Beside her Robert propped himself up on one elbow and watched, and for a reason she didn't understand that made her laugh even more.

'I'll have you know that most men are offended when they are laughed at in bed.'

But when she checked his expression there was a smile there, a flash of teeth in the low light, and so she flipped onto her side to face him.

'Why are they offended?' she asked, and despite her best intentions she snorted again.

'Do you really have to ask?'

Alice bit her lip, but the corners of her mouth still tipped up.

'I reckon I do.'

'This ... bed sport is a matter of male pride, I'll have you know. If a lady laughs afterwards, it tends to mean we've done it wrong.'

'Oh,' she said, thinking that it was hard *not* to laugh after everything that'd just happened. What were they supposed to do next? The idea of getting up in the morning and putting on regular old clothes and going to breakfast like everything was normal was ridiculous.

And how was she going to look at anyone now? Most would know what they'd been up to, and then ... Did Elizabeth know about this sort of thing? Lord, she hoped Elizabeth didn't know things like that about her own brother, and she decided to never discuss it with her.

The thought of *that* conversation happening made her laugh again, and when Robert wrapped an arm around her waist and tugged her up against him she turned her face into his shoulder and smiled against the crook of his neck.

'If you're worried,' she told him earnestly, 'I don't think you did it wrong. Even if you did, I promise to lie for you if anyone asks.'

He laughed outright at that, his arm tightening around her in appreciation before he let her go.

'I certainly hope that is never a question that comes up in conversation.'

He seemed happy enough to be flopped across the bed, and so Alice decided it must be over for the time being. She hadn't any idea if a person only did it once a night, or more, but she'd just have to learn as they went on. She'd have thought it was only once, but he wasn't sleeping yet and nor was she.

Alice adjusted her position carefully, not wanting to bounce him around when he looked so relaxed. It was going to be unusual sharing a bed. Even in her little house she'd never had to share her lumpy old mattress with anyone.

Robert grunted and then surprised her by gathering her back up against him, silently encouraging her to lay across his chest.

She imagined that everyone else in the homestead was sleeping by now, and the men who worked the land all day and lived in the outbuildings would be long asleep, too. The window was cracked ever so slightly open and through it she heard the sounds of night: the chirp of some insect or another, and the soft rustle of breeze through leaves.

It was only the two of them awake, and—after what they'd just done—it was surely the most personal she'd ever been with someone else.

When did married people ever sleep if they had to fit in time for *that* as well as everything else that went into a day?

That brought on a new worry. 'I'm supposed to stay in here tonight?'

Robert shifted underneath her, dislodging her from the spot she'd claimed against his chest, pushing up high enough to give her face a thorough inspection. Alice was well glad of the low light, because she knew immediately she'd said something else silly and wrong.

'I wasn't planning on forcing you, if you'd rather have your space. Your old room is—'

'Oh, no,' she said quickly, sensing she'd given him entirely the wrong idea. 'No, I meant—well, Mister Farrer, that I wasn't ... I forgot to find out earlier if I'm *supposed* to stay here.'

Those arms went back around her, and with a little encouragement she was laying across him again.

'I'd rather not be addressed so formally in bed,' he said, sounding amused about it. 'My Christian name will do nicely. And yes, I think you should stay. I want that.'

'I don't think I snore.' She would surely have been told by her father or her brother at some point.

She felt his smile against the tangles of her hair. So much for those careful curls Mrs Adamson and Bessie had been so intent on fixing for her that morning.

'That's good to know. I don't think I do, either, if you're concerned.'

No, she couldn't imagine he'd be a snorer, but even if he was, Alice reckoned she'd be happy to share the bed with him all the same.

'One good thing about me—*my* size is that I won't use up much of the mattress.'

'You might be a restless sleeper. Throwing yourself around and stealing all the covers—and the space.'

'I'll try and stay still then.'

'Take as much space as you need. If it becomes a bother, I'll simply rearrange you.'

'I'll try all the same.'

'The deal is already sealed, Alice. You've no need to sell yourself to me.'

She decided to stop arguing. Winter was on top of them, so it might make sharing a bed ... cosy...

'The first time is always a little awkward—uncomfortable, perhaps,' he said, and it took her a couple of moments to realise what he meant.

'I suppose I'll get the hang of it soon enough.'

She might not understand why people did ... *that,* what they'd just done together, all the time, with all the rolling and funny noises—and the *poking*—but she could understand that touching part. That'd been nice. She'd rarely had anyone touch her in her life before.

Robert's chest expanded and relaxed underneath her, and if she pressed her ear a little further down she might hear the steady beat of his heart. It was amazing to think that until an hour ago she'd only ever seen him with a collar up to his earlobes.

'You can ask questions, you know,' he said.

'I think I'll be savin' those questions for another time.'

'If you're sure.'

'I am,' she said immediately.

Right before sleep pulled her under, Alice couldn't help but wondering who Robert Farrer had been behind the church hall with in his life before. Not Annie Wilson, for certain, but there had to have been *someone.*

Chapter 13

'Tell me about England,' Alice asked as she and Robert walked arm in arm down Monaro Street, completely respectable and happy as they had ever been together.

'What in particular do you want to know?'

It wasn't the first time she'd asked him the question, and he'd come to realise that she liked to collect little snippets of information, as though she were forming a mosaic of him. It didn't seem to bother her what little snippets he shared, as long as he shared. Sometimes he found himself telling her of a long-buried memory, one that could still cause a pang for his first home. Other times, however, it was a silly little anecdote that came to his mind first.

Either way, Robert found he was happy to talk.

So far he'd told her of English country winters, of long nights followed by mornings with dustings of snow. This time, he told her of that one terrible winter where men and boys alike had used shovels to dig their way through feet of snow simply to get out of the house.

'It makes here seem hot,' she said once she'd laughed at the image he'd conjured, of a little boy version of himself battling with an implement as big as he was, determined to do his part.

'It certainly does.' In Barracks Flat it was one of those winter days that made the season seem idyllic. With the sun out, it was as warm as early summer in Cumberland.

'I'd love to see snow. I mean, I've seen it on the mountains a few times, but never up close. Is it like hail, or different?'

'Different.' He thought it over. 'Mushier. It makes the oddest noise when you walk on it.'

She peered up at him from under the brim of her unfashionably large bonnet, one she favoured as much for working in the garden as she did for trips into town, and he caught a glimpse of her eyes before he looked away to help her across a pothole in the road.

'Would you ever go back there?'

'To England? Possibly one day, but only to visit. Not for a time though, not until Endmoor and the viticulture business can survive without me.'

Which might be never, but that afternoon he chose to be an optimist.

A sudden thought struck him. Was she concerned he might? His wife needed her horizons broadened, definitely, but he guessed she was rather tied to the land, even with its arachnids and outlaws and all the other less savoury aspects of life in country New South Wales.

'If you mean would I return to England to live,' he continued. They were at the end of the road, where Monaro Street hit the water and the bridge, and the river walk veered off to both the left and the right. 'Then no, it wouldn't be possible now.'

He was far too tied to his life and responsibilities in Australia.

He turned them left, eastwards and away from the grand Wright house that faced the river on the west. Ducks waddled along the riverbank and glided across the water, their little community punctuated by the occasional large frame of a black swan.

'But do you *want* to go?'

What he *wanted* didn't hold the relevance it had a short time ago. With each decision made in the past few months he'd tied himself more and more closely to the land. From Elizabeth's return home, to the plans with John, and now a wife ... He wasn't his father, and he'd not be taking off back to England.

Robert waited for panic to hit. It was a delayed realisation that he was bound to the tablelands now, but all he felt was a bloody-minded determination to succeed.

'I couldn't say, just as I can't promise all of my memories of the place are accurate. I was only a lad when I left, and when I went back to study it was in London, which is far from my family's home. Most people are guilty of being too romantic about the past, I think. With a bit of time it's very easy to forget the unlikeable parts of a situation when they're thousands of miles away.'

'I think that about me—*my* family sometimes,' she admitted absently.

Before he could respond to that someone behind them sneezed loudly, and multiple times. A true sign spring wasn't too far off, Robert thought wryly. Church that morning had been accompanied by a symphony brought on by a premature attack of hay fever.

'One thing I keep rememberin' about my family, though ... I fell in the river once, when I was really small. Everybody thought I was too tiny to play cricket with them, so I decided to go to the riverbank on me own. Ian had to dig me out, and by then I'd travelled through the water to the other end of town.'

That stopped Robert in his tracks. His mind filled with all sorts of dreadful images of a small blonde girl flailing about in the fast-moving Murrumbidgee, her legs tangled uselessly in her skirts.

'I did not know that.'

Alice made a dismissive sound, waved to someone on the south bank of the river, a man leading a horse towards the bridge, and tugged at Robert's arm to keep him going.

'Why would you? You needn't sound scared about it. As you can see, I didn't drown. Afterwards Ian taught me how to swim, how to stay afloat should it ever happen again. It was a good thing someone planted all those weeping willows 'round here, because if I hadn't got tangled in them, I would've sunk.'

They noticed the lady in front of them at the same time, a finely dressed creature coming from the opposite direction, small daughter in tow. It was Mrs Johnston, one of the society wives and one of their wedding guests. The woman had attended both the church and the reception that came afterwards, even though her presence at the celebration was definitely under sufferance. She'd not tried hard to hide it.

Robert watched the woman's step falter as she realised whom she approached, and saw the tell-tale sideways look that said she was trying to decide if she could duck across the street without appearing too obvious with her snub.

Naturally, his wife tugged him on, undaunted, and the other two had little choice but to stop.

'Good afternoon, Mrs Johnston.'

The other woman momentarily appeared horrified by his wife's gall, but recovered well enough.

'Good afternoon.'

The barest of niceties exchanged, the lady was ready to be off already, but Alice had the Devil in her and gave the woman's little girl a wobbly approximation of a curtsy.

'And to you, too.'

Predictably, the girl was oblivious to her mother's dilemma, and took great, giggling delight in returning the curtsy, thankfully even wobblier than Alice's.

And then it all was over and done with and Alice led him on their way again.

'I think the lady's growin' fond of me,' she said, poker-faced.

***

The rain arrived three days later, as did Robert's book on Catholic saints.

The downpour came unexpected and suddenly, overnight as was the custom in the tablelands, and it seemed to suit Alice's mood. After the initial surprise, and—at times—joy at her new situation, all the worries had settled back in like old, unwelcome friends.

The book, however, came when there was nobody else about except for Alice, delivered by a man on a horse, the beast's hooves kicking up chunks of new mud as it cantered away, leaving her in possession of a brown-wrapped package with her husband's name on it, and more curiosity than she thought she could contain.

As for Robert, he was off somewhere far out on the edges of the property, having mentioned something about visiting and warning the Ngambri and Ngunnawal settlements about interlopers on the land while he was away.

Briefly, stupidly, she considered rushing out there in the rain to find him, to share her news. She'd seen her husband handle a gig, and thought she might manage it on her own if necessary, but common sense finally got the better of her. Instead she sat, mending—there was always mending—and allowed herself to be driven increasingly mad by the endless ticking of the expensive clock on the mantle.

Elizabeth was in town for some reason or another. She'd seemed reluctant to explain it to Alice, and so Alice had not asked.

She didn't eat in the dining room, as she would have if there'd been anyone else about to dine with. Instead she was content with a tray by the fire, enjoying her little cocoon of comfort.

The package sat opposite her, where she could see it whenever she looked up from her stitching, slowly but surely driving her mad with curiosity.

The first message arrived from Barracks Flat, delivered by a soggy stockman back from town, informing her Elizabeth was to stay the night where she was, thanks to the bad weather. The second message was delivered not long afterwards, by another man hovering in muddy boots on Endmoor's doorstep: that Robert was to stay the night in one of the small huts along the property and be back in the morning.

'Damn,' she said quietly, once the man was out of earshot. How was she meant to last that long not knowing what the package might be able to tell?

She continued to sew, and then when she was all done with that she wandered the house, dusting things that really didn't need it.

The sun had almost completely gone down when Alice's patience ran out entirely.

Wishing she were a better sneak, she carefully untied and unwrapped the book—she'd been certain what it was as soon as it arrived—and was gratified to find it the Catholic tome she expected.

Had Robert not, after all, told her on their wedding day that he'd ordered it? Had he not implied it was to help *her?* Would he mind if she unwrapped it? She knew he wouldn't, but she still hesitated another moment before opening the cover.

She had to know, especially if it was to help the lot of them. She just had to.

***

'It's September,' Robert's wife told him gravely when he returned home late the next morning, ready for a wash and a hot meal, Hutton at his heels. The storm was long gone. She hadn't even waited in the house for him but was there at the gate to the west when he came over the rise.

Bemused, he bent to kiss her cheek, and then drew back to offer her a grave look.

'That's optimistic of you, Alice, but despite appearances, it's not spring yet.'

She made a noise of frustration and then waved his words away.

'No, I mean Januarius. It's a feast day. On the nineteenth.'

He looked at her. 'The book arrived.'

'Yesterday mornin'. Sorry, but I opened it.' She paused. 'I needed another one of your Latin books to help me understand it. Um, *The Latin Dictionary?*'

'A *Latin Dictionary?*' he corrected, wincing. 'Good God, I still own that thing? The number of times while studying I swore I'd burn it at the first opportunity...'

'Well, now I'm glad you didn't.'

Robert took her hand and set off for the homestead.

'All this time, I was thinkin' it must be in January. I was thinkin' that maybe I'd just misheard Ian.' She glanced up at him. 'I was thinkin' we were on a wild-goose chase, but I was too embarrassed to end it.'

'So, we have a date,' he said thoughtfully, aware of how tense his wife's hand was in his own. He looked down at her.

'When did you hear of this event, anyway?'

She became tenser still.

'Alice?'

'When I ran into me brother back at the old house in May,' she admitted, and attempted to tug her hand from his own. Robert held fast.

'What? When I took you there?'

He received a jerky nod in response.

'And you said nothing about it? Why? Alice?'

'I was scared.'

'Of me?'

'No!'

She trudged on faster, forcing him to speed up to keep up with her.

'No,' she said again. 'Of *him*. Of who he might have with him. Of what he might do if I told you he was there.'

'Alice, I can protect myself.'

'I know,' she said immediately, in a placating tone better suited to a mother than a wife, in an attempt to smooth his pride. 'Robert, I know that. But that night, that first night when the men came to the house, there were so many of them. I didn't know if Ian'd brought them back. I just wanted to get us both out of there.'

She looked up at him, and then quickly away. She hadn't a hat on, and the sunshine had turned her cheeks pink.

'I'm sorry, Robert.' It was a guilt-ridden mumble that would turn even the hardest of men forgiving.

'What do you think your brother intends to do on this date, on the nineteenth of next month?'

'I dunno exactly, but he thinks he's goin' to help make a lot of money.'

That didn't sound good.

'He might've given up on it by now,' she added, not sounding convinced. 'I've not seen him since.'

'All the same, I think I'd better pay a visit to the magistrate,' he told her, and she nodded vigorously.

They came up to the house via the western façade, and let themselves in the back way.

'Alice,' he said to her before they parted in the hall. She stopped and watched him with wary eyes.

'I'm not angry you didn't tell me.' He understood family loyalty, even if it was severely misplaced in her situation. 'But if you discover anything else, please tell me.'

She seemed agreeable to that, and Robert went to wash.

God help her, but he feared for her safety around her own brother, let alone around whomever else was lurking out there in the bush.

***

It was only once he was clean and changed that Robert discovered the book wasn't the only thing that'd come addressed to him the day before.

A letter with the direction written in a flamboyant hand gave him pause, and his stomach lurched as he saw its origin.

South Australia. There was only one reason anyone would be contacting him from there.

'You bastard, Tom,' he muttered under his breath once he'd read the contents. The man had got his way manipulating and ordering Robert's life, and suddenly correspondence had resumed, like some sort of reward.

He could've done with an hour's nap in a decent bed, but now had three visits to make before the day was out. One to the magistrate, one to John Stanford, and one to the office of Thomas Wright.

Chapter 14

Alice hadn't a clue what was wrong with her.

Weeks had passed since the wedding, and the many sudden, surprising changes that came with being Mrs Robert Farrer had settled to an extent Alice felt she was able to catch a breath. Waking in a man's bed each morning was ... warm, even if Robert left it before her as often as not. By necessity she had been early to rise her entire life, but some mornings Robert rose too early for even Alice to appreciate.

Maybe that was the problem, though. It was hard to trust something that seemed too wonderful to be real.

'I might go for a walk,' she said to the dining room at large the afternoon both Farrers had returned, which earned her a gasp of surprise from Elizabeth, the only other person there. They'd still not left the table after lunch, but her new sister-in-law was already sketching. Robert had promised her vines to paint in the near future, but for now it was gum trees. There were always plenty of gum trees.

Now, Elizabeth looked at Alice as though she'd lost her marbles. It was still raining steadily enough to drive sane people indoors.

'You are joking, aren't you?'

She had a point. After a sunny start to the day, the storm had blown back over.

The direction of the wind changed, and the rain seemed to come heavier than seconds before.

'Maybe just a quick stroll.'

What she *was* sure of was that she wanted to be outside. It wasn't usual for rain to last so long in a part of New South Wales known mostly for sunshine and drought, and it was raising an urge in her to be out in it. Because surely the poor weather wouldn't reach her inside this time, unlike at her old house, where a rainstorm always meant puddles inside and buckets on the floor. Endmoor wouldn't dare do anything as undignified as leak.

Alice excused herself before anybody might think to stop her.

Common sense won her over in the end, and she put her coat on and resorted to shivering on the veranda instead of tramping about in the elements like that poor fellow out on the town road. She could barely see him as he passed, head down and limping.

She leaned her hands on the railing, shivering a bit more at the cool water puddling along the wood. The sight of the wedding ring on her finger still astonished her every so often; she could still hardly believe her new situation. Lifting her face up to the sky, she decided the clouds looked angry right then, like they had a point to prove.

Whatever that point was, Mother Nature sure was making it. Alice had never been one to fear storms. She'd not been one of those children who hid under the covers at the appearance of thunder and lightning. Now, though, the whole world was cloaked in a grey haze, making it difficult to make out anything clearly more than a few feet in front of her face. Puddles were forming indiscriminately, and far off the animals huddled under trees. Alice imagined she could smell the soggy sheep from where she stood, but it had to be her overactive imagination.

It was the sort of wretched day she hadn't seen many of recently. The rain came down so fast and heavy then that she could hardly see the trees at the other side of the carriage loop. Every so often the wind splattered big, fat drops across the veranda and her clothes with such power and noise.

She wondered if her old house was flooded. She wondered if the small vegetable patch was surviving. And then she realised it hardly mattered.

'There you are!'

She was surprised into a laugh as Robert snagged the back of her coat and tugged her away from the railing. She turned at his urging and submitted herself to a thorough inspection.

'The way Elizabeth put it, I thought I was going to have to go back out in that and dig you out of flood waters. You're a tad soggy around the edges,' he informed her gravely, brushing at a raindrop and catching it in a rivulet halfway down her cheek.

'I'm all right.'

'Why are you standing out in the rain?'

'We don't see the stuff very often.'

Sometimes, just sometimes, she still felt shy with him. It wasn't the social differences between them—not exactly. It was more that they'd gone from nothing to everything so fast she'd no bloody idea how to cope with it.

She looked back out into the storm, trying to make out figures in the mist. 'Robert, it might be nothin' but there was a man limpin' down the road a little while ago.'

'Limping?'

'Yes. He was headed in the direction of Captains Flat, which I guess isn't that odd, but in this rain, and on foot...'

'I'll keep a lookout for him.'

The rain went on, drumming on the corrugated iron above their heads.

'Is something the matter?' she asked eventually, because he'd made no move to go, and she could just about feel the tension in him.

'No, oh no. It's just that I thought I'd warn you we'll have visitors tomorrow.'

'In this rain?' she asked to cover her immediate stab of apprehension. *Visitors?* Hadn't she had enough of them at her wedding breakfast? Wasn't that enough for the season?

'Alice, you know as well as I the rain won't last another day. Not in this part of New South Wales.'

'Who's comin'?'

He smiled faintly. 'Brace yourself: it's your favourite person.'

Alice groaned, and then groaned again for good measure.

'Oh, *Lord,* Robert. The fellow won't want me there anyway. I might ... I might be deathly ill tomorrow mornin'.'

'Well it's a good thing then that they're expected in the afternoon. I'm sure you'll be fully recovered in time.'

She elbowed him in the side. 'They?'

'Yes.' His tone had changed. 'The reason you'll want to be here tomorrow is because I've been warned Tom Wright is bringing his daughter.'

***

With Elizabeth there to help the conversation, the visit wasn't as excruciating as Alice had anticipated.

Mr Wright was inclined to ignore Alice, and she was more than inclined to let him. Anyway, it gave her a chance to listen to him talk about himself—nonstop—and it was almost entertaining to hear his pompous chatter. Despite his airs, the man's way of speaking was hardly fancier than her own.

'Could it've been a group of Aborigines passing through?' Mr Wright said in response to a comment from Robert she'd not heard. 'If so, I'm sure it's nothin' to worry about. They'd move on in time and—'

'It wasn't Aborigines,' Robert said with absolute certainty. 'They couldn't possibly be stupid enough to leave a fire still smouldering like that.'

The older man leaned forwards and heaped his plate, sitting back to nibble thoughtfully, his moustache moving in a circle with each chew.

Alice wished she could find her voice and ask questions, but she'd gone as shy as a church mouse, and it was infuriating her. She wasn't meek. When'd she become meek?

She sneaked a sideways look in the other direction, accidentally colliding gazes with Mr Wright's daughter. The other woman smiled tentatively, and Alice tried for a smile of her own, and then—thank God—Robert said something about the weather, and she had an excuse to look away again.

It was easier, she decided, as she sipped tea and declined to eat—not wanting crumbs on her mouth or dropped on her frock—to listen to the father than to try and converse with the daughter.

Because Miss Wright terrified her.

Oh yes, she'd heard of the lady before. Of course she had. Only, never before had she got so close to her, and never before had she the chance to see that rumours of her beauty weren't exaggerated. Actually, they hadn't been complimentary enough.

Movement to her left, where the lady was perched, caught her attention momentarily. Miss Wright bit into a small cake and then turned to listen to something Elizabeth said. Not a single crumb dared to fall as she ate.

Alice was in awe of her. She was dark-haired, blue-eyed, and perfectly formed, and Alice didn't want to say a word to her in case it was the wrong one. Stuck beside her, in a new frock of dark green, for the only time since her betrothal Alice wished she'd chosen a more extravagant wardrobe.

She felt scrawny, faded. And suddenly such trivial things mattered to her.

And yet her stomach growled; she'd been too busy that morning—and a little nervous—to eat, and now here she was rumbling loudly in a roomful of people. Did anybody hear it? Were they simply being polite by not reacting?

Oh well, she decided. Better to have crumbs in her lap than a band playing in her belly.

She edged forwards in her seat and reached for a cake.

Outside a dog yelped suddenly, right at the moment she got the piece of her choice between her fingertips. Juggling with the thing before it was startled right out of her grip, Alice gave up on daintiness and devoured it in a couple of quick bites.

'Martha,' the lady's father began in a tone that at once was chiding and indulgent, 'did you really have to bring the dog?'

It'd been a surprise for Alice that the first visitor to descend from the barouche that afternoon hadn't been human. A dog that was striking in its similarity to Hutton seemed thrilled to be there, and had turned Robert's dog ecstatic. And judging by the way the two heelers greeted each other, they were well and truly acquainted already.

Miss Wright glanced at Robert before responding. 'Well, they *are* siblings, father. Lysander wanted to pay his brother a visit.'

Wright scoffed. 'Such nonsense.' He winced when both animals barked again somewhere nearby, but he smiled at his daughter as he said it.

'They're brothers?' Alice asked, looking from Robert to Elizabeth, and finally to Miss Wright.

'From the same litter,' Elizabeth explained, and a short silence followed, until Mrs Adamson came in and asked if they needed anything else.

'Mrs Farrer?' she asked when nobody else immediately replied, and Alice looked up in surprise.

Of course, she realised. She was the missus of the house now—more or less. Even though she didn't know these people she was expected to be their hostess. Even though she was the youngest there by years, she was meant to know everything she was supposed to do.

Feeling her face heat at her failure to realise it immediately, and knowing without it being said that she'd just failed some sort of test, she ordered her shoulders not to slump.

With two sets of Farrer gazes on her to go with the two Wrights, she managed to dig up a smile from somewhere.

'No, thank you. We're fine.' She looked to her sister-in-law for confirmation.

'We are,' Elizabeth echoed, and that was that.

***

Robert couldn't have been more relieved when Tom Wright indicated it was time to go. Allegedly the visit was an apology of sorts for missing the wedding, but it was one every person in the room could have happily done without.

They all rose as one, but Miss Wright lingered as her father walked on ahead, and then lingered longer when his wife followed with Elizabeth, who glanced back and met his eyes with what Robert could only call warning.

'Robert,' Martha said to his turned back, and manners won over. Tom's daughter's feet were all but dragging in her attempt to stay behind, and—with a sigh—he realised he wasn't going to escape the conversation.

'I should not have brought the dog,' she said in a distressed, hushed tone. 'I am so sorry for that. I'd not thought about how it might seem ... What your wife might think of it.'

His wife. Robert wasn't sure what Alice thought of the dogs, if anything at all, but it was odder to hear those words from Martha Wright than it was hearing the housekeeper address Alice as *Mrs.* He hadn't any idea how much longer it would be before it began to feel normal to him, how much longer it'd be before it didn't all seem like some strange dream.

He almost opened his mouth then, to give her an explanation of his marriage. She would have been as shocked as the rest of Barracks Flat when she heard about it, and he doubted she knew much about what her father was up to. He caught himself, though. He and Alice didn't owe explanations to anyone.

The father's voice echoed down the hall, and Robert knew he'd doubled back, calling for his daughter as he returned to the drawing room.

'It was nothing, Martha,' he told her quickly. 'Nothing to worry about.'

Her lovely face lifted up to him, those eyes no man could help but notice so very, very blue in the afternoon light. Whatever it was she was expecting from him, Robert was determined not to give it. He was happily anticipating the removal of anyone named Wright from Endmoor for the remainder of the day, and then he might finally be able to relax.

She must have read something in his expression, because whatever words she'd been about to say died on her lips before they were spoken.

Closing her eyes briefly, she looked away when she opened them again, and then led him from the room.

Robert wondered, as they said their goodbyes, why the daughter had to come on a visit that had seemed to serve little purpose, other than for her father to laud his victory over him.

And Robert asked himself if he *did* feel a sense of defeat. It was impossible to not appreciate Martha's delicate, feminine beauty, and even as that bloody barouche made its way home he was aware of her posture, of the dark curls he caught a glimpse of as the vehicle turned for town.

Lysander, the runt of the litter at birth, sat with father and daughter as they left. When he'd been given to Martha, Robert had considered him the least feminine, and least suitable of pets, but the puppy had been transformed since then, gentrified. For all his frolicking with Hutton earlier in the day, he now perched half on his mistress's thighs, practically a lap dog.

'Heaven help me,' Robert muttered.

Had it been Hutton heading into Barracks Flat instead of Lysander, he would've run alongside. In fact, there his own dog went right then, keeping pace with the vehicle, attempting to herd the thing like it was a sheep. Heelers weren't lap dogs, and not for the first time he wondered how Martha's had managed to survive in a proper, decent, town household all this time. Perhaps there was some poor servant tasked with walking the fellow several times a day, through frost, heat, and hail.

Robert shook his head in amused disbelief at the whole situation.

He watched longer than he should have as the vehicle disappeared from view, the sound of the barouche and the horses that pulled it echoing through the countryside longer than he could see it.

He realised he was frowning, and quickly cleared his expression.

Only ... Despite all of her parents' ambitions for their overly attractive daughter, here she still was. She'd not disappeared up north, nor south to fashionable Melbourne. She had not married someone grand and important.

And here *he* was, newly married to someone who couldn't have been more different to Miss Wright if she tried. Fate was a strange thing.

After a while even the sounds of his visitors dissipated and the countryside returned to its usual state. Robert heaved a great sigh and then went to retrieve Hutton from the gate.

Chapter 15

It had never occurred to Alice to question Robert's reasons for marrying her. She knew it wasn't because Cupid had come to call, and suspected strongly he'd done it for some business reason or another, but if he was willing—and she was willing—she'd called it good enough and left it alone.

She'd thought they'd go on and make the best of it. The Farrer family seemed like a reasonable bunch, and she knew nobody who'd married for anything as ridiculous as love, except perhaps Mr and Mrs Adamson, who seemed to like each other more than was usual.

Alice called herself more than content, and threw herself into her gardening and her reading, and into learning how to run a household. Thank the Lord Elizabeth was there to help with that.

And she threw herself into understanding all the private matters between a husband and a wife, doing her best in that aspect, too. She had to convince Robert they'd be all right in the long run, but she found that even playing Lady of the Manor was exhausting when she was working so hard on it.

It was one afternoon, when she was inspecting an order from town, that Robert brought her the cat.

'Good afternoon.'

She'd heard him coming. The homestead's wooden floors tended to announce new arrivals when the house was quiet, and—for once—the house was still. However, she'd been trying to decide how much meat Endmoor would need for a week, and it really was rather important she didn't ask for too much steak, or not enough.

'Good afternoon,' she said distractedly. There were still the next week's menus to worry over.

She bit her lip and waited for her husband's footsteps to fade.

How many beans would be eaten? Did anybody even like beans? Alice shuddered; she sure didn't.

'*Mrow.*'

All right, that sound didn't come from a man. She had to look now.

'That's a cat,' she said when she turned. And not just any cat, but a speckled one of an indecipherable colour, somewhere between brown and grey, and one that—to Alice's untrained opinion—looked rather large.

Robert looked at the animal in question as it flopped in his hands, and then bent to put it down on the ground. After a pause, the creature moved off to a corner to investigate a scent Alice couldn't detect.

'It is,' he said, straightening and brushing fur from his hands.

'Whose is it?' She didn't recall seeing it before, but maybe it was from the stables.

'Um, I thought she might be yours? That is, would you like her? She belonged to an acquaintance in town, but he has a couple of small children who were too fond of prodding at her, and *she* wasn't overly fond of it. I thought, maybe...'

Alice watched the cat stretch halfway up the table leg and reach a paw out to investigate something or another.

'It's a she?' She hadn't a clue how to tell girl cats from boys.

'So I'm told.'

It really was an ugly cat, poor thing. Alice wanted to tell Robert to take the creature back where he'd got it from, that she didn't need romancing with second-rate animals, but then an image formed in her mind of naughty little children with prodding fingers, driving the creature mad, and her words died before she got them out.

'I don't know anythin' about cats, Robert.'

'We can all muddle it out together.' He came up beside her and they watched the cat lose interest in the table leg and move on to the woodpile in the corner. Maybe she'd be good at catching spiders, and mice...

It wasn't like Miss Martha Wright's dog, and Alice was glad of it for a number of childish reasons. In fact, there was nothing special about the cat, a most average creature and not fancy enough for a lady's lap.

Alice decided she liked that about her. Yes, she thought, she'd keep her.

'What do I call her?'

'Whatever you want.'

'Do you reckon cats ever answer when they're called, like dogs?'

'I doubt it. I think cats do whatever they wish, whenever they wish it. So choose a name as ridiculous as you please.'

'Gertrude,' she decided.

'Gertrude?'

'Yes.' The cat edged a little closer to them. 'I'd have picked Emma, but I'm—'

Oh, she'd not meant to say that aloud.

'You're what?'

Alice felt herself go red; she shook her head.

'Oh no you don't. Tell me what you'd planned to say.'

'Can't remember.'

He laughed. 'That is absolutely the worst lie I have ever heard from you!'

'Oh, fine. I was only going to say that I'd rather save the name Emma.'

The cat found a patch of sunlight and settled down in it.

'Save it for what?'

She gave him an incredulous look. 'You know what for, Robert. For if we ever have a daughter. If you like it, that is.'

He went silent long enough that she began to worry. When he eventually spoke, his tone had changed.

'You're right. It'd be odd to name our daughter after a cat.'

***

'Well,' Alice told Gertrude when Robert was gone, called away to some important thing or another, 'we'd better learn to get on.'

She was going to befriend this large, scruffy mess of a pet whether it wanted her or not. She'd not fail with her gift of a cat. It felt like a test.

She regarded the animal pensively from across the room. Gertrude seemed disinterested in friendship right then, or—worse—disinclined. Alice had never had a *pet* before, and suspected they required a different sort of approach to a chicken or a cow.

'Hello?' she began uncertainly, edging closer. The animal was very focused on the cleaning of a paw. 'Cat? Gertrude?'

When that achieved nothing, she knelt slowly, in increments so as not to startle her from the room before they'd even greeted each other.

Muttering quietly about the hindrance of her new skirts, she finally reached her knees.

Gertrude paused and took a good look at her through round, yellow eyes.

'Hello there,' Alice tried again. She extended a hand, holding it there, hovering between the two of them long enough her arm began to ache. She tried a smile.

The cat studied her a long time before lowering the freshly cleaned paw, rising, and approaching.

When they were within inches of each other Alice closed the distance, her fingertips coming to rest upon Gertrude's head. The fur was a good deal softer than she'd been expecting.

She received a bored look for her efforts, but just as she was about to pull away in defeat the cat butted her head against her fingers, once, and then again, and Alice patted her some more.

It was all over in moments, with Gertrude retreating to her spot in the sun to resume her bath, but it was progress.

Before she left the room, Alice turned back once.

'We'll do, Gertrude. We'll be a fine pair.'

***

The days of rain had momentarily transformed the landscape of the valley. For a little while everything grew at an almost alarming rate, and everybody on the station found themselves very busy dealing with the changes. For a couple of days there was even the occasional patch of green in amongst the dusty browns in the paddocks.

Weeds shot up alongside everything else, and Alice donned her gloves and worked until her hands ached. She tried to be done by midday each day, tried to be inside at the height of the afternoon when even the winter sun became blinding and tanned her skin.

It also meant, with Robert riding off most days, and Elizabeth off somewhere with her paints and canvases and making the most of the countryside's transformation, she could claim the library as her own for an hour or so each day.

And that was where she found herself one Wednesday afternoon, along with her cat.

The rattling and clattering of a wagon on the drive took Alice by surprise. It made her jump and lose concentration on the instructional book of ... *Lord,* she wasn't even sure what she was reading. There was only so much time in a day a person could spend bettering themselves before it became deathly boring.

Marking her page in case inspiration took hold again later, she set the book aside and rose from the chair, wandering the length of the shelves, searching, searching ... As long as whatever she chose next had no passages on food budgets, stain removal—or *the Bible*—then she'd be happy to read it.

More clattering came from outside. They'd received a delivery of some sort, judging by the snippets of conversation that floated to her through the cracked-open window. The library was perfectly located so that it was warm even on most winter afternoons, and Alice planned to take a couple more private minutes before she headed off to the kitchen to discuss a thing or two with Mrs Adamson and find some scraps to throw to her chickens.

There. She found a couple of books with fanciful words and patterns on the spines, and lit up like a child at the sight of them. Perhaps not everything in the library was designed to be instructional.

It took a few dozen seconds of grunting and fiddling to manoeuvre the first one, *Black Beauty,* out of its place.

'Horses!' she said once it was done and she had the green and gilt cover in her hands. Maybe not ... Setting it on top of her sombre housewives' manual, she reached up for the next thing with an elegant cover, and it was then that gravity took over. She had only just closed her hand around something with a bright red spine when a second and then a third book came tumbling quickly after.

Alice cried out and sent up a quick prayer that nothing in the avalanche would bop her on the head. It didn't, but because she had rotten luck, it wasn't only a handful of books that dropped, but all the other bits and pieces that'd been stacked there on the shelf with them.

Having caught books in each hand, and a third with her knee pressed against the cabinet, she slowly manoeuvred until everything was either back on the shelf or safely—undamaged—on the rug.

'You could help, you know,' she told Gertrude, who'd stirred at the onslaught of bumps and thuds and shifted positions on the chair, 'instead of just watchin' *me* do it.'

Were those yellow eyes laughing at her? Alice rather thought they were.

Pulling a face at the cat, she put the books she'd been after on the desk and then knelt to pick up the rest. There was something that looked painfully religious, and beneath it a couple of well-worn pieces Alice bet were from Robert's student days.

A picture addressed to Elizabeth had drifted under one of the table's feet. She retrieved it and peered at it closely, smiling at the image. It was of Robert, who sat alongside a handful of other fellows in a photographer's studio in London. He was by far the handsomest of the lot, she decided.

After studying it for a long time, she set it aside to show her sister-in-law later.

She thought she was done cleaning up her mess, and was ready to lift the cat into her lap and settle in her husband's chair to read, when she stepped on something.

'Oh no,' she said when she lifted her foot again and realised she'd trod on a collection of letters, tied in a bundle with a bow. She picked them up and inspected them for damage, hoping they weren't anything too important.

'Oh no,' she said again, and swore quietly when she noted the distinct imprint of her shoe on the top one, and hoped that the little tear in the corner had been there before she'd got at it. If she'd had slippers on instead of sturdier shoes from outside, it wouldn't have happened.

These weren't new letters, she realised once she'd finished worrying. They were a little bit worn, and had collected a bit of dust in their time on top of the shelf.

Curious now, she shifted the bow aside enough to make out an address written in a lovely, curly hand, as neatly done as though it had been printed. It looked like a feminine hand.

Gripped with the exciting notion it might be correspondence between the older Farrers back in England and their children in Australia, Alice lifted the top envelope a little, squinting into the gap between it and the next letter, hoping to discover if she was right.

So far neither Robert nor Elizabeth had said much about how their parents reacted to the marriage. Maybe they were sparing her the outrage, she didn't know. Perhaps it was better not to know. And yet sometimes she couldn't help being inquisitive.

Doubly curious now, she removed the ribbon entirely, and turned the top missive over.

'Oh,' she said as her vision narrowed to a point.

'Oh,' she said again when she checked the next envelope beneath the first, and found the same name, written again in the same elegant hand.

Plop. Alice jumped when Gertrude dropped heavily off the chair and onto the wooden floor, making a beeline for the open door. The cat might have left her alone then, but she was waylaid by a scent of some sort behind the door.

The clock on the mantle seemed to increase in volume, the ticking enough to drive her to distraction. The sounds of Gertrude's claws on the floor were a reminder Alice could be discovered any moment. She wasn't doing anything wrong—not exactly—but she was quite sure she was on the verge of snooping.

She went to the door, closing it almost to, waiting a moment with her ear at the space, waiting until she was certain there was nobody close by.

With a peek out the window that showed her plenty of sheep but no Farrers in sight, she finally took the seat the cat had vacated, and took the first letter between two trembling hands, hesitating only a moment before opening it and unfolding the paper with dread.

Dearest Robert,

You have no idea how much I have missed you.

Maybe she should have expected it. Perhaps she should have suspected it when they sat in the drawing room only days earlier, everybody acting painfully formal and polite ... and yet somehow it still came as a surprise. Maybe if she hadn't been so bloody worried about getting crumbs on her skirts she might have noticed there was more tension in the room that day than there should have been.

She finished the first letter, and then hesitated only a moment before moving onto the next, wholly unable to stop.

The second letter was much the same as the first. Miss Wright told Robert about all the things that had been happening in town since she'd last written. Alice remembered that dreadful day the river flooded, the one that was written about on the paper in her hands. She'd been there for it, worrying just like everyone else that the water would come all the way up Monaro Street and engulf everything around them.

Once she was done with the second letter she forced herself to replace it—and the first one—in the pile, and fumbled with retying the bow. It was dreadful of her to have read any of them at all, but she could at least try refraining from reading the rest. Besides, she didn't want any more news. It'd not do her any good to continue.

Why hadn't she known? Somehow Alice hadn't guessed that Miss Martha Wright had once been a good deal more to Robert Farrer than a business partner's daughter.

'No wonder...' she said aloud to the now empty room. Something more interesting than old letters had drawn Gertrude away, through the crack in the door. She couldn't even hear the clicks and clacks of the cat's claws anymore.

Rising, she did her best to restack the shelf as it'd been before, and then she turned to inspect the rest of the room, eyeing the shelves opposite her for any other piles of secret correspondence. The clock wouldn't stop ticking.

'No wonder,' she said again, 'he got me the bloody cat.'

***

Alice was unsurprised but disappointed when Robert reached for her that night. The newfound tension between them, the uneasiness she hadn't completely been able to disguise at dinner, had broken for a few happy moments when he'd come to the bedroom and caught her checking for spiders under the covers.

'My goodness, Alice. I hadn't any idea you still did that.'

She'd arched a brow at him. 'You'll be regrettin' it the day I don't check and it's *you* who gets bitten.'

'Spiders wouldn't dare come in here, I promise,' he'd declared, and she'd rolled her eyes at the arrogance of it.

'I might stop that one day,' she'd told him once she was satisfied they were the only two in the bed. 'But not yet.'

He'd shaken his head with a smile and then extended a hand to her when she climbed in, his arm going right around her waist.

'Hmm,' she said, not sure how she felt about it. Oh, sure, she didn't *not* want to do what he had planned; once she'd overcome the weirdness of the act, she'd learnt Robert wasn't at all bad at it. Only ... now she'd always be wondering who he had in his head when he was doing such things. No, there might not be any spiders in the bed that night, but it sure felt like there was more than one woman.

'Robert?' she asked mid-kiss, grappling for a distraction. 'Are those paintings in the bedrooms of England?'

Her husband paused briefly, looking up from where his hand traced a pattern up the side of her, and answered with barely disguised impatience.

'They are. In fact, they're of Cumberland, where my family still lives.'

'And sheep in England have black faces?'

'Some of them do.'

His hand continued on its exploration. Alice kept her eyes on the ceiling and thought about green grass and English villages and odd-looking creatures—anything better than worrying about whose mouth her husband imagined he was kissing, or whose breast he pictured taking in his hand.

She'd not let herself forget that neither of them married for love.

'Keep going,' Robert encouraged a few minutes later, and she realised she'd come to a stop.

He rolled so that she lost her view of the ceiling, taking her with him until she was atop him, one knee on either side of his hips, and she decided she'd better focus on what they were about. And not on his first betrothed.

Time passed, but the man didn't seem interested in rushing things.

Alice's legs began to strain with all the effort the position required. 'Robert, this is bloody hard work!'

He cracked a laugh but didn't relent, and so Alice dug up the reserves of her strength and bent to kiss him, alternating delicate kisses with more urgent ones as he moved inside her.

She'd make the most of the situation. He wasn't the only one with an imagination, she thought as heat roiled inside her.

'Golly,' she said up into his face when he rolled them again without breaking the connection, 'how'd you manage that?'

'I do have some talents,' he whispered, and she closed her eyes against a sudden wave of melancholy. It struck so fast she'd no chance to disguise it.

***

Robert stopped suddenly, and Alice snapped her eyes back open.

'What's wrong?' he demanded.

'Nothin'.' She arched up to him, but he'd have none of that. Withdrawing from her, he rolled them so that they faced each other. The mood had changed so fast it felt like a terrible case of whiplash.

'Nothin',' she said again, and tried to pull him back for another kiss.

He might have let the lie stand then, might have let the whole thing continue to its natural conclusion, had he not seen the grim determination on her face.

It wasn't the type of look a man wanted to see, as though the entire act was something to be endured.

He steadied her with a hand on her hip and injected sternness into his tone.

'Alice, tell me the truth.'

She sighed. Bit her lip. And looked away.

'Robert...'

'Yes?'

'I think I'm not feeling very well.'

'Why didn't you say anything?'

He was up in an instant, sitting back on his haunches. Was she paler than usual? The light was too poor to tell. When he pressed the back of his hand to her forehead she made a sound of frustration and batted it away.

'It's not that bad,' she said.

He left the bed and dug around until he'd produced his shirt and her gown, and then—to a chorus of grumbles from his wife—dressed them both before pulling the blankets up around her.

'I'd not have said a thing if I'd known you'd fuss like this,' she said while he stoked up the fire.

He replaced the poker with a clatter and returned to her, worried, but also glad she'd enough energy left in her to argue the point.

'Here,' he said, bringing the blankets all the way to her chin.

She didn't much like that; he could see it in her eyes. 'Get in the bed, Robert. It's not catchin'.'

He did so carefully, and then turned on his side to face her and kissed her forehead.

'What do you need?'

'Nothin'. Absolutely nothin'. Let's just sleep, all right?'

She turned her head away, her fair hair a tangle across the pillow. He'd have combed his fingers through it, but if she was ill she needed rest more than she needed grooming. After a long while, he knew she slept.

Robert took longer about it. And when he finally did drift off it was with a realisation at the back of his mind.

In those final moments before she'd closed her eyes, Alice had seemed more angry than ill.

No, he thought as his body was pulled under. She wasn't angry, she was *resigned.*

Chapter 16

Alice brooded over her discovery more than she wanted to. Oh, it wasn't all the time, as there was usually someone else around, and there were plenty of other things to do. But it hovered there on her mind.

She hadn't the right to be annoyed with anyone about it. A person couldn't change their past. And back when Robert Farrer had been pining for Miss Wright, the chances of a Farrer marrying a Ryan were much the same as Alice's were of marrying Prince Leopold.

Only ... she suspected she had a right to be annoyed about those letters, seeing as he *still* kept the bloody things.

'Alice?' Elizabeth said, possibly not for the first time in the past few moments.

'I beg your pardon?'

Feeling rude, she put aside the petticoat she was mending—gardening and her new garments didn't always go well together—and forced herself to focus.

'I said that I am expecting another visit from Martha Wright soon. The weather has improved, so she might ride out with her father this week.'

'Oh. That's nice.'

It was going to *have* to be nice, because it was something that'd be happening a lot. In recent days Alice had figured out that Elizabeth and Miss Wright weren't just friends, but were *close* friends and had been for a very long time. It explained a lot about everything, about Robert...

And privately Alice worried Elizabeth resented her for taking Martha's place, for ruining the natural order of things. Not that her sister-in-law ever showed it, she was too nice for that.

'She'll be going away for a week or so after that, and thought to stop by on the way. To Goulburn,' Elizabeth added when Alice had nothing to say about it.

She nodded, because it was polite to do so. It was something, at least, that she'd get *a week or so's* reprieve from the world's most beautiful woman.

A week or so where Robert wouldn't have a chance to spot her in town, or in church, or *in his own drawing room.* It wasn't much, but it was something.

She went back to her petticoat, tutting at how jagged the tear was; it'd come about through a combination of an enormous thorn and Alice moving with too much speed when Hutton paid her an impromptu visit.

She couldn't marry the Prince anyway, she remembered suddenly. He'd carked it last year, *and* he'd had a wife at the time.

And while she stitched in a neat line she silently chastised herself for being too curious for her own good. Sometimes life was easier for the ignorant.

***

Miss Wright returned on a Tuesday.

She visited alone this time, as Mr Wright took off to Heaven only knew where once he'd deposited his daughter at the door. It was all Alice could learn of it from her position, hidden behind an overgrown wattle bush to the side of the house.

It was no different a day to any other. The morning started off with frosty air, and then it turned sunny and warm enough to sit outdoors. At least, Alice preferred the outdoors, but her husband's first fiancée was a proper, pale, delicate sort, and she watched the woman disappear into the safety of indoors and never return.

It was a mean thought, but one that struck Alice before she could call it back.

When the barouche appeared Alice had been lost in her work, happy enough with her day. It'd taken an extra moment for her to notice the sound of approaching horses, her focus was so much on the garden. Rising from where she crouched, she tugged off her work gloves in a hurry.

When she peeked over the budding yellow flowers and saw who'd come, she'd panicked. As she buried her face in her hands and groaned, one of those words she'd tried to keep to herself since her wedding escaped her mouth. Sometimes there just wasn't a politer way to say it.

It wasn't an unexpected visit. She'd been prewarned by Elizabeth. However, the reality of sitting through another one of those teas was a little different. More uncomfortable silences. More worrying about crumbs on her clothes. More wondering what comparisons Robert was making when he looked at the two of them sitting there, side by side.

And so, when faced with the reality of it, Alice did exactly what the lady of the house shouldn't ever have done: she hiked up her skirts, put a hand on top of her workaday straw bonnet and dashed off in the direction of the trees.

So much, her conscience told her as she hopped over a rock, dry grass catching in her stockings, *for her newfound maturity.*

She used the best of her energy to get past the house, only giving in to exhaustion when her breath came in painful gasps, when she was sure there was enough land between herself and the drawing room windows that nobody inside would pay her much notice.

She passed her old cow, who watched her with mildly interested eyes, jaw working as she chewed, and—idiotically—paused briefly to wave at her, and then she was off again.

What she hadn't realised until she picked up the pace again, was that she'd been followed.

'Oh, Hutton,' she said in dismay at the sound of an excited bark. She stumbled to a stop and readjusted the ribbons of her hat, and turned to order him home—not that she thought the dog would follow her directions.

Only, she saw double.

Two dogs had been taken up with the excitement and run after her. Hutton was one, and the other ... oh, she knew the other.

'Go back, Lysander,' she told the fellow, but he merely watched her with interest. Or maybe he was waiting for her to do something else stupid.

She pointed. 'Back that way. Back to Martha.'

He looked at her hand, and then back at her face.

'Please?' she tried.

Of all her bloody luck, she couldn't even find a stick to throw to distract them as she completed her escape.

Weren't these heelers bred as working dogs? How'd Robert manage them? Desperate, she tried a rock—a pebble, actually. The two creatures merely watched it fly over their heads before turning their attention back to her

Of all the things she didn't need to happen right then...

'If you get lost, Lysander, we're all going to be in so much trouble.'

The dog appeared disinterested in the warning. In fact, he seemed quite pleased with himself.

Alice hiked up her skirts again. She'd be damned if she worried about being ladylike for dogs.

'I'm movin' on now. If you follow me, you'd better be quiet about it.'

Alice walked; the heelers continued. Twice more she tried stopping and sending them back. Twice more they sat obediently and listened to her tirade, and then walked on when she did.

She checked back every now and then, watching the undulating land gradually swallow up the house until she could only see its chimneys. Soon she'd hit a bend in the river, and she thought she might sit there a while. How long did these social visits ladies made last?

If Elizabeth and Miss Wright were old friends, they probably both fancied a chat without her anyway, she reasoned. Many things couldn't be said otherwise. Even so, she'd need a good excuse for when she got back. If only her mind weren't blank right then.

Hutton, nose to the ground, moved a few steps ahead of her, all but disappearing a time or two in the long grass.

'Watch for snakes,' she warned him, not that he listened to a thing she said. 'And spiders.'

Onwards they walked. Up ahead Alice made out the silhouette of a single rider along the road, passing the property and disappearing and reappearing through the trees. Of course, once the dogs also saw him they took it as an invitation to run faster, up ahead to investigate.

'Oh, lovely,' she muttered as she dashed after them, panting a little with the stress of too much activity and a strong new corset. 'Now I'm going to lose her bloody dog for certain.'

It became a choice of running or complaining, so she shut up then and lifted her skirts higher still, trying for speed as a pair of wagging tails disappeared into the trees by the river up ahead.

Alice dived in after them. She broke through the mess of the bush much more suddenly than she expected, and might've fallen down the incline if she'd not put on her brakes so fast.

'There you are,' she said when she caught up to the sounds of scratching and scrambling in the undergrowth, puffing under the added weight of her dress, and pressing a hand to the stitch in her side.

Hutton and Lysander regarded her for all of a second before they were off again, obviously thinking it was part of the game.

'Good Lord,' she muttered.

But already she could see the glint of water through the trees, and a few more steps on she heard the rush of the river. It was full for once thanks to all the recent rain, and running at a good speed.

She could hear the yips and barks but not see their owners. She took a couple more steps.

And before she was ready for it, the ground gave way to the riverbank in a hurry.

Alice's feet slipped out from under her, and she was pretty sure she said something else unladylike on her way down.

***

As soon as she'd recovered from the shock, Alice concluded that while the trouble she'd landed herself in this time might not be dire, it was still trouble.

Yes, it was true she'd slipped partway down the riverbank and now perched on a pile of wet leaves. It was also true that a wrong move would topple her into the water; but she wasn't planning on making a wrong move.

She'd twisted her ankle a bit, but it wasn't the end of the world. Half a day and she'd be walking just fine again, if not running. She'd already done enough running to last the rest of Eighteen-Eighty-Five.

On the other hand, she was a small person and so fitted quite nicely on the little ledge. The sun was out and it was not that cold sitting where she was. She might stay there until dinnertime and not be too sorry about it.

This was a fixable situation, but humiliating should she be discovered.

She shifted gingerly, not because of the pain, though there was that, but because she wasn't yet confident the ledge she'd slipped down onto was as sound as it ought to be. A tumble into the Murrumbidgee seemed unlikely, however she didn't know if she could make it back up.

The little dog noises that'd been punctuating the afternoon changed. Naturally, neither one of them had considered rescuing her. Once Hutton and then Lysander had come to the path above to get a good look at her, they'd lost interest and moved on to other things. Now though, the yapping became full barking, and the scratchy sounds of the silly beasts investigating their surroundings became almost deafening.

All the signs pointed to a new arrival, and she didn't want whomever—or *whatever*—it was that was about to find her seeing her flipped on her arse in the dirt.

Filled with new determination, and with a big heave of newfound energy, she gripped the ends of a weeping willow, launched up from her perch, nearly fell straight into the water, swung precariously for a moment, and then righted herself enough to scramble back up the way she'd come.

She landed on all fours on the dirt path, and then pushed herself to her feet, favouring one over the other as she headed back towards the trees.

The barking grew more excited still, and she rushed to put herself to rights, dusting and straightening in anticipation of a visitor. She brushed some leaves off her bum and hoped there wasn't as much dirt on the back of her as she suspected. She twisted, trying her best to see but failed quite miserably.

It was the deep chuckle that alerted her to the fact she was no longer alone.

Automatically frightened, she spun too fast, stumbling badly enough to twist her ankle all over again and nearly fall to the ground.

Letting out a cry of surprise, she grasped the nearest thing, which happened to be a rather prickly shrub. If only she'd not abandoned those gloves.

It was John Stanford who finally rescued her from her own incompetence, steadying her with a casual grip on her arm, and it was John Stanford's chuckle she'd heard that'd startled her in the first place. No wonder Hutton and Lysander were excited; everyone and their dog liked the man. Not even Alice was immune.

A few steps behind him was his magnificent horse. He had to be the rider she'd seen.

'Mrs Farrer,' he said formally once she was more or less upright. He completed the greeting with a doff of his hat. 'You're a long way out.'

'Mr Stanford.' It was still strange to hear herself called Mrs *anyone,* let alone *Farrer.* 'I am out with the dogs, as you see.'

His eyes flicked to them, and—too late—she realised the second dog was a complete giveaway. Mr Stanford struck her as a smart chap. He'd know whose dog it was, why it was so far out of town, and why Alice was tramping about in the trees instead of taking tea with her guest.

The only thing he didn't know was that *she* knew. He'd been keeping Robert's past betrothal a secret, just as everyone else had been. She didn't doubt for a moment he'd known about it, and now she was terrified he'd feel sorry for her.

'Still,' Mr Stanford said in a deceptively casual tone, 'the exercising of dogs does not explain why you are this far away from the house.'

'I got lost?' she tried, making him snort in a way more like her brother than her husband.

'On a near-straight road you've lived along—what—all of your life? With at least one animal who'd be able to lead you straight home if you requested it? Somehow I doubt that's the truth, but you may have your secrets if you must.'

'Hutton would take me home if I asked?' She eyed the dog dubiously. 'I'll try that next time. The other one sure wouldn't listen.'

'You've a bit of dirt on you,' he observed casually, still smiling a little, but not—she didn't think—judging.

'Tends to happen when you take a tumble down the slope. Bloody stupid bush,' she added, wishing swearing didn't come to her so naturally.

'I beg your pardon,' he said after a moment's consideration, looking her up and down. Inspecting her. 'You didn't hurt yourself, did you?'

''Course not.'

She was beginning to feel as foolish as she deserved to after running off like that, and her husband's closest friend was frowning.

'Yes, I think you've injured something.'

He looked pointedly to where she gripped the awful plant, and then more pointedly at her boots, hidden as they were beneath her skirts. She was standing crookedly.

'It's nothin'. I'll have you know I'm not as clumsy as I seem to be every time we meet.'

But then she ruined her show of bravery by easing down onto the uneven stump of a fallen tree. It was a relief to be off her feet.

'Indeed,' he said after a pause, like he was weighing up whether or not to call her out on her lie, 'but we seem to be meeting in the bush rather more often than is normal. It's not safe out here, Mrs Farrer.'

His eyes flicked briefly behind her, around her.

'Not at the moment at any rate.'

'What d'you mean it's not safe?' Had they not caught the men involved in the murder? Was Ian already back?

'Mr Stanford? What do you know?'

He regarded her for a bit, and Alice felt more and more ridiculous the longer he looked. Clearly he didn't want to upset her with scary stories, but if there was danger around, she thought she needed the fright.

He also looked like a man who didn't want to upset her delicate sensibilities. Alice sighed. She'd interrogate Robert later, see if she could break him to talk. She doubted it'd work.

'You could help me, I suppose,' she said grumpily and extended her hand to him.

'Of course.'

He helped her to her feet with a lot more strength than she expected, murmuring a smiling apology when they nearly collided, and pointing to a spot on her skirts where she'd collected some twigs during her escapade.

The dogs, apparently deciding to behave now someone more important had turned up, circled the two of them with interest and stuck snouts into the debris of leaves and sticks on the ground. John glanced at them.

'So ... the dogs escaped, did they?'

'As you can see.' Alice quietly tested her ankle by adding a little more weight. She'd survive.

She watched him study the bush again, his eyes focusing briefly on a place in the distance, one of the fields half visible from their place in the trees.

The bush seemed still if not quiet; there were always too many birds for that. King parrots flashed bright red and green in amongst the dull colours of the trees. Nothing seemed amiss now.

'I see Lysander is leading Hutton astray with his poor town manners. I could've sworn I saw a rather splashy barouche heading out this way earlier, which would explain his presence.'

He smiled as he said it, as though they were in on a secret together.

Hesitantly, she replied. 'I didn't even know what a barouche was until Mr Wright started visitin'. I s'ppose I'm meant to be impressed.'

'Oh, you certainly are.' He tucked her arm through his. 'You're sure you're all right? I could put you on the horse.'

'I'm not much of a rider. It's better I walk.'

He had to notice her uneven gait, but ignored it for the time being, slowing down a bit and lowering his voice to a conspiring whisper.

'That fancy vehicle of Wright's is from Shanks and Co in London, he'll have you know.'

They'd reached his horse and he smiled a tad as he untethered the creature and took the reins in one hand. Mr Stanford made a noise halfway between a whistle and a click, and the two dogs fell into line.

He then offered her the crook of his arm again, and they set off.

'I've never heard of Shanks and Co,' she admitted when she began to feel some comfort with her companion.

He chuckled, blue eyes sparkling when they met hers.

'To be honest, nor have I. I'm certain it's a very grand production company, though.' He chuckled again. 'Or perhaps not, and he's banking on us never discovering the truth.'

Alice was grateful for his help when he hefted her up and over a log.

She looked up at him again, this man who was her husband's friend. She wandered what he thought of her, especially when there was Miss Wright to compare her to. It made her worried, because she wanted him to like her, and to *accept* her.

'You truly don't think we're safe out here?'

'I do not know,' he said softly, thoughtfully, when she thought maybe he wouldn't answer at all. 'However, I'd rather be safe than sorry, especially with Robert Farrer's wife with me.'

'I'm not so sure Robert Farrer'd mind.'

Immediately, she wished she'd not said it. She sounded petty and childish.

'You might be surprised.'

They were back on Endmoor land now, and there was the house up ahead. Alice forced herself to keep on limping forwards as the traitorous dogs bounded on, happy to be headed home, as though they hadn't just done their best to be away.

She would've happily taken the rest of the afternoon to complete the walk back, but the man with her had to have somewhere else to be. And it was high time she started being more sensible about things.

'I don't know what Wright's about, dragging his daughter out here nonstop,' Mr Stanford said almost to himself, as if he'd read her mind. He patted her hand where it rested on his forearm. 'You may have to learn to ignore the man. You're going to be seeing rather a lot of him, and his favourite activity seems to be making others uncomfortable. I suspect you'll rise to the occasion.'

Maybe one day she would, Alice thought. *Only not today.*

Smoke spiralled from a chimney of the homestead; from the angle they approached it seemed an even more important building than it did from the road. Despite her newfound resolve to be sensible, Alice felt her stomach flutter as they continued their approach, reaching the edge of the scrubby mess of the bush and stepping back into the styled English gardens of the homestead.

She twisted to look up at Mr Stanford and he raised his eyebrows in query.

'What would you have done today if you were me? When you saw the barouche arrive, I mean.'

'Firstly, I'd not have married Robert in the first place, and not be in your situation.'

Alice scoffed, and his expression softened.

'If you'll keep it a secret between the two of us, I'll confess: I'd have run, too.'

'I know about Robert and Miss Wright. Only, Robert doesn't know I know.' She'd had to tell someone. Anyone.

There was a significant pause, long enough she thought he hadn't heard her right. Alice didn't think she had the courage to blurt it out again.

'Do you not think,' he began after some consideration, 'that if there was a long lasting attachment between your husband and Miss Wright they'd be married now?'

Alice shrugged. She wasn't in any mood to be reasonable. Hurt was too close to the surface of what she'd felt for days now.

Mr Stanford was intent on explaining, however. 'Your husband is usually right about things, unfortunately, though I'll never admit it to him. Take our new business venture, for example. There I was, ready to have a go at making syrah, but he insisted on riesling, was correct in his choice, and now here we are.'

'Oh don't you worry. As things're now, I've no intention of tellin' him he's ever right either.'

Her husband's friend laughed at that, and then turned serious again.

'Giving her that heeler mightn't have been the wisest thing Robert's done, considering how things ended,' he said. 'However, I wouldn't call the ownership of a dog a sign of everlasting love, Mrs Farrer.'

He was suddenly arrested by the dog in question up ahead. Lysander had taken a particular interest in one of the trees, and Mr Stanford tried his best to change direction, to direct Alice's attention away from the situation right when the fellow lifted his leg. Even Alice knew there was no polite way to describe the dog's behaviour, and it surprised a giggle out of her.

'Don't know much about dogs. I'm good with chickens and cows. He gave me a cat,' she whispered when Lysander was done. 'I named her Gertrude—no, don't laugh, I know the name's odd. She's a bit cranky sometimes, but she'll do for me. I only wish she hadn't been given in guilt.'

He said nothing to that, but she felt his friendship radiating from him. It was a comfort. They continued on in silence until they were near to the house. Alice's ankle ached, but she said nothing about it.

Of all people, it was Mrs Adamson who appeared from the house then, hands on her hips while she took in the new arrivals. Whatever conclusion she came to Alice had no idea, but with a nod she left them to it, disappearing back through the door.

'Do *you* have a dog, Mr Stanford?'

'I do. Unlike Robert's, mine is a large barbarian with powerful muscles, as is befitting a man such as myself. I've no need to herd sheep, you see, unlike certain friends I associate with. And so I chose a dog to reflect my personality and position.'

Delivered with so much snobbery and such a ridiculous tone, Alice laughed at him. She glanced up at his answering chuckle.

'You are not a snob, I think.'

'You think that?' He sounded wounded. 'I'll have to work harder on it then. Square your shoulders now and how about we go in to confront the intruders.'

***

Robert was out in the old cottage with Mr Stanford when Alice finally worked up the courage to make her second confession of the day.

Miss Wright was long gone. Alice had only had to sit through some ten or fifteen minutes of her company before her father came to collect her. Alice wished she could find a reason to despise the lady. She wished she weren't a nice person, as she—unfortunately—seemed to be.

Now, she looked up from her blasted Latin book.

'Elizabeth?'

'Yes?' Her sister-in-law was sketching something, and Alice belatedly thought she shouldn't interrupt her. Oh well, it was too late now, and Elizabeth was waiting.

'If you got your heart broken, would you keep letters from that person?'

Oh, Lord, Alice thought. There was no backing out now, because it was clear Elizabeth understood immediately.

'Oh no. You mean my brother kept them?!'

'Keep your voice down!' Alice whispered urgently. Panicked, she rose and half-limped to the door, pressing it firmly shut, knowing too well how much sound echoed around the house. Just in case, she pressed her back against it, palms flat against the wood, as if it would keep snoops out.

'I didn't go lookin' for them or anythin'. I was in the library and they toppled out. Of course, I shouldn't've opened any of them, but I couldn't help me—myself. I just couldn't.'

Elizabeth sighed, shook her head, and looked sad. 'If I'd known about those letters, Alice, I would have said something about the past straight away. As for Martha...'

'You don't need to say anythin'. What happened, happened.'

'Yes, but still ... I was waiting for Robert to, but I think I should have said something earlier...'

'You can't give up your friend. I mean you *shouldn't.*'

'That's very generous of you. However—'

'Elizabeth, I'm *feelin'* generous this afternoon. Let's just leave it at that.'

Chapter 17

August turned into September without any fanfare. Spring had been coming on gradually for a fortnight or so, and the wattle was already out in full, bringing bright patches of colour to the landscape, dotting the valley with brilliant yellow.

Alice knew—had been told when anxiety had driven her to ask time and again—that the magistrate had requested extra assistance from further north just in case her worst fears came to be, that it was because Robert himself had delivered the warning about the outlaws that the town was taking the threat seriously.

She also knew, though Robert wasn't aware she did, that the assistance was still to arrive. The possibility of bushrangers in the region meant no other settlement was willing to offer them help when they were concerned with protecting themselves.

She'd heard more than once that the railway brought wonders and chased away criminals. It was a little harder to chase down a locomotive than it was a man on foot or horseback. If it was true, then Alice wished the workers would hurry up and finish laying the tracks, but the whole thing was still years off.

She stopped in the hallway to straighten a painting—one of Elizabeth's—and to pluck a few dead leaves off the arrangement in the vase beneath it. They crumbled in her hand and she carefully dusted the remnants into a little pile on the side table. Later, she'd clean it up properly, but right then she'd something else on her mind. Fiddling with her wedding ring, she tried to calm the rapid beating of her heart.

She was in need of a little bit of courage right then, because she could hear shuffling papers and knew her husband had reached that point in his day where he was winding down. He'd be clearing his desk now, and be off in search of his meal soon.

Alice needed to get into that room before he left it; and before she turned into a chicken again.

Using the tip of one finger to tap the painting just a smidgen more to the left, she decided it was as perfect as she was going to get it, and so she forced herself to move on.

Robert had removed his jacket, and stood tall and handsome in the room, oblivious to her arrival. It was a bit of a bother, because Alice couldn't find the words to get his attention.

What would things have been like, she wondered, if what she'd read in those letters had come to be? Would he be happier now, married to his first choice? Would he smile when he turned and found her there?

There was no way to know, and not much chance of undoing what'd already been done.

Because fancy words had never been part of her vocabulary, and especially because she was too nervous to think of a better way to phrase it, Alice simply took a step into the room and spoke the truth without subtlety or tact.

'I know about your fiancée, Robert.'

It was like the sentence echoed, the day suddenly seemed that quiet. Maybe, she thought, she'd have been better off never saying a thing about it.

The problem was that she suspected Elizabeth would say something soon if she did not. And it was better, she reckoned, to be in control of who found out what, and when.

Robert had stilled. Alice dreaded the look she might find on his face when he faced her, and wished she'd stayed outside the room, minding her own business and crushing leaves. Turned out, when she got a look at his expression she couldn't read it anyway.

'Who told you?' he asked, and at least he didn't try and deny it.

Bracing herself, she stepped properly into the room. 'The letters, Robert. Nobody told me; I found 'em.'

'The letters?'

Why was he parroting her like he didn't know what she was on about?

'I didn't go lookin' or anythin' like that. I just found 'em by accident. All right, I admit that didn't mean I had to read the things, but...' She still couldn't figure out what he was thinking. 'I just *had* to read one or two, you know...? I had to know what they were about.'

'Where are they?' he sounded stilted and just plain strange, and Alice sighed and pointed to a spot behind him.

'There, with *Black Beauty* and *Tom Sawyer.* I put them all back, in case you're wonderin'.'

'Alice, I had no idea that I still ... No idea. *None.*'

'All right, well. I thought you should know, you know, that *I* know. So you don't need to keep hidin' it, or whatever you were up to. And I really did only read two.'

The voices of Elizabeth and the housekeeper reached them then. This wasn't a time for such a serious discussion; they'd places to be and there was a meal to be eaten.

'We'd better go an' eat,' she said, and left the room.

***

Robert hoped he wasn't a coward. However, the evening unfolded without a single chance to talk to Alice about her revelation. And then, when after dinner he'd left his wife and his sister alone long enough to finish a letter that needed to be sent off in the morning, he'd returned to find only Elizabeth still in the room.

'Where's Alice?' he'd asked, and received a curious look and the information that she'd taken herself off to bed.

She'd only got half an hour's head start on him—maybe less—but when he entered the bedroom that night he'd found her doing a half-hearted attempt at feigning sleep.

'Alice,' he'd begun, and felt the tension vibrating off her.

'Alice,' he'd tried a few more times, clasping her by the shoulder.

Her response to that was to snore, which was hilarious and frustrating in equal measures. His wife didn't snore, just as she'd told him on their wedding night. And, he learnt then, as he tried to find a way to make her sit up and talk to him, she was a fairly terrible actress.

But he'd left her alone then. Not because they weren't ever going to discuss Martha Wright, but because if she was that desperate for her space, he'd give it to her ... for the time being.

They'd slept on opposite sides of the bed that night, mostly because Robert found himself experiencing an odd sensation: fear. He hadn't a clue if getting close to her after what she'd told him would get him thumped, or if he'd see that resigned look on her face again as she let him do whatever he wanted.

Alice was out of the bed at some ungodly hour, leaving him to wake up alone. When he finally tracked her down later in the morning she was outside, in an apron and gardening gloves and discussing vegetables with the housekeeper.

And so he'd taken himself off to the library to find those letters for himself.

They were just as she'd said, and the pang he felt of ... familiarity? Disappointment? Whatever it was, it was a pang all the same at seeing them, at the memories they brought back that he'd worked hard on forgetting over the past five years.

Why hadn't he said anything to his wife? Had it really just slipped his mind? Or had he assumed she already knew? Mostly, he thought it was something he didn't want to discuss anymore, especially not with the woman who—in one way or another—had taken Martha's place.

Shaking his head at himself, he returned to the letters. He read a couple, and only a couple, just like Alice said she had done. And then he put the little pile back together and wondered what he was supposed to do with them next?

He thought about it a long time as everything fell into place. All those odd behaviours and funny looks from Alice over the past few days. All those inexplicably uncomfortable silences where there'd been chatter and jokes and gentle teasing in the past.

It probably also explained the little limp she'd developed—and vehemently denied having—but he still hadn't a clue how that part was connected.

Bloody hell and damn.

Now, it was late morning and both Alice and Elizabeth had an appointment in town, and there was no way Robert was letting them go without him. Not now, not now it was September and the roads potentially dangerous. He could not ask them to stay home, of course, because he didn't own Elizabeth, and he knew Alice well enough to be certain she'd make her own mind up on the situation no matter what.

Was he overreacting about Ian Ryan and the others? Was Alice? It was likely. They might be somewhere completely different by now, making their mischief in a place less prepared for them.

He readied himself for the outing, foregoing the heavier coat now winter was over, and then went to find the others. It was Alice he found first, dozed off in the dining room with her face resting on her folded arms, and a gigantic book open on the table in front of her.

Robert stepped into the room and noted she was dressed and ready to go, and that her hat was waiting at the other end of the table.

His footsteps must have broken through her dreams, because she stirred at his arrival, and then came awake quickly at the realisation she wasn't alone anymore. She sat up straight, her hair in something of a state of disarray, one cheek red from where it had been pressed against her arm.

She looked first at him in some confusion, and then he saw her mind kick in. *Yes,* he thought. *This is the first time we've been able to talk since you told me.*

'I swear I hadn't any idea those letters were still here,' he told her quietly and without preamble.

She studied him a good, long time, and then got to her feet, running a hand over her hair.

'What time is it? We can't be late for the Salvation Army.'

'We've time. Elizabeth isn't even—'

'I can hear her coming now.'

Robert moved to her and shifted the book aside.

'Alice...'

'There's not time for this talk now, Robert. I have to...' she touched her hair again and muttered in annoyance at all the escaped strands. Risking a slapped hand, Robert ran his fingertip gently down her reddened cheek; it was creased in spots from the lace on her sleeve.

'Alice ... I swear I'd no idea.'

And if he *had* known, what would he have done about it? Somehow—and shamefully—he couldn't see himself tossing the letters into the fire, or disposing of them in any way. It was a time of his life that had lasted years, beginning with a courtship between two people too young to think sensibly, and turning into a betrothal as though it was the most natural thing in the world.

Martha Wright was connected to a huge portion of his life; more than half of it, in fact.

Did he still love her? He told himself not.

'I believe you.'

His wife's softly spoken words took him by surprise.

'You believe me? That I didn't know?'

'Yes, I do.'

'As easily as that?'

She touched her cheek where he had, seemingly annoyed with the creases she discovered there.

'I saw how you looked when you saw those letters, Robert. You didn't know they were there. But, the thing is—' she shook her head. 'The thing is that I told you everything I could think of before we married, except about seeing Ian that one time. You should have told me *this.*'

Before he could make another apology, she smiled sweetly.

'But it's no real problem now it's out. It's not like we married for love, is it.'

'Alice...'

Elizabeth came into the room, and his wife dropped her voice to a whisper.

'Not now.'

***

While Alice and Elizabeth met with the town's most respectable and discussed the distribution of clothing and food and other charitable activities, Robert dropped by the magistrate's, and then sent a telegram to Adelaide.

He met his wife once she'd finished her meeting, leaving Elizabeth to linger and catch up with friends.

'I can come back for you later,' he offered when he found Alice standing in the midst of a small crowd, head held high and eyes bright as she carried on a conversation like a Farrer wife trained to play the part of Mrs Bountiful.

'Oh, no,' she said, and took his arm firmly in the kind of closeness she'd been avoiding for days.

'I think,' she began once they were free of the building—and the curious eyes—and wandering more or less aimlessly. They'd ended up on Monaro Street, as usual. 'It would be a good idea to not to have a grudge about this.'

Robert didn't need to ask what *this* was.

'Just like that?'

'Well, not quite that simple, but—'

He would never hear what her *but,* her condition on her forgiveness, was, because a stagecoach rounded the corner at that moment, and if Robert hadn't grabbed her quickly she would have been run down by the horses.

'My God!' he said once they'd stumbled aside. Alice coughed on a mouthful of dirt and dust but quickly recovered.

The coach travelled a few dozen more yards before it skidded to a stop, the horses rearing up and neighing, dangerously agitated. One of the doors swung open a way, and then shut again with the sudden change in momentum.

'What in the world is—*Alice!*' he made a grab for her arm when she would have taken off after it, but she whirled back to face him, shaking her arm free.

'It's *September,*' she said, reminding him, and then took off again.

There was no stopping her, so Robert jogged after her, and then overtook her. He was one of the first to reach the vehicle, save for a man who'd emerged from *The Dog and Stile* and was doing a half-decent job of steadying the horses.

It was a Cobb & Co coach, he realised as he reached it. It should be transporting passengers from other towns, from the cities further north. It would have come to them via the Great South Road, a route that was largely abandoned and largely exposed to anything—and *anyone.*

'God,' he said under his breath when he reached the driver's box. The man was slumped to one side.

Others were arriving fast now, drawn by the unexpected excitement and stepping right in to do what they could.

'I'll take him,' he said to whomever was nearest; he didn't take the time to look. The man was bleeding from somewhere, badly enough it was visible even from Robert's viewpoint on the ground. 'Are there any passengers?'

The man behind him hopped up on the step and glanced in the window.

'It's empty in there.'

A murmur came from the injured driver, 'They all jumped out before the bridge and took off.'

Robert wasted no time. Knowing it was going to be hell for the fellow, he hoisted himself onto the step and dragged the driver by his jacket until he was close enough to pull from his perch. The angle was awkward, and Robert worried he was doing even more damage with his actions, but the spooked horses wouldn't hold steady for much longer and he couldn't well do much for the fellow in his seat.

They rocked badly for a moment as the vehicle moved a couple of paces forwards and then another one back, and it was only through sheer bloody determination that Robert kept both his grip and his footing. Legs braced, arms straining, he found his balance again and then, with the weight of someone at least his own size over one shoulder, he hopped backwards onto the dirt, hoping to God that he didn't land in a pothole and break an ankle.

As he landed, knees buckling under the weight, the driver stoically gritted his teeth and refused to cry out, but the movement had exposed the extent of the wound he clasped. Robert let go of him, and he slumped in the dirt. Through so many layers of clothing and dust it wasn't possible to see clearly, but he had the dreadful suspicion the wound had been caused by a bullet, and Robert knew with sinking certainty that Alice's worst fears had come to truth.

Good God, he thought once more as he inspected the man from various angles and tried to figure out how to lift him again, *don't let Ian have been the shooter.*

'This will not be fun,' he warned the moment before he planted a boot in the dirt, tucked a shoulder under the driver's least injured side and hefted. There was no point in prolonging the process.

This time the man, a grizzled, stubbly, prematurely aged fellow, did cry out, but there was nothing for it. Ignoring the loud swearing, Robert stepped back from the coach, looked around and made a choice. Marching him over to the newly laid pavement beside the shops, he deposited the man onto the cleanest spot he could find, and set to work.

There was nothing for it but to tear at the bloodied clothing right there, in the middle of the street. The physician's office—just like the police barracks—was too far away to carry a fellow over to for help.

'A bullet wound?' he asked as he freed the man from one side of his jacket. It was a slow process, made more difficult by the groans and flinches each movement earned.

'Sure was. Damn, this bloody hurts.'

Robert's jaw hardened. 'Where did it happen?'

He received no answer; his patient's eyes had closed.

A shadow fell over them and a man, not much more than a boy, emerged from the shop he'd stopped in front of, eyes taking in the manic scene with disbelief. Robert glanced at him, discerning the chap wasn't about to swoon at the sight of the blood.

'Can you find me a knife?'

The kid was gone in an instant.

With the man losing consciousness, it was far easier to remove the other half of the jacket.

'Here, Robert.' Alice appeared at his side, kneeling on the hard ground and offering up her shawl. Bunched in her hands, she pressed it against the driver's side when more blood welled.

Robert stole a quick look at her face, saw that her colour was pale but her expression was steady. He inclined his head in thanks.

The kid returned with the requested knife, and Robert took it with a murmur and began to work on the seam of the injured man's waistcoat. The shawl was steadily turning red. That bullet likely hadn't come out, and it needed to if he was any judge of anatomy.

'Oh Lord, Robert. What more can I do?'

What he wanted his wife to do was be away from the grisly sight, even though she'd not flinched at the scene so far. Looking up briefly, taking in the chaos of townsperson after townsperson emerging from houses and shops, all of them moving *towards* the danger, he came to a decision.

'Be very careful of your safety, but see if you can find me the physician.'

'All right.' She was up on her feet and gone immediately.

Robert gave up on removing more clothes and simply pressed the shawl against the wound even harder. He hoped both that Walter Dunn was home, and that his wife ran fast.

Chapter 18

Alice slipped between two men who ran in the opposite direction, and then dodged a pony someone had parked in the middle of the street and abandoned in all the excitement. She focused on the sounds of her feet kicking up dirt with each step, because it was a lot better than thinking about all that blood...

A police constable dashed past on the other side of the street, and someone screamed in distress. They were a little bit late, Alice thought as she hopped over a discarded glove, landed on a foot mostly healed from its last misadventure, reached Mrs Hobson's shop, and crossed the road.

It was happening, she thought with frustration as she passed the post office and then reached the end of the street, turning right at the park. A nursemaid walked with a couple of small children, the largest of the two carrying a ball and chattering away as Alice passed. Further off a man strolled, his large dog bounding off after a stick. They'd not yet heard of the drama only around the corner.

Despite her warning, and despite her idiotic hope her brother would've come to his senses in the past few months, it was happening all the same.

She hopped up onto the pavement to avoid a horse, and dashed past the magistrate's house to the newer structure beyond. Pounding on the door, she grunted with impatience when there was no immediate answer, and stepped back enough to look up at the building's second storey, squinting in a search for movement at any of the windows.

'Come on, hurry, hurry,' she muttered, and then knocked on the door again.

She didn't know much about wounds, but she was certain that driver'd been shot. And if they were shooting at stagecoaches again, then Barracks Flat's violent history was coming back to haunt them.

'*Hurry,*' she said more loudly as she rapped her knuckles on the door again. 'Come on, come on.'

And then suddenly it was pulled open. Alice nearly fell through it in surprise before righting herself and finding herself face to face with Mr Dunn himself.

'You're needed,' she said, and then gasped for breath. 'Gunshot on Monaro Street.'

The physician dashed back with her the way she'd come, he carrying his bag, and Alice hugging spare rolls of bandaging to her chest. The man moved fast enough that a time or two Alice struggled to keep up, but desperation kept her feet moving, even when she thought she'd no breath left to move *with.*

***

Once relieved of his position with the driver, Robert found himself standing uselessly in amongst the onlookers. Alice had disappeared somewhere at the request of Mr Dunn to collect water, and he hoped Elizabeth was still occupied with the charity, because he was loath to drag her out into the middle of all of this.

He looked down at his hands but saw no blood on them, not a single sign of what he'd just been doing. Such a short time had passed since Alice had left the meeting, and yet it seemed like it'd been hours.

In amongst the growing crowd, Robert caught a glimpse of fine scarlet fabric, a flash of movement between the duller browns and greys of the others gathering around.

The woman—for it was a lady's dress that'd caught his attention—appeared again, a little further along, and this time Robert changed his direction, moving back towards the stagecoach.

'Mrs Wright?' he called out, even though the din on the road carried his words away before they'd even reached her.

With so much chaos around nobody was paying the woman much attention, but the fineness of her clothes and the way she stood apart from the others ... Something was very wrong if such a lady had moved towards the stagecoach instead of away from it.

Moving faster, he tried again. 'Mrs Wright?'

The woman stopped when she hit a barricade of onlookers, and then pulled a face and dived into the fray, physically separating one person from another in a display of strength Robert didn't know she had.

He moved a young lad aside himself and kept his focus on his former fiancée's mother as she came to another barrier in the crowd and all but stamped her foot in frustration.

'Robert, what's wrong?' Alice had reappeared from somewhere.

'I don't know.' However the dread that was building deep in his belly was warning him of something he didn't yet understand.

Throwing propriety to hell, he walked faster and closed the distance until he could grip the older woman's arm, and then bent to speak directly in her ear.

'What's the matter?' He kept his tone low but steady, feeling the tension that ran through Tom Wright's wife, tension that reminded him of a panicked animal about to bolt. 'Who are you looking for?'

She swivelled to look up at him, and her eyes were dark and wide. Robert didn't know if she'd even recognised him, but she didn't pull away.

'The coach came from Goulburn,' she said in a clear, even voice, and then looked back towards it.

Goulburn. The understanding hit Robert with a jolt.

'It came from Goulburn? Are you certain of that?'

'Yes.' She surged forwards then, but her progress was again hindered by the avid onlookers. Robert heard her mutter of frustration, and he bent to speak to her again.

'Mrs Wright, there were no passengers.' He'd been told that, hadn't he? But even as he said it he stepped forwards too, using his bigger hands to break a pathway through a cluster of tightly packed shoulders and gossiping heads.

'How do you know it's from Goulburn?' he asked over his shoulder to the woman who followed. His voice sounded disturbingly calm even to his own ears.

He forced his way through a narrow gap and felt the firm pressure of a hand gathering the fabric of the back of his coat, felt the tightness of the grip

Martha's mother had on him even through the layers.

With another push and another shove, they broke through to the other side of the crowd, and Robert regarded the large stagecoach with trepidation. More often than not the vehicles were stacked with luggage and heaped with people. Even so far into the country, he'd expect to see more signs of life...

The grip on the back of him grew tighter still for a moment, and then the lady released him, taking a faltering few steps ahead before she turned back his way. It was the look on her face that finally convinced him she wasn't delusional but terrified.

'I came into town to meet her this afternoon,' she whispered.

***

Once she'd delivered the physician and his bandages to his patient and found the requested water, Alice had all but been declared superfluous, and she'd stepped back from the commotion as people older and more male than her muscled their way in, determined to be seen being part of the biggest excitement the town had seen in years.

Frustrated, Alice stood back, watching the drama evolve around her. The shakes were coming on, a late reaction to the surprise, and even though the afternoon was warm, she suddenly felt the loss of that shawl.

She'd caught up with Robert only very briefly before he'd been distracted by someone else. Unlike him, she hadn't the height or power to keep up in the crowd, and eventually had stepped back from him.

She had to find something to do or else the shakes might take her over entirely, but right then she was being engulfed where she stood. Nothing brought people out in droves like blood and danger.

Getting up onto the tips of her toes, she looked this way and that. Nobody paid her much attention, so she ducked around to the other side of the stagecoach and muscled her way through the growing crowd, sneaked past a man or two who didn't even seem to notice her go by. Because of her size it was easy enough to manage.

The coach was unmoving now that someone had dealt with the horses. There were splotches of old mud kicked up in a spray along the side, and the paint was cracked in a place or two, thanks to the extremes of the weather. Alice stretched up even higher in search of Robert or Elizabeth or even Mr Adamson, but her view was obstructed by the carriage's immense height.

Grunting again, she was about to edge further around, hoping to find a familiar face at the back of the vehicle, when it lurched suddenly. It dropped on the opposite side under someone's weight as they hopped up.

'Robert!' she called uselessly when she saw his face appear through the window on the other side, but someone jostled the coach in that instant, and she was forced to take a step back. If everybody was going to insist on crowding around until the bloody sun set, she'd crawl under the vehicle in a minute. It was high enough, and it seemed an easier way to make it back around to where she wanted to be.

She was contemplating doing just that, weighing up how much damage it'd do to her reputation, when the coach's door came level with her face, and she noticed something she hadn't before.

A neat, clean hole had been made in the door's centre. It was a little hard to see at first because of the dark colour and the angle of the shadows, but now Alice stared at it, comprehending, but not understanding.

The driver *had* been shot then, she concluded. But he couldn't have been shot by *that* bullet, not unless he was directing the horses from inside a cabin.

She couldn't understand it, but the energy of the crowd changed then, a hush coming over them. Again, her husband's face appeared through the window opposite, but she was too short to see much.

'Robert!' she called again, more loudly now, wondering what in the world he was up to.

He might even have heard her that time, she thought, because he looked up suddenly. But it was at that exact moment that a woman began to scream.

Chapter 19

Robert knew what he would find when he opened that door, but that didn't mean he was prepared for it.

The sight of Martha Wright collapsed in a heap winded him.

He became aware of the screaming coming from behind him, and knew that the mother was going to be of no help to them now.

Leaping up onto the step, he held either side of the doorframe and tried to see where the injury was, what had been done to her. Her pale face was unmarred, and one foot had emerged from her skirts, the light stockings marked with a few red speckles of blood.

Urgent now, he hauled himself inside the space and ran his hands along her, just as he'd done to another unconscious woman not long ago, just as baffled as to what'd happened to this woman as he'd been with the other.

Martha was not on the seat, but on the floor, and it was no wonder she'd not been seen.

Good God, he wished the mother would stop her hysterics. It'd help nothing, and it was fast breaking through his forced calm.

'Bloody hell, Robert.'

The voice came from the other side of the compartment, and he looked up, startled to see his wife had inexplicably appeared through the other door. She leaned in further and assessed the scene in an instant, drawing in a quick, sharp breath.

'I'm sorry, Robert, I shouldn't've used those words.' She'd hoisted herself onto the ledge on the other side, and was now taking in the situation with reassuring calm. She lowered her voice. 'There's a bullet hole in the door on this side.'

It was a nightmare of a thing to be told, and confirmation of what he'd already suspected. Robert knelt awkwardly on one knee and braced a shoulder against the doorframe, willing his hands to stay steady as Mrs Wright's screams dissolved into general hysterics and he searched for the daughter's wound.

'I can't see a thing in here,' he muttered. Alice heard it and made a sound that matched his own frustration. 'I've got to get her out of this coach.'

She nodded.

'Let me help.' She was already crawling into the space on hands and knees. 'Grab her legs an' I'll get her arms.'

He didn't have time to question her strength, and he didn't even contemplate leaving Martha in the stagecoach; the place was cramped and dark, and—he was quickly discovering—was smeared with blood.

They managed, somehow. Robert gathered as much of her as he could, arms around her skirts at the tops of her legs, and braced himself for another awkward descent.

Hands came from behind him, steadying him as his leading foot struggled to come free of the step and navigate its way to the ground. Opposite him Alice made use of her small form and climbed entirely into the space, shuffling her way through, managing to scoop Martha up beneath the shoulders and move her across in difficult increments.

When the two women were close to the compartment's opening, Robert let go and grabbed Martha around the shoulders, and then stepped fully down onto the ground, hopping once as her unconscious form flopped against him, and then finding his footing.

The crowd parted for him this time, and he marched her directly across the street, not waiting for permission or direction as he made a choice in an instant and barged his way into the Hobsons' shop. Mrs Hobson was already there, holding the door for them as she ushered them inside.

He swiped ineffectually at the bench to clear it of its clutter, and then put Martha down on top of it. Out of the coach there was no mystery as to where the blood was coming from. He hissed at the sight of the wound on the right side of her body and tried to think what danger she was in, what parts of her had been damaged inside.

He looked around for something to treat her with as Alice also entered the shop and came up to stand beside him.

'Robert, I haven't another shawl. We need something to...' she grabbed at her skirts, and looked like a woman about to tear her petticoat to pieces when some other lady—Robert was too distracted to see who—offered up an apron. It seemed clean enough, and there wasn't time to check further as he bundled it up and pushed it against the wound. Unlike the driver, Martha did not even stir.

Robert gritted his teeth and tried not to think about the implications of that.

'Get Walter Dunn,' he said to Alice, who right then seemed to be almost the only rational person in the vicinity. The driver, he'd dealt with with distance. He'd not known the man. This ... this was something different.

Alice looked over her shoulder. 'Robert, he was busy with the other—'

'Get him anyway.'

She didn't argue, and again she was off, shoving gawkers aside in her haste.

He was aware that the people who still surrounded him were offering all kinds of advice. Robert ignored all of it.

Had Alice been unable to find the physician earlier, he would have taken a risk treating the driver himself. He knew a thing or two about treating injuries, had learnt over the years. It was better than nothing, and sometimes it was all they had in the bush.

The driver was one thing; Martha Wright was entirely another.

He tried to not think of the woman in front of him as *Martha,* as the girl he'd known since she had her hair in plaits down her back, the one who'd loved to come to Endmoor so often because she was able to do all the abominable things—as she'd put it back then—with the Farrer children and John that her parents would never allow at home.

He tried not to think of her as the young lady she'd grown into, when one day he'd realised she was far more than just his sister's closest friend, when she'd turned from a pretty child into an extraordinarily beautiful young woman.

He tried not to think that, despite the assumptions of many, it was far more than her appearance that changed things between them back then. How, when she wasn't busy trying to please everybody, she was a friend to him, one with far more passions and interests and dreams than she was ever given credit for. How she'd made him laugh...

And then there was the day she'd broken off what was between them. What had survived her parents' meddling, their secrecy, and even his years studying in England had all been ended in an instant. Robert wouldn't think about how he'd cursed her for her weakness back then, for her blind obedience to her family at a time he'd thought she would reject *them* for *him.*

He tried not to look at her face, at the pale, gloveless hand that rested alongside her body. It, like her stockings, was dotted with a few speckles of blood, and he wished he could wipe them off but he didn't dare release the pressure on her wound.

***

'Martha!' Elizabeth appeared, crossing the floor to step into the space Alice had left. Robert pressed on the wound harder.

'I heard something out there,' she said, immediately producing a handkerchief from somewhere and wiping at the dots of blood. 'I heard, but I'd hoped...'

'Is she alive?' she asked in a small voice after a lengthy pause.

'She is.' *For now.*

'Robert,' his sister said, her voice shaky as she swiped at her cheeks, 'your coat.'

Detached from the situation—even from himself—it took him a moment, maybe longer, to realise what Elizabeth meant.

The coat was as good as ruined, just as Alice's shawl was. It mattered nothing to him, but as the door was again flung open and this time Walter Dunn came through it, he backed away when ordered and then realised it would serve nobody any good for him to be seen like that.

He kept his eyes on Martha as he stripped it off and bundled it up.

'What became of her mother?'

'She was out on the street, refusin' to budge,' said Alice who'd just returned. 'But just now Mrs Hobson has steered her off somewhere.'

He nodded, reluctant to leave the space when the physician and his assistant ordered it, but there was nothing more he could do.

***

It seemed like an age had passed, but almost nothing on Monaro Street had changed. The crowds were reluctantly dispersing, but many still lingered. The sun was still up, and doors along both sides of the street were still open, filled with curious workers. And, at the other end, the stagecoach still stood in the centre, the horses gone, like some sort of haunted monstrosity.

'They've gone after them,' Alice overheard someone say, 'chasing the bastards back towards Goulburn, back the way it happened. Reckon they'll be caught by morning.'

She thought that was a lofty, optimistic take on the situation, but she'd too many other worries right then to tell them that.

'Robert,' she said, gripping one of his hands with both of hers to capture his attention, 'what should we do?'

He stared down at her like he hadn't any idea who she was, and she pushed away the annoyance and disappointment.

'Robert,' she said again. 'We've gotta do somethin'. Is it too dangerous to go home?'

He visibly shook himself from his stupor and stood straighter.

'I'm armed,' he told her, which wasn't a surprise, but she hadn't known for certain. 'We'll go.'

The moment his mind was decided he began to steer her towards where their carriage waited.

'Elizabeth,' he said when they reached her, and then he took his sister's arm with his free hand, 'we've got to get back to Endmoor.'

Elizabeth was taller than Alice, and—right then—stronger. She dug in her heels and gave her brother an incredulous look.

'Home? What about Martha? We can't go now.'

'We must.' He had only moderate success in dragging her—and Alice—a few steps, and then she shook herself free and rounded on him.

'Are you *mad,* Robert? This is *Martha,* not just anyone.'

He stared hard at her. 'Yes, and if you think Tom and his hysterical wife'll be letting any of us anywhere near her in the coming hours, you're mad. We have to go home, Elizabeth. We have a household to protect.'

Tears glittered in Elizabeth's eyes, but she only raised her chin and stayed silent. There was truth to Robert's words, Alice knew. She also knew that the more distance they put between themselves and town, the direr the situation would seem.

But Robert was right.

'We've gotta go, Elizabeth,' she said quietly, praying she'd not be snapped at or told to mind her own business.

'All right,' her sister-in-law said, turning to Alice when looking at her brother any longer seemed to be distasteful. 'All right, we'll go.'

They continued on for the coach and Mr Adamson, who held the reins in a tight grip.

'This is bloody awful,' she whispered to the older man before stepping up inside, pausing a moment to look back at the crowd that still milled around the street.

Alice didn't think Robert heartless. He was never that. And she got her proof when they all squashed up in the carriage, all three of them on one side together, and she saw her husband's hand shaking where it rested on his thigh.

She didn't know much about how he felt, not when it came to her. She didn't know if she was a welcome sight right then, when his real love was hurt—maybe even dying.

But that shake did it.

She clasped his hand as they rattled along, and he allowed that much.

But it wasn't enough.

The unevenness of the road might've knocked them all from their seats a time or two if they hadn't been so squashed in. Instead they fell this way and that, first against one window, and then against the other.

Robert kept his gaze cast out to the passing bushland, as Elizabeth did on the other side.

Her husband's fist clenched and unclenched beneath her fingers, and Alice released it and got an arm around his shoulder instead.

They turned past the last building of town and set off into the countryside, and she lifted her other arm and put that one around Elizabeth.

It wasn't comfortable, but someone not connected to Miss Martha Wright had to be strong that afternoon, and Alice was the only one left.

**

'I guess you could stay here overnight.'

Alice spoke for the first time on the journey home when the spire of St John's disappeared from sight as they reached the bush. Robert only became aware he'd been looking back when his wife's voice brought him back to the present.

Concentrate, he ordered himself. It wouldn't do to finish the day with yet another disaster.

'What do you mean? Stay in town? It'd achieve nothing, Alice.'

She was silent long enough that it drew his gaze to her face. She worried her bottom lip between her teeth and then lowered her arms to tug at her gloves, gaze down in her lap.

Robert's gloves were gone, ruined. *Martha...*

'Well, maybe not for Miss Wright, but for you?'

'No,' he said immediately. 'No, it won't achieve anything for me.'

He fixed his attention on the countryside rolling out around them. By the time they'd got into their own carriage and turned for Endmoor, the Cobb & Co coach's passengers had started appearing in town, rattled, minus a few of their possessions, but apart from scrapes and bruises unharmed. The men who'd attacked them were long gone.

It was a relief, but only a small one. If they were sensible, they'd take what little they'd stolen and move on from the area, but he had a suspicion they were more ambitious than that.

And then there was Martha ... It felt traitorous to be travelling away from the Wright house right then, but what else was he supposed to do? Stand about in the street, waiting for news? There was much else that needed doing that night.

'But,' Alice continued, 'how will you know if anything ... changes...?'

'Someone will inform me eventually. Remember they've no reason to come running to me with the news first.'

She didn't need to say anything; her disagreement radiated off her and filled the half-inch of space between them.

'She's not my fiancée anymore, Alice. Nor anything beyond an old friend.'

'It doesn't matter now, does it?' She pressed closer to him. 'It's not important.'

She was right about that.

When they reached the homestead he handed her down the step and realised small tremors ran through her. He'd been too preoccupied before that to notice. He didn't release her when she was steady, instead squeezing her fingers gently until he was certain he had her attention.

'I swear, I'll find out if your brother had a role in this, and do my best by him.'

He'd not the faintest idea if he could successfully extricate Ian Ryan from true criminal charges, or even if it was morally right to do. First he'd find out the truth, and hope his brother-in-law was as stupid and lazy when it came to bushrangering as everything else, and that the charges would be minimal.

For Heaven's sake, the man was his family now, something he'd barely considered before.

'It's not that,' Alice said quietly. His staff were beginning to emerge from the house and the outbuildings, and their time for private conversation was all but over.

'What it is, then?'

He studied her face beneath her bonnet.

She sighed. Shrugged. Her voice was quiet in response.

'I don't know. Let's go inside and we'll ... What do we do now?'

He put a hand to the small of her back and guided her up the steps. His housekeeper had emerged from somewhere, and looked utterly startled by his dishevelled and likely bloody appearance.

'We'll prepare for danger. And pray,' he added when he couldn't think of a single useful thing to do. 'And we'll hope that the next news from town is that Martha is improved.'

***

It was dusk when Alice managed to escape the Farrers' notice and pick her way through Endmoor's grounds, moving slowly despite her desperation to reach her destination. She was not familiar with the path, and it dipped and rose here and there. Everywhere she stepped there seemed to be another rock in her way, or another bush to catch her skirts on.

The note that'd been waiting for her when she returned home was in her palm, folded into the smallest square she could make it. It was for only her eyes, not even for Robert's.

So focused on her destination, she stumbled over her own toes and muttered an admonishment to herself as she found her footing again. Maybe it was the worry settling like a lump low in her belly that was making her clumsy.

She'd laced her boots tightly, and been sure to wear her stockings this time. She stomped loudly on the ground with each step; it was meant to scare off the snakes, even if she worried it would draw attention from humans.

She had other options, she thought. Most of the girls her age, those she'd counted as friends back in the past, back when her father had still been alive and occasionally helping her with the things that needed doing, most of them had taken off in the years since. Some were married. Some, she knew, were already mothers. Many worked hard jobs with long hours, in towns and cities.

She'd never quite been able to make herself leave in the past. She was too close to the land around her, and to the home her mother had created for the lot of them, crumbling about them as it had been in recent years, despite Alice's efforts. She'd been planning on climbing up and doing something about the roof before winter set fully in, but there seemed little point in the months since. She had no expectations of ever being back.

Before Robert, she'd thought to put her head down, take care of things, and stash some coin away to improve her life a little more in the coming years.

And now? Now she'd finally found the courage to do what she ought to have done in the past? Now ... well, she'd Robert, hadn't she? And Elizabeth, when it came to that. And the Adamsons, and Bessie, and Bertie. Even Mr Stanford. She had so many people in her life now, and didn't know how to break away from them.

She should've, she told herself silently, taken off before things had got so complicated. It was going to be a lot harder to do now, if it came to it.

The sun would set soon, would be down by the time she sneaked back, and she didn't relish the thought of making this same journey without light to guide her way. Above her the sky was turning a brighter and brighter shade of orange, and the sun, unencumbered by clouds, was blinding in its intensity, in the minutes before it dropped behind the hills.

Alice kept her head down and prayed she'd not been spotted.

And so, when she came across her destination more suddenly than she expected, she stopped abruptly as a jolt of fear hit her square in her centre. Up ahead no smoke rose from the small shelter's chimney, and as she noticed that fact, Alice was jolted again.

What if she'd missed him? The thought set her off walking again, rushing now.

The door to the hut opened before she reached it, and a tall, slim man appeared in the entrance.

Alice's step faltered, and she pressed her hand to her chest to try and stop her heart from beating quite so fast. It made the packet inside her bodice crinkle, which reminded her of why she was there. It gave her the motivation to keep walking.

'I thought,' she said when she was inside the rapidly darkening hut, forcing her eyes to make out the guilty-looking figure of her brother, 'that you might've come to your senses in the past couple of months.'

'I didn't rob the coach, Alice.' His voice was so familiar, but also brought with it a very familiar frustration. No, she amended silently, not *frustration* anymore. Pure, bloody anger.

'Why should I believe you?'

'I didn't!'

It didn't matter. Not really. He was still part of it in some way.

'Two people got shot. One of you lot shot a fancy lady from town, and nobody's goin' to forget it.'

'I heard the driver'll survive.'

'And that makes it better?'

He shook his head, and had the grace to look uncomfortable.

'What about the fancy lady?'

Alice shook her own head. 'Why'd you keep fallin' in these holes, Ian? Why not just do what other folks do and stay on the right side of the law?'

He looked belligerent, but then he sighed and stepped back.

'Don't know, Alice. But it's too late to change now, isn't it?'

Alice thought not, but she'd not come out at sunset to repeat a conversation they'd had over and over in the past. She sneaked a hand inside her coat and felt around clumsily, hoping she wasn't revealing things a brother ought not to see. Her fingertips found a corner of paper, and she tugged and tugged until she had the money free of her frock.

Almost, almost, she didn't hand it over, but she was quite sure money was the only thing that Ian would respond to. It was worth the sacrifice if it worked.

'Me savin's from ... before ... It's not much, but it'll get you out of town.'

It was the money she'd kept when she'd had hopes and dreams of leaving Barracks Flat, back when she'd never've dared dreamt of the life she had now.

Her brother took the packet and opened it, flipping through the cash before looking back at her. She understood what he was feeling. He wanted that money badly. But what was left of good in him remembered it was bad to take money from his little sister. It was embarrassing to do so.

'You know you must leave here, Ian. You know that, yes?'

He sighed again, and she was almost inclined to feel sorry for him. But not quite.

'I sure do now.'

She turned to go.

'Alice?'

She paused on the threshold and looked back, a question in her eyes.

Almost nothing that day had shocked her more than when he thrust the envelope back out to her.

'It's not mine to take.'

She looked at the money, held out between them. 'Just take it and use it to go away. A long way away.'

And then he came closer and took her hand, putting the money into her palm. Reluctantly, she closed her fingers around it.

'Can't be caught with that much money right now. People'll suspect me then for certain.'

Chapter 20

By the time the sun set Miss Martha Wright was alive still, if not awake and talking. That was the news John Stanford brought out to the house a few hours later, when he arrived on horseback, armed, and with a bag of provisions large enough to keep him comfortable for a few days' stay at Endmoor.

Robert's old love had been moved to the Wrights' house, which Alice knew was a big, two-storey place near the river, the kind of household where nobody wanted for anything, and the family was hiding away behind those expensive walls from busybodies and gossipmongers. If she'd a chance of recovering, there would be the best place for it.

Alice felt an acute pang of sadness about the whole thing. It was nothing if the lady didn't live, but she couldn't help thinking beauty like that shouldn't be marred by bullets. It went against the natural way of things.

She wasn't envious of the lady anymore. Not in any way.

'I'll spend the night here, and we'll start the hunt in the morning,' Mr Stanford said. 'We ought to warn the Ngambri people, and see if they know anything we don't.'

Alice's innards plunged at the thought of the two of them rushing off to play vigilante. She didn't want them shot. She didn't want anyone else shot, but it was time for this to end one way or another.

'The driver—who is badly hurt but expected to survive, by the way—swears the shooter is the same man on the *Wanted* posters in town. He couldn't have had a terribly good look at the chap before he was shot, but I'm inclined to believe him.'

Mr Stanford turned to her then, expression grave. Alice braced herself for what she already suspected.

'While nobody's said he was part of what happened today, more than one person is saying they recognise one of the men hanging about the outskirts of town as the fellow who used to deliver the milk.'

Ian, in other words.

Alice felt like she'd been stung by something. 'Who's saying that? How many people?'

Did it really matter? Once one person started the gossip, it was bound to spread. It wasn't as though the people of Barracks Flat would be discussing anything else in the coming days.

'It's not important,' Robert's friend said softly, but everybody in that room knew he was only saying it to be kind. Of course it mattered.

Alice willed the pounding in her head away.

'We all knew Ian was a fool,' she said, trying to keep her chin high, but it wasn't easy. 'We knew it already. It's no secret.'

She tried a small smile for Mr Stanford, but it felt wrong to give one to Elizabeth, considering what'd just happened. Robert, though ... Alice couldn't even bring herself to look straight at him.

Instead she devoted a ridiculous amount of time to fussing over Gertrude, who'd wandered into the room midway through Mr Stanford's update and arranged herself in a big ball in the middle of the floor. It seemed even the cat wanted to lounge about in company that night, rather than taking off into the darkness to stalk the shadows.

Servants came and went. There were a lot more people about the house that evening than usual, and it didn't need saying why. Mrs Adamson came to the threshold and took Elizabeth away for some reason or another; Alice was too distracted to notice why.

After that she sat there alone, listening to the men murmur to each other while Gertrude gave herself a thorough wash.

As the discussion continued around her something important crystallised in Alice's mind. The room was well heated, perhaps even a little overhot with the fire so strong and so many people about, but in those minutes she felt cold on the inside. Her world became small as the solution to many a problem presented itself to her in all its awfulness.

'I'll be goin' off to bed then,' she said, rising before anyone could voice their objections. The men both rose out of manners that still bemused her.

She looked hard at Robert, trying to read his mood, but not confident enough to make assumptions.

'With me gone the two of you can discuss ... whatever manly things you obviously don't want to say in front of me.'

First, however ... she surprised him utterly by stepping up to him, chest to chest, and on her toes in an attempt to meet his height.

'Do *not* get hurt. Do *not* get shot. And *don't* do anything foolish because you think it's heroic. All right?'

He clasped her to him for a long moment, releasing her only when she pulled away.

'I'll try my best, Alice. I'll try my best.'

She gave both men a stern look before turning to go.

'Alice,' Robert called after her, and when she looked his way he seemed like a man about to apologise and tell her she was welcome to stay.

She smiled and felt a traitor, and hated herself for it.

'In truth, I'm tired. And you two ought to discuss guns and such. I am really sorry, Robert, about Miss Wright. I reckon I have to say it 'cause Ian never will.' She got herself on the other side of the threshold before anyone responded to that.

'Good night.'

Robert and John left soon afterwards, John turning in one direction, and Robert in the other. They were to meet some of the other men from town, Alice had learnt from the discussion earlier. It seemed that it took an actual robbery, and two people being shot, for people to take the threat as seriously as it should have been from the start.

She went to the window of her old room to watch them disappear into the night. The moon shone brightly, reflecting off the corrugated iron above the veranda, allowing her to watch Robert and his horse until the trees swallowed them up.

Only then, when she knew they'd not be back in the near future, did she return to the bedroom she shared with

him, take down a bag and begin to
pack.

***

Alice stashed her things and then
went about the process of sneaking out
of the house. It wasn't hard. Elizabeth
had thrown herself into a frenzy of
cleaning up her art supplies, almost
silent while she waited for news of her
friend. The household staff were on
edge, waiting for anything that might
come by that night.

Because she couldn't simply stand
around making up her mind about
whether she'd stay or go, she drifted
to the veranda, and then took the steps
down and continued beyond it. Nobody
wanted her crusading, going after the
outlaws, wherever they were, but she
could at least stand guard of Endmoor.

The clear sky was lit up with a
thousand stars—maybe more. She
looked up at them a long time, listening
for anything wrong in the night. But in
the end it wasn't her hearing or her
sight that picked up on the danger; it
was her nose.

Smoke.

Alice whirled, searching, wondering. It wasn't smoke from a chimney, it was more than that, and growing fast. Suddenly the stars didn't seem so bright, nor the night so clear. She picked up her skirts and dashed around the side of the house. It was when she reached the back of it that she caught sight of the growing orange glow.

'My God,' she said.

Someone gasped, and she turned to find Elizabeth behind her.

'It must've just happened,' she told her. 'We've gotta do somethin'.'

The two women watched in shock as a stockman ran past with a bucket of water, his panic and speed making him lose half of the contents along the way. The closest outbuilding to the house was burning fast.

'We've gotta do somethin',' she said again, and surged forwards. She made it a step and a half before a rough hand caught her by the arm.

'Mrs Farrer, stay back.' Mr Adamson's voice was as rough as his skin, and she turned to him in desperate bewilderment.

'But, if there's a fire it could spread to—'

'This is no normal fire.' Two more men ran past them from the stables, buckets of water sloshing madly.

'Oh, I know. An ember caught in the chimney, most likely. But if the grass around it catches, too—'

'That's not what I meant. That fire's burnin' from the outside in.'

She realised his meaning immediately. Bumps broke out across her skin and something prickled at the back of her neck. 'Someone set it on purpose?'

'I've no doubt of it.'

He released her and began to stride away, pausing only to point at the house.

'Stay in there until I know it's safe.'

Alice might have argued more, and on another night, under other circumstances, she would have held her ground and made her case.

But this was fire, on dry, dry land, and she wasn't going to hold everyone up while she debated the merits of her taking part.

'We'll go to the kitchen,' Elizabeth said, relenting before Alice could get the words out. 'We'll find things to fill at the well.'

Alice trotted after her as they retraced their steps, and for a reason she'd not know when she looked back on it, she glanced behind herself as they passed through the main hall.

Her feet skidded to a stop.

A silhouette of a man moved by the window at the other end.

Tall, unfamiliar, and skulking about when every other man on the property battled the blaze, she froze where she stood, barely daring to breathe as she watched it—him—edge around the front of the house.

Iciness, a particular kind of fear she'd not felt since April, slipped through her, but determination also came with it. She'd a job to do here, and right then she was the only person able to do it.

But there was more at stake now, not just her little house in the bush.

Keeping her focus on the fellow, she backed up, praying and then praying some more that the floorboards wouldn't creak and give her away. She silently cursed her voluminous skirts, knowing she was so easily seen through the windowpane beside the door.

She shuffled back another step, and then another. The man, the intruder, had stopped moving entirely, his back flattened against the glass.

She ought to shout for help, Alice thought. But there was nobody around except Elizabeth, and she couldn't...

Another step and she came into contact with the entrance to Robert's office.

With a big breath for luck, she dropped to her knees and crawled into the darkness. Thanks to her eternal curiosity, she was well acquainted with where her husband kept his old cricket gear.

She might be making a grave mistake, she worried once the bat was in her hand and she'd crept back towards the front of the house.

'Stay where you are, Elizabeth,' she said as loudly as she dared when she passed through the kitchen. There wasn't time to see if her sister-in-law followed the order, and Alice slipped out the back door and darted around to the left, taking a breath with each corner she turned.

It was the final corner before the front of the house that she found the mysterious man. He'd backed away from the window a few steps, and held something suspicious in both hands, but it was too dark to make out the particulars of it—or him.

Whatever it was he held, the bat was bigger, and it gave Alice a touch of confidence. She'd simply creep up his way, and then use the element of surprise to take care of matters.

She was about to do that when a second figure appeared.

Alice pulled back with a short gasp, and scanned the darkness beyond the house for any more men. Nothing else stirred; nobody else came forward.

She couldn't take on two men, could she? Or, maybe...

The second man moved again, and this time she noticed the limp.

***

Robert didn't know what he expected when he searched the hut on the fringes of his property, but what met him when he approached it from the front and pushed the door open without warning was Ian Ryan, alone, the sparse space neat as a pin and the fire already extinguished. A small lamp gave off the only light, but the place was too small for any other men to be hiding in the shadows.

Years. It must have been two years at least since he'd last got a good look at the man, and he *was* a man now, not the boy he'd first been when they'd given him a chance at Endmoor. Grown now, if still lanky, he was too old for the antics he'd pulled in his earlier years.

There was only one reason Robert wouldn't grab him then and turn him over to the authorities to do with him whatever they would, and she was back at the homestead, hopefully doing exactly what he expected her to: staying safe.

The brother's reaction to Robert's appearance was a fraction too late. By the time he'd stirred from his nap in the hard wooden chair and reached for the rifle beside him, Robert was fully inside the hut and staring the fellow down.

'Don't even think about it, Ryan. We've things to discuss and I doubt you want my murder added to your list of crimes. Surely not even you could be so foolish.'

It took him another couple of seconds, but then the man relented.

'Took your time about findin' me,' he finally said, trying only half-heartedly for bravado.

'Well ... It's been a busy day.'

'Is she dead?' The man looked ragged. Red-eyed and scruffy, with unevenly barbered stubble that wasn't quite a beard, it didn't much look like the criminal lifestyle was treating him well. Robert searched for anything of Alice in the man's face, and was relieved to find it only in his eyes. Brother and sister weren't alike in looks then, either.

Troubled for a number of reasons, he looked away a moment before fixing him with a hard stare. He wasn't going to discuss Martha Wright with this man.

'Are you here alone?'

''Course I am. I'm no genius, but I'm not stupid enough to be bringin' those men onto Farrer land.'

'Hmm,' Robert said, inclined to believe it. 'Did you play a part in it? In what happened this afternoon?'

'No! Bloody hell. No, I didn't even bloody know about it until it was done.'

Robert shifted his weight, leaning against the small, dusty wooden table that dominated the tiny space.

'And you found out about it then ... how?'

As though Robert was the magistrate himself, Ian Ryan cracked then. He gave names and locations and talked of future plans of the other men. He almost spoke faster than Robert could keep up with, but he filed as much of it as he could away in his memory, for he was also inclined to believe his brother-in-law on this. The fellow was a hopeless liar, and clearly not the slightest bit loyal either to the bushrangers—or his sister.

He'd act on this information, and soon. And he'd hope to God that this was the true story.

'Here,' he said when the chattering finally died out. He reached into his coat and retrieved a small bag.

'You need to leave this place, leave New South Wales, preferably. There's enough in here to get you away from the region.'

Grey-blue eyes far too similar to Alice's glared back at him.

'I'm not takin' your bloody money.'

'Take it ... and get yourself out of this area before it's too late for you.'

'I'm not touching a pound of it. But you're right on one thing: I'm gettin' out of here as soon as I can.'

Robert held the money between them a fraction longer, until it became clear the man was serious.

'Go to Queensland,' he said, tucking the bag away again. He'd had his chance with it. 'It rains more than here, but it'll be warmer in the winter months.'

Robert needed to be gone from there.

'*Januarius*,' he said, and then took another step inside, forcing the younger man back.

His brother-in-law's eyed widened slightly, and then he nodded slowly.

'We're onto the lot of you. The magistrate is, too. Make sure you're gone before sunrise, Ian.'

Ryan fidgeted. 'Is she dead?' he asked again.

'I can't say. If you're a praying man,' which Robert seriously doubted, 'I'd be praying right about now. For *her* first, but also for yourself.'

Robert glanced at the man's swag, bundled and ready to go, over in a corner.

'I thought you'd have been off by now. I see the others have already made their start. They'll not get far, you know. The secret's out.'

'I know,' Ryan muttered, and then squared his shoulders. 'Oh, I'll be off in a couple of minutes. I reckon I'll try a little harder to stay away from the noose for the time bein'.'

Robert inclined his head and resisted asking the fellow if he'd finally come to his senses. No point in antagonising the man when they were so close to being rid of him.

'Mister Farrer?'

'Yes?'

'If your mates are goin' after the men headed to the houses west of Barracks Flat, they're goin' to miss someone.'

He tensed; questioned the truth of it. 'Who?'

'There's a third chap headed for the Baxter house on his own. Figures he can manage that one alone, not get much in the way of resistance. Come an' go before they even know what's hit them and all of that.' He fidgeted again. 'He'll be on his way over there now.'

Robert mentally calculated the path out to the property. 'This fellow's name?'

'Wakefield. James Wakefield.'

He nodded his thanks and put his hat back on his head, taking a couple of steps to the door before a memory niggled. He stopped and turned back.

'Oh, and Ryan? One more thing.'

The other man groaned quietly, and Robert nearly reminded him not to push his patience. He'd met with extraordinary luck so far.

He fixed him with a stare. 'You sister's necklace. What became of it?'

The man rose immediately and dug about in his things before removing something and rising.

'Take it,' he said, closing the small distance between them and dropping a sliver of metal into Robert's palm.

Well. That was simpler than he'd expected.

'So, she's still livin' with you then? Me sister?'

'As she's my wife now, she certainly is.'

The brother hadn't known. His reaction was immediate, and of disbelief. Robert held his gaze steadily while Ian sputtered under his breath, and then enjoyed the surprise that widened his eyes when he realised it wasn't a joke.

'Well, hasn't she done well for herself.'

'I've done pretty well for *myself*, I'd say. If you're looking for a favour from this, it isn't the time.' *It'd* never *be the time.*

He scoffed. 'I thought as much.' He grabbed his swag and swung it over one shoulder. 'That's all then?'

'I suppose it is. But, Ian? If you do one sensible thing tonight, make it this: stay away from my house.'

***

Not one word about his sister's welfare, Robert thought as he rode away, careful with Skirmisher on the dark trail. Not a single one. While he'd be eternally grateful Alice's brother had prevented her from drowning that day years ago, he couldn't help thinking it was the man's only saving grace.

Except, perhaps, the information he'd been given now.

Robert wasn't foolish enough to take it at face value, and he didn't follow the path exactly as Ian Ryan had told it, but he thought it was advice given in earnest. Noise carried far in the night, and somewhere not too far off he could hear the sounds of men crashing their way through the bush. Ducking to pass under the low branch of a tree, he heard a possum send up a warning call—protecting her baby from man and horse—before they hit open pasture. The Murrumbidgee was visible beyond it, the rippling water catching in the light of the moon.

He brought his horse to a stop and simply listened, waited. There was something unnatural nearby, something that belonged nowhere near the road to the Baxter property in the middle of the night.

Robert withdrew his weapon and cast his senses out.

It was easy to find this Wakefield character in the end. The man moved with carelessness through the night, a man on a mission with no thoughts of being caught. Robert followed him a while, until he reached the point he knew the man would try and cross, where the river narrowed enough to make it an easy enough swim.

He was maybe twenty yards from the chap before he became aware he wasn't alone, and then Robert rounded him, cutting off his route to the riverbank at the exact moment he looked ready to bolt.

'Good evening,' he said as he pulled up in front of him, sliding easily from the saddle. Good Lord, the top of the man's hat struggled to reach Robert's shoulder. This would be easier than expected.

'If I were you, I'd reconsider crossing that water tonight.'

***

Take out the strongest one first.

It was advice Alice drew from God only knew where as she sprang into action, running ahead and swinging the bat at the exact moment the first intruder would've used his weapon to force his way into the house.

There wasn't time for finesse—or moderation.

Thud. It only took one swing, and it was done, the impact of it reverberating through her arms.

The intruder dropped to the ground, and did not rise again.

'Oh, bloody hell,' she muttered, immediately in a panic. She'd not meant for the blow to be quite *that* hard.

But there wasn't time for fainting yet, because the second man had seen, and was charging at her, despite his bad leg.

I think, Alice decided rather too late, *I oughtn't underestimate men with limps.*

'Thank Christ,' she said heartily and in all earnestness as two of Endmoor's men finally arrived on the scene armed with rope, all too eager to belatedly play the heroes, and ready to truss the intruders like tomorrow's dinner.

She stepped back and let them deal with the second man. Taking out one was more than enough for her for one night.

'Bloody hell,' she said again when Elizabeth appeared at her side, 'I didn't know I could do that. Wait a moment ... I didn't kill the fellow, did I?'

The first man wasn't moving. Actually, he'd have to be dragged away, feet clunking and bumping along the ground, no doubt. He was completely out cold.

Her vision swirled, filling with images of her impending arrest for murder, and—bracing herself for anything—she nudged the chap with the toe of her boot. *Did* he move then, or had she only imagined it?

'No, I don't think so,' Elizabeth said, taking Alice's arm and squeezing gently.

Bertie rushed past then, too, his lanky frame supplemented by determination as he joined in the fray. The lame captive put up quite the fight, but with the butler's help the stockmen subdued him. He sputtered and swore the entire time.

Elizabeth made an unimpressed sound. 'They're not so tough now, are they?

'That one'll be even worse when he's behind bars,' Alice said, also unimpressed. She crept forwards.

'In all honesty,' she asked him when he was trussed and trapped, 'what were you expectin' to come of attacking Endmoor tonight?'

She received no answer; hadn't much expected one. The unconscious man stirred a little as he received a similar treatment, turning Alice wobbly with relief. He wasn't dead, then.

She realised she still held the cricket bat.

'I ought to keep this,' she said, contemplating it in the low glow of the homestead's lights. She could've used the thing all those nights ago, back at her old house. It was a damn sight more useful than that little knife she'd had then. She could've clobbered each and every one of those men chasing her in April, but then she'd not be where she was now.

'It might come in handy,' Elizabeth agreed. 'Every now and again you might want to use it on my brother's hard head.'

They laughed at the same time, a relieved reaction to a tense night.

Alice lifted it again, swinging it like someone had bowled her a ball. She'd not played cricket in years.

'No, not for Robert. Not yet at any rate. But it might come in handy in the future.'

She ran her hand down the smooth surface, remembering the horrid *thud* of the thing when it made contact with its target, and then came to her senses. She'd not be clobbering anyone in the future if she could help it.

'How's the fire going?' Elizabeth asked one of the men as he came by again, another bucket filled and ready to go.

'Under control now, more or less. Don't worry, Miss.'

The air still smelt like charred wood, but beyond Endmoor's rooftop they could no longer see that frightening orange glow.

Alice turned to Elizabeth. 'We should go in. There's no point waitin' out here and shiverin' in the dark.'

***

It occurred to Robert before he even reached the gate that he shouldn't have lingered to talk to the magistrate. Endmoor was lit up from nearly every window as he approached it. The veritable crowd he saw gathered outside, and the scent of smoke in the air as he left the road and began his approach to the house, told him he'd missed some sort of excitement that night.

'Good Lord,' he said under his breath, urging Skirmisher on, the sense of satisfaction that had wound around him seeing the outlaws apprehended, of seeing Ian Ryan disappearing into the night, even with his pockets insufficiently lined, dropped away from him in pieces with each step of his approach.

Had he left the women with enough protection? Had they miscalculated how many men were involved in the crime? Had he left the household exposed to danger?

He was a fool, and one who right then was ready to keel over in fear.

It was Mary Adamson's silhouette he recognised first, unmistakeable in size and form, the voluminous skirts a giveaway.

He retrieved half his breath at the sight of his sister next. She stood off to one side, head bent in discussion with Bessie.

And yet the vice gripping his chest continued to squeeze as his eyes still searched, and searched...

Whatever had happened at the house was significant enough to draw everybody on the property out well after midnight, and he didn't miss the relief in the shout of greeting he received when Old Adamson finally noticed his arrival and started down the drive to meet him.

Robert brought the horse to a stop and dismounted onto unsteady feet.

'What's this about?' he called before he met the man, leaving the horse to investigate a bush, and striding ahead alone.

'We've had our own bit of excitement here. Didn't want to be left out of things, did we?'

Robert scanned the small crowd up ahead.

'Where's my wife?' The man wouldn't be joking if there was still trouble, surely.

Adamson frowned as he followed Robert's gaze.

'Not a clue, actually. She was here a moment ago.'

'Was she all right? What happened?'

They approached the house as the other man filled him on some of the night's dramas. It was enough to make Robert weak in the knees and shudder with belated fear. He'd thought he'd left the homestead well protected. He'd thought they could get to the men before they got to Endmoor.

Entering the house on his own, he wandered the halls, peering into rooms, and finding them empty.

Finally, as a last resort, he went to the kitchen and found her there. Alice was alone and mumbling to herself—and inexplicably contemplating a cricket bat in her hands. The cat sat on the bench beside her. Or, rather, half on top of her.

He'd heard she was fine, and he'd believed the words when Adamson had said them, but seeing it for himself was an entirely different matter.

Robert paused in the shadows and watched as she set the bat aside on the table and gently ran her fingers along Gertrude's fur.

'You're far too heavy for playin' the lap cat, I'll have you know,' she said. 'You're nearly the size of a sheep. But you don't know that, do you? You think you're small, and that this is comfortable. So I'll allow it, *for now.* It'll spare you the embarrassment tonight.'

He fell in love with her in that moment. Completely and without condition.

Robert had no idea what to do with that new knowledge, but the realisation nearly made him stagger.

'Alice,' he said softly, and her head snapped up and found him as he entered the room.

She smiled then, and it was unguarded and relieved, but then she removed the cat from her lap, stood a little awkwardly, and studied his face. The smile slowly faded.

'Oh,' she said, her voice a little odd. 'There you are. You're late, Robert, but at least you're 'ere in one piece.'

And then whatever scold she'd been building up to was cut short as she paled suddenly, swayed once, and—before he could make a grab for her—dropped in a heap at his feet.

Chapter 21

Alice was sitting up before Robert could even reach her.

She rose fast, pushing on her hands as he knelt beside her and took her firmly by the shoulders, though she didn't seem to need the support. In fact she didn't sway at all. Hell, she already looked recovered.

It didn't stop a tremor from running through him.

'Alice, my God...'

Pale blue eyes turned on him, gone fiery with incredulity.

'I fainted!' she said, and sounded furious about it. It seemed she was as swift and practical about fainting spells as she was about everything else in life.

He kept his tone low, comforting. 'So you did.'

'I can't believe I fainted.' She was thoroughly disgusted. 'It must've been because of that man I had to whack earlier. For a few seconds back there I was certain I'd killed 'im. Seems shock came on later than I expected.'

Robert stilled—forced calmness and sanity into his tone.

'The man you had to ... what?'

As she explained her night to him, Robert let go briefly, testing her steadiness and ascertaining she was too annoyed with herself to keel over again. She continued talking as he got his arms under her and rose with her in them, too full of outrage to protest being carried.

He took her out of the room and into the surprisingly deserted corridor, turning away from the voices of the others and towards their room while horrific ideas of what might've happened that night when he'd left his wife and sister alone filled his mind.

'And then,' she said, telling the story as though it wasn't going to drive him to a heart attack, 'I sneaked up behind him with that bat of yours, and right at the moment he would've turned and noticed me—'

'Good God, Alice, you shouldn't have done any of that.'

'Maybe, but it worked, didn't it? Sorry, by the way, for taking the bat from your cabinet.' Her arms tightened around his neck. 'But by then I was so angry that those men'd come *here,* that I could've beaten ten of them, I reckon.'

He reckoned she might be right.

He reached the threshold and paused, gazing down at her cheeky little face.

'I should have been here. I swear, Alice, I'd thought I'd left you with enough protection or I'd never have—'

'Oh, that,' she said with a scoff and a flap of her hand. 'It should've been fine, but then someone set the old outbuildin' on fire, and so...' She struggled against his hold until he let her down on the bed, and then huffed out a breath between tight lips. 'It's all over now, and the men're watching the rubble in case, you know...'

In case an ember reignited and the whole of Endmoor was burnt to the ground, she meant. If Robert hadn't enough trust in Adamson and the others he'd be out there now himself, watching the place until the sun rose and the last of the smoke cleared from the ashes.

However, he had someone to watch over for the rest of the night, especially considering what Bessie had whispered to him when he'd entered the house just now, cheeks all pink with distress.

Hoping she'd stay put for the time being, he started off across the room, and was reaching for a cloak his wife had draped over the dresser when she spoke again.

'This is all very mortifyin'.'

He whirled.

'*Mortifying?* Alice, you—' he stopped and shook his head hard and fast and only once, and then he was back in control. 'Alice, I should have been here. I'm never going to forgive myself for it.'

'I think,' she said, earnestly, 'that if you'd been here it would have been worse. They could've hurt you.'

She studied her hands as she spoke, and Robert eased the cloak aside enough to find the small bag he knew was hidden there. He worked hard to maintain his temper at the sight of it, but it was a hard thing.

'Here, let me help you,' he said in a reasonable voice when he caught sight of her twisting and turning this way and that, attempting to free herself of her gown.

'I really am better, Robert,' she told him once he was done.

He again moved over to the corner. This time, she watched him closely, suspicious now.

'Yes, but humour me. We've a few things to discuss, and now I have an excuse to make you stay and listen.'

It got her hackles up, he saw that and concealed his amusement. She reached for the laces of her boots, muttering something about dirt on the counterpane.

'What've I done now, Robert? If this is about takin' that man out with the bat, I've no regrets on that front, so you'd better prepare yourself to be—'

'Hush, Alice,' he said, sitting on the bed beside her, making the mattress dip just enough that she rolled against his side. She plucked a leaf from his coat, and he nudged her with his shoulder.

'Secretly, I'm impressed about that, but if you're determined to win over the ladies in town you might want to give *me* credit for doing it.'

'Never.'

He kissed the top of her head and rose. 'I thought not.'

Robert was well aware he had an avid—if weary—spectator as he stripped out of his coat and boots and made a valiant effort of removing the dust from his hands and face. He heard her own boots hit the floor as he draped the coat across the back of the chair and then dipped his hand into one of the pockets, curling the necklace in his palm before turning back to his wife.

Her eyes widened when he returned to her side and he let the locket drop, the chain pinched between his fingers. The piece was too well-loved and the metal of too poor quality for it to glint in the light, but Alice's expression lit up at the sight of it in a way it had not ever done with any of the prettier baubles she'd collected over the past few months.

She sat obedient and still as he unfastened the clasp and fixed the necklace around her neck.

'Where'd'you find it?' she asked as the locket settled into place against her chest. She lifted a hand to touch it, her fingers tracing the small nicks and dents.

'I didn't find it so much as requested its return.'

She swivelled, turning wide, astonished eyes on him. 'You saw Ian.'

'I did.'

'And he'd not sold it?'

'He hadn't.' It wouldn't have fetched much—if anything—but there was no need to share that with her.

She shook her head in wonderment. 'I've been surprised more times this year than in the whole rest of me life.'

***

Alice had long ago resigned herself to never seeing the thing again. More than once she'd tried her best to call up a memory of her mother's face, seeing as the pendant—all of her mother that was left—was gone, but she'd been too young and her memories too hazy to form a proper image. Even now, touching the locket, she saw only flashes, hints in her mind, and that was all.

'I can't believe he kept it.'

Biting her lip, she refused to let herself cry. Instead, she stared hard at her husband, hoping her face wouldn't give her away. He'd moved off again, and was digging far too close for comfort to where she'd stashed her things.

'What's that you're doin' over there?' *Oh, but she knew.*

He bent and retrieved the bag, and Alice's belly dropped.

'Robert ... I swear that I was—'

'Going to leave us? Leave me?'

'No! Well, maybe. Dependin' on what happened, you know? I thought it better to have options.'

'Options!'

That seemed to do it; the man upended the paltry contents of the bag between them on the bed. All right, he was angry, and Alice couldn't blame him, but he had to understand.

'Robert, what if it all went wrong tonight? Would you want the Ryans around, draggin' you and Endmoor down? What about Elizabeth? What about John? What'd it do to them?'

He sighed then, and with an invisible whoosh, all the ire went out from him. After scrubbing his eyes with a hand, he fixed that attention squarely back on her.

'What *Ryans?* Ian is gone now, left town for good I hope, and you might recall an event that happened not all that long ago. The one where you became Mrs *Farrer.'*

'Don't be so pedantic. You know what I meant.'

'Yes, I do know. And I think that if you try such a thing again I'll have to barricade you in this house until I can make you see sense.'

He sat beside her again, on top of the things he'd upended, and picked up one of her hands, toying with her fingers one at a time.

'You know this marriage of ours? It mightn't have come about in a regular way, but that doesn't make it any less of a marriage. It was never meant to be temporary, Alice. And the longer it goes on, the more I can see I married the right woman after all.'

He paused, and took her measure before saying the rest.

She waited.

'I married the right woman,' he finally continued, 'even if she *is* prone to bouts of ridiculousness.'

Well. This wasn't the scold she'd been expecting. Alice shifted until her head could rest on his shoulder. It wasn't a soft cushion for her cheek, and he still smelt of horses, but she didn't mind.

She stayed that way until she could feel much of the tension go from him, until he began to sink back against the headboard, relaxing slowly, slowly. And then she lifted her cheek and kissed him where it had been.

'Robert?'

'Hmm?'

'Two things. First: I swear I'd already decided not to go. It was just done as a final ... well, it was just in case there was an emergency, if things turned out different.'

He nodded, and she didn't know if he believed her or not, but he didn't argue with her about it.

'And the second thing?'

'If you dare try and lock me in this house I'll go get your bat and whack you with it.'

Obviously he didn't believe her threat because he snorted at that and oh, what a relief that he found it funny when she thought she'd earned herself a verbal walloping for packing that bag.

He rose then, and she watched him strip out of most of his clothes, draping them around the place. There wasn't much light, but she knew an exhausted man when she saw one. Mister Robert Farrer was in need of some sleep; rather a lot of it.

Soon. There was a little more that needed saying first.

She patted the mattress. 'Tell me about tonight. Only the important things, and then later you can tell me the rest.'

And so he returned to her, put his arm around her shoulders to draw her in close, and told her.

'All right,' she said when he was finished, and despite her curiosity, she didn't ask a single extra question. There'd be time for that in the morning. 'All right.'

'That's all?' he asked her, all bristly chinned against her hair. 'No interrogation?'

He leaned into her palm when she brushed it down his face, and she paused to cup his jaw.

'Tomorrow, you tell me. I trust you, so sleep now.'

It was then that she remembered one final thing.

'Robert?'

'Mmm?'

'Did you check the bed? For arachnids?'

He put his arm around her waist.

'I did. Did you learn that word in my ghastly old Latin book?'

'Maybe. Are you lyin' to me about the spiders?'

'Mmm. Maybe.' He pulled her closer still.

Alice resisted the urge to tug the covers back and take a look for herself, snuggling in instead, enjoying the closeness. She'd take the risk with the spiders, she supposed. Just this once. And anyway, there were other things moving under the covers then, things that were a lot warmer and more welcome than an arachnid, and not as likely to bite.

'What d'you think you're doin'?' she asked as his foot rubbed against her leg in a way that certainly wasn't accidental, and slipped her hand inside his nightshirt in response, finding the now-familiar warmth of his chest, feeling his muscles flex against her touch.

'You should be asleep by now. Endmoor won't be takin' a holiday tomorrow, no matter what happened overnight.'

'If you're worried about that,' he said in a perfectly reasonable tone that was in stark contrast to what he was about, 'then what are your hands doing?'

Alice hadn't the willpower to snatch them back.

She hiked a knee around his thigh, enjoying the heat of him.

'I wasn't the one out in the bush. Honestly, Robert. You've gotta be tired. Rest.'

He buried his face into the tangle of her hair, and his sneaky fingers found the hem of her chemise.

'Soon,' he told her, and pulled it higher. 'Later.'

***

Alice woke first.

Love you, Robert had finally whispered as he'd drifted off a few hours before, and she'd simply smiled and then rested on her favourite spot on his chest as he fell fully into slumber. He'd better bloody mean it, she thought with a small smile, because she loved him right back.

His arm around her middle had relaxed as sleep dragged him away, but each time she'd tried to move to her portion of the bed, he'd stirred enough to tug her back in place.

As ever in the bush, some creature outside was crashing about and calling in high tones, but Robert slept through it. Likely it was another possum. No other animal she knew had such a spooky call. And no burglar she knew of—not even a drunken one—would be so careless as to make so much noise.

She felt ... safe. Completely safe for the first time in her life, and the awareness of it kept her awake and wondering instead of settling down to rest. What a bloody mess the night had been, but in the end everything seemed to have worked.

What now? she wondered, drawing back from Robert one more time simply for the fun of having him pull her back. The way she saw it, the only person who couldn't be happy now—apart from those criminals who were rotting in a cell in town—was Miss Wright.

She frowned.

That odd creature outside started up with its horrid cackling again, and she decided she'd be giving up on rest for the remainder of the morning. When the sun came up she'd get back to work on those roses, she decided. Then she'd deal with the vegetable patch, if Mrs Adamson was in a mood to allow it. And, if she could muster the motivation, and manage not to fall asleep from the boredom, she'd get back to learning her Latin.

Who knew? One day it might come in use for a second time in her life.

She eased out of her side of the bed very slowly, slipping free without waking her husband, feeling the absence of his warmth keenly as she reached for a shawl and stepped away, trying not to make a sound.

Dawn wasn't far off. The restlessness of the bush told her as much.

Ian was out there somewhere ... She hoped by now he was a long, long way away.

*＊＊

Despite everything, Robert slept. It was the softest of sounds, a whisper of movement and a stirring of life in the room that finally pulled him back over the precipice.

He stirred and opened his eyes, registering that hours must have passed, and became aware of a couple of things at once. One was that dawn was all but broken. The other was that his wife was not in the bed with him. The place beside him was cool to the touch.

He noted the bedroom door was open a little, and spied Gertrude asleep by the fireplace, a speckled ball of fur.

'It's so pretty out there.'

Alice's voice helped him locate her over by the window. She'd her back to him, but must have heard him stir. He propped himself up on his elbows and studied her.

'Prettier than usual, or prettier because of the relief that last night is finally over?'

As was his wife's way, she took the question as a serious one, and considered it before giving her answer. Robert spent the time appreciating the way the morning light cast her hair in silver and gold.

Finally, she shrugged. 'Can't say. Come and see.'

He was already on his way, swinging his legs over the edge of the bed and pushing to his feet.

When he reached her, she edged sideways so he had an unobstructed view. The entire valley was lit in a spray of pinks and golds, spreading out from a point over the Brindabella Range and stretching out to touch the sky above them.

'Prettier than usual,' he decided. He tugged lightly at the ends of her hair and then rubbed the strands between his fingers, watching the colours grow even richer while Alice fell suspiciously silent. He could all but feel the thoughts radiating out from her mind.

'So,' she began, 'it was worth it, then? Last night? All of this?'

'I'd say almost everything that has happened these past months was worth it.'

'Even if it means Miss Wright ... No, you needn't answer that.'

No, he need not. There'd been casualties in the past weeks, but Martha had suffered the worst of it.

And yet he couldn't leave it unsaid.

'Alice...' he cupped one of her hands in both of his as he gathered his thoughts.

'What *was* with Martha Wright is long over, as it ought to be. I realise now that if I'd wanted to be with her I'd have found a way around her father—and I did not. Whatever it was I felt for her these past few years was nostalgia, the loss of a dream. I'd too much time to myself, I suppose. Too much time to feel sentimental about something that never was.'

'Why'd you two end it?'

'Because her father has bigger ambitions for her than to be the wife of a landowner in the tablelands.'

Alice seemed confused. 'But she's still here.'

'I know,' he said, voice laced with irony. 'I'm not sure all of Tom Wright's plans work the way he wants them to. Not from lack of trying.'

She watched him in silence as he turned her hand over and traced a pattern across her palm.

'If our positions had been opposite, I would've put up a bloody good fight to stay betrothed to you,' she said so fiercely he squeezed her hand hard in gratitude.

'The memory of discovering Martha wounded in the street will haunt me, but—*Alice*—that's not love, and I need you to be certain of that.'

She seemed to accept that, and turned her focus back to the sky. There was more to say, but the morning was too beautiful for it. There'd be time later.

'Look at it now, Robert. If I had Elizabeth's skill, I'd paint it.'

'I could buy you some paints and you could try. And I know my sister would happily share hers.'

She laughed at him and shuffled even further to the side. He reached out and tugged her back.

'Come back here. There's room enough for both of us.'

Because he could, he moved her closer still. She came to him in little shuffles until she realised what he wanted and slipped right in front. Wrapping his arms around her middle, he pulled her back until they were touching from head to toe.

'This is better. You're small enough that I can see right over you.'

He received a grunt for that. 'I'm not so sure that's a compliment.'

'It's not exactly an insult, however.'

He smiled when she covered his hands with hers at her waist and squeezed, adding a little pressure with her short fingernails as punishment.

'You think I'm too short?'

'I think you're exactly the height I want my wife to be.'

She made an inelegant sound at that but let it go, and Robert decided there were definite advantages to the difference in their size. Such as the way her soft breasts rested against his arms when he wrapped them around her...

A figure moved past the window: Adamson heading back to the house. If he'd left the remains of the hut then the fire danger was over.

Alice rested her head back against Robert's chest.

'I tried to give Ian me—*my* savin's, so that he'd go,' she whispered. 'It was all the money I brought with me from before.'

His arms tightened briefly, and he bent to brush his lips across the top of her hair before he replied.

'He wouldn't take my money either, if you're wondering.'

'So he's not entirely bad then.'

'I suppose not.'

'He's just *mostly* bad. A hopeless cause.'

The sky changed again, the colour about to give way to the bright blue of the day. The mood was all but broken by a flock of a few dozen cockatoos streaking—*shrieking*—across the sky, followed by the calls of a dozen currawongs. The white-tipped black birds darted past them, and in and out of trees, in pursuit of each other.

'*Lord,* they're loud.'

Robert had to agree. His ears were ringing. 'It's that time of year. You can always tell spring has arrived when the currawongs start behaving like recalcitrant children.'

'Robert?'

'Hmm?'

'That word you said just now...'

'Recalcitrant? In this instance it means they're a great big bloody pain in the arse,' he explained, answering her unasked question.

She laughed, and then turned her pale gaze back on him. 'Thought so.'

She rested her head against him, for once not in a hurry to be off anywhere in particular.

'I won't paint it, but I reckon I'll remember it a long time.'

Epilogue

'D'you see that?' Alice asked, her voice as bright as the sparkle in her eyes and the flush in her cheeks.

They stepped away from the other parishioners, done with church for the morning, leaving Elizabeth to make her way down Monaro Street to pay her visit to the Wright household. Martha would recover—eventually. Until then she was closeted away, hidden from view from all but her closest of family members and friends.

At the gate John lifted a hand to Robert in farewell and then guided their newly arrived German guests off in the other direction, lost in animated conversation. Tom Wright had honoured his deal, and there was every reason to believe this newly arrived man, this riesling expert from the Rhineland, was everything he'd claimed to be.

'I saw it.' Robert offered his arm, which his wife took with glove-splitting, bone-crushing enthusiasm.

'I made it so they spoke to me like an equal, an' I reckon they couldn't've liked it much.'

'What makes you think that?'

She didn't bother honouring the question with an answer, but a glance down at her face, lips pursed against a smile, and he knew she was harder to offend than a little snobbery in town.

'I think you're growing on them, Alice. Give them a while to come down off their high horses and you'll see.'

'If you say so, Robert,' she responded with the long-suffering tone of a wife of several decades, not several months.

He *had* seen. He'd seen his wife conduct a conversation with some of the worst sticklers for propriety—all on her own, as he'd been caught in a conversation with the magistrate at the time—and had seen her come out of the discussion triumphant.

'Robert?' Alice's tone had changed.

'Yes?'

'Do you know where Ian went? Where he *really* went, I mean, not a pretty story to make me happy.'

They'd not heard from—or *of*—the brother for long enough that it could only be a good thing.

'I have my ideas,' he began, 'but nothing certain. North, I suppose. He might not have too much sense in him, but I think he knows to stay away now.'

He watched her closely as she thought about that, subconsciously matching her steps to his, moving them along as one. They'd reached the riverbank, at the place where the Murrumbidgee curved, creating a grassy space favoured for picnics and impromptu cricket matches. More than one ball had been lost to the water over the years.

A couple of swans glided by silently, the water glistening on their jet-coloured feathers. Alice watched them until they were out of sight, and then smiled unexpectedly, disarming him completely as she seemed to as her regular custom.

'He'd better stay away. We've too much to do to worry about him at the moment.'

And they did. At home and elsewhere, with the Intercolonial Trades Union Congress coming up in October. Alice would get her first experience of the world beyond the tablelands.

'Is he really from Germany? Your new man?' she asked as she glanced back towards where they'd left the town's newest resident and his wife. It was too early to be certain, but Robert was of the impression the man would be a godsend for the lot of them.

'*Johann...*' Alice tried out the name under her breath, her footsteps crunching on the gravel path alongside his own. 'I didn't know what a German man would be like—don't think I've ever met one before.'

They reached a break in the trees and she tilted her face up to the sunlight. 'He's all right, even if I don't know what he says half the time.'

'He spoke German to you?'

'No, I mean all those things he says about makin' wine.'

'I've no doubt you'll learn the terms as we go along. I promise it will be much less painful than learning Latin.'

'It'd better be,' she said darkly.

Smiling, Robert tucked her hand a little more tightly through his arm as they continued on their way. The winter chill had long ago given way to lovely spring days, a respite before the smothering heat of summer made walks outside difficult to bear.

''Course I can't say for certain, but Robert, I really think he knows what he's doin'.'

Which was deeply reassuring, as Robert happened to agree. He watched as his wife paused to bend and pick a couple of bluebells.

'I'm glad you think so. As long as he is as competent when it comes to all things viticulture, he could be from Siberia and at this moment I'd struggle to take issue with it. In fact, he could be some sort of charlatan—an actor, perhaps—and I wouldn't mind much as long as he helps us succeed in the next couple of years.'

'I think you'd mind in that case,' she pointed out, and they both paused to watch a carriage pass on the river road.

'If he *was* an actor,' Robert said thoughtfully, 'he might know the words to your *Pirates of Penzance.*'

He saw the memory of a past conversation come over her face.

'It's not "my" *Pirates of Penzance,* Robert. I've never seen it.'

Which was going to change in the near future, but that was a surprise for her birthday a few weeks away. Despite all the work that lay ahead for Endmoor, Robert was still absolutely determined to have a honeymoon of *some* description, late though it may be. And he'd be taking her to the Theatre Royal whilst in Sydney for the congress.

There was a lot to look forward to.

Once the vehicle was past, Robert bent to kiss her cheek. She put up only the smallest of protests when he moved his attention, briefly, to her lips.

'You'll be ruinin' me newfound respectability,' she told him in a grave voice when he pulled away.

Naturally, his response to that was to heft her higher and kiss her better. Alice allowed it—momentarily, and then pulled back, hands on his shoulders.

'Stop it, you oaf. What happened to all your fancy manners?'

He released her, letting her feet touch the ground again.

'Someone must be having a bad influence on me.' He knew he sounded wholly unrepentant.

Alice lifted her chin.

'I've no clue who that someone might be,' she said, and he grinned.

'I'll behave until we're home. Do you want to take the carriage, or leave it for Elizabeth, and walk?'

'Walk,' she said decisively. 'There's no danger now.'

'No, there isn't.'

'And it's a beautiful day.'

'It is. Shall we? Come on, then.'

And he turned her away from the water and towards the bush.

Thanks for reading *The Landowner's Secret.* I hope you enjoyed it.

Reviews can help readers find books, and I am grateful for all honest reviews. Thank you for taking the time to let others know what you've read, and what you thought.

Sign up to our newsletter romance. com.au/newsletter/ and find out about new releases, must-read series and ebook deals at romance.com.au.

Share your reading experience on:

Facebook

Instagram

romance.com.au